AMBUSH!

"Yankee Thunder," the radio operator said. "Our helo's been delayed."

Rainey snatched up the microphone. "Yankee Thunder, this is Dogma One. We have wounded personnel. Need immediate extraction. Just send that helo A-SAP!"

Rainey returned the mike to Houston and said, "They're regrouping. Probably moving up into the hills around us so they can fire down when we make our break."

"What about our dead and wounded?" Sergeant Golez asked Rainey.

"We'll carry the wounded. We'll have to leave the dead behind and come back during daylight."

"Janjali and his men will chop up the bodies. We cannot leave them here."

"Then we'll die trying to carry them out."

"We won't get very far either way. Somehow, Janjali knew we would be here—"

At that moment, the thump of mortar fire sent Rainey and Golez dropping to their bellies and covering their heads. Before the first blast subsided, a pair of fragmentation grenades went off, nearly in unison, and someone shrieked.

"Dogma One, this is Dogma Two!" called Doc. "We're being overrun! Repeat, we are being overrun!"

Also in P.W. Storm's
FORCE 5 RECON series

DEPLOYMENT: NORTH KOREA
DEPLOYMENT: PAKISTAN

FORCE 5 RECON

DEPLOYMENT:
PHILIPPINES

P. W. STORM

AVON BOOKS
An Imprint of HarperCollins*Publishers*

This is a work of fiction. Names, characters, places, and incidents are products of the author's imagination or are used fictitiously and are not to be construed as real. Any resemblance to actual events, locales, organizations, or persons, living or dead, is entirely coincidental.

AVON BOOKS
An Imprint of HarperCollins*Publishers*
10 East 53rd Street
New York, New York 10022-5299

Copyright © 2004 by Peter Telep
ISBN: 0-06-052355-7
www.avonbooks.com

First Avon Books paperback printing: August 2004

Avon Trademark Reg. U.S. Pat. Off. and in Other Countries, Marca Registrada, Hecho en U.S.A.
HarperCollins® is a registered trademark of HarperCollins Publishers Inc.

Printed in the U.S.A.

10 9 8 7 6 5 4 3 2 1

"Certainly there is no hunting like the hunting of man and those who have hunted armed men long enough and liked it, never really care for anything else thereafter."

ERNEST HEMINGWAY

"People sleep peaceably in their beds at night only because rough men stand ready to do violence on their behalf."

GEORGE ORWELL

Acknowledgments

My editor, Michael Shohl, has given me insightful and invaluable guidance during the coarse of writing this series. I have been very fortunate to work with him.

Jim Newberger, dear friend, writer, paramedic, and military enthusiast, provided many suggestions for the story and characters, as well as critiques that were as helpful as they were amusing. Once again, his contributions are deeply appreciated.

Author's Note

While this is a work of fiction, I have endeavored to faithfully portray the Marine Corp's Force Reconnaissance community, relying upon information made public via the internet, via the many texts on the subject, and via email exchanges with the Marines themselves.

That said, there remain weapons and tactics employed by Force Recon Teams that are not described here in deference to national security. Some of what you read is the product of my imagination, but every word is meant as a tribute to those brave men who serve as the eyes and ears of their commanders.

P. W. Storm
Orlando, Florida
Force5recon@aol.com

FORCE 5 RECON

DEPLOYMENT:
PHILIPPINES

01

Sergeant Mac Rainey was on the hunt, and that meant bad news for the guerrilla fleeing down the jungle trail.

A group of fourteen men from the Abu Sayyaf Group (ASG) had just raided the rural town of Tipo-Tipo. The terrorists had stolen money, food, and medical supplies, and had shot and killed three farmers who had made the unfortunate mistake of standing up to the bandits. Rainey, his Force Recon Team, and a five-man team of Filipino Marines had fast-roped into the town from their Huey slick choppers. As they had questioned the locals, two meatheads armed with AK-47s and clad in nondescript green fatigues had darted from a perimeter hut and sprinted for the jungle. Evidently those geniuses had not been able to escape in time with their ASG buddies, so they had made their move, splitting up once they had reached the tree line. Rainey had charged after the guy on the left, sending Corporal Jimmy Vance after the other one.

The familiar *crack* of gunfire resounded about thirty yards east of Rainey's position. Before the echo died, Vance's report sounded in Rainey's earpiece:

"Dogma One, this is Dogma Four. First bad guy is down but alive, over."

"Roger that, out," Rainey replied breathlessly into the boom mike at his lips. He ducked under a limb, smashed through the leathery leaves of a mass of rubber plants, and found himself in ankle-high mud as yet another limb blocked his path. He shoved the branch aside, but it slipped from his fingers and snapped back, scratching his painted face and pulling at his bush cover.

Just as he flinched, a round exploded from the terrorist's rifle and sliced through the branch, coming within a few inches of his cheek.

Reflexively, Rainey bounded to his right while leveling his M4A1 carbine and squeezing off a three-round burst toward a coconut tree, the bad guy's most likely point of cover.

As the shots echoed, Rainey hunkered down and squinted through his rifle's night-vision scope—

To watch his prey book off toward the next cluster of trees. Rainey panned for a shot, his reticle sweeping over the man's glowing silhouette before he lost him. "Damn it." He lowered the rifle and bolted to his feet.

Heart thundering, hamstrings ablaze, he fell into the

bad guy's trail, foliage now blurring by, the shadows heaving up with a life of their own. For a moment, he heard only his breath, his heavy footfalls, and smelled only the stench of gunpowder hanging in the humid air. He caught a glimpse of the terrorist, saw him vanish down into a gully ahead.

Rainey rounded the next cluster of rubber plants and began to descend. The gully swept out across a long bank of mud and rose up, about fifteen yards ahead— where his bad guy was just ascending the opposite wall of weeds and dirt. The man suddenly turned, jamming down the trigger of his AK.

The popping stung Rainey's ears as he hit the deck and the rounds scissored through the fronds behind him. At once, the nearness of death rocketed him back to the recent past, to that morning in the delivery room with Kady. Just a month ago their first child, James, had come into the world.

"It's a boy! A beautiful baby boy," the doctor had said.

Rainey had worn the widest grin of his life. "My son . . . I'm going to teach him how to be a man."

But *he* needed to be a man now. A Marine. He had a job to do. But Kady and James also needed him . . .

Honor. Courage. Commitment. Core values. *Corps* values. Had Rainey forgotten them after nearly seventeen years of service?

No! Where is that scumbag? There!

But don't get too close.

A baby boy needed him now.

But so did the United States of America.

He forced all the fear and bullshit from his mind and willed himself across the gully. He reached the wall and barreled right up to where the ground grew level. He shot his gaze left, right, peered hard into the dark pockets of jungle ahead and detected a glimmer, just a glimmer—but it was enough.

Running again. Hard. Hard as he could. Shoulders tucked in, his rifle warm and ready.

He was back on the hunt.

"Dogma One, this is Dogma Two, request sitrep, over."

Not now, Doc. Rainey couldn't blame the Navy corpsman for being concerned, and, of course, Glenroy "Doc" Leblanc, AKA Dogma Two, had no way of knowing that his team leader was narrowing the gap on bad guy #2 and had no time for a little encrypted coffee klatch.

The canopy of brown and wilting palm fronds abruptly opened, permitting the full moon's shimmering light to fall upon the terrorist.

Remarkably, as luck or fate or God would have it, the bad guy tripped over a bulging root and fell onto his gut. He clambered to his hands and knees, but Rainey was already in range.

A series of warning shots leaped from Rainey's carbine and blistered a path beside the terrorist. He would've shouted *Halt!*, but Rainey knew that not all members of Abu Sayyaf understood English. Some members spoke Arabic, while others had learned English or Filipino (based on Tagalog) or even one of the eight major dialects.

Besides, bullets were a universal language.

Unfortunately, the meathead was as dense as the lead rounds that had torn into his path. He got onto his haunches, turned, prepared to fire—

Rainey blinked, glanced around the delivery room. "How does it feel to be a father?" Kady had asked.

Blinking again, Rainey took aim, shot one of the thug's kneecaps, then he shot the other. The young fool collapsed to a carpet of withered palm fronds, clutching his legs and screaming his ass off.

"Dogma One, this is Dogma Two, request sitrep, over."

Panting, Rainey neared the thug, arms steeled, fingers poised over his carbine's trigger. "Two, this is One. Second bad guy is down but alive. I need you to treat this guy and get him out of here. Firelight One? Request two operators to assist my corpsman. My GPS coordinates are as follows . . ."

After Rainey read off the numbers and finished up with Doc and Team Firelight's sergeant, he kicked away the terrorist's rifle, then shoved the muzzle of his carbine into the back of the guy's head. The olive-skinned man wore a black bandanna and had a series of strange tattoos running like ebony vines across his neck. "You speak English?"

"Yes," the thug gasped. "Fuck you!"

Rainey made a lopsided grin. "No, that's 'Fuck you, *Sergeant*.'"

"Every American on Basilan is going to die."

"Dogma One, this is Dogma Three," came Lance Corporal Bradley Houston's voice over the tactical frequency. "Be advised we have found the mayor, but, uh, you'd better get back here, over."

Rainey would reprimand Houston for letting his emotions leak into the airwaves. The radio operator and San Diego native loved to make bad jokes and play up the drama of every situation, but despite those foibles, he had shown his mettle time and again. Once a cocky rookie, Houston was now, for the most part, a hard but humble veteran. "Roger that, Dogma Three. Will return your location A-SAP, out."

Within a few minutes, Doc and the Filipino Marines from Team Firelight arrived and tugged off their Night Vision Goggles. Doc towered over the Filipinos, who had said they had never seen a man as tall and muscular as him.

"Haven't lost your touch, I see," Doc remarked, tugging off his bush cover to reveal his bald head, smooth as satin.

Rainey pursed his lips. "He almost got away."

"What? *Almost* counts for something?" While the two Filipino Marines held the prisoner, Doc rifled through his ruck to produce trauma bandages. "Good guy, bad guy. I treat them all: Doc's jungle medical service. Would you like some morphine to go with that malaria?"

The corpsman's jovial tone was lost on Rainey, who kept replaying the moment in his head. "Hey, Doc?"

The corpsman lifted his brows.

"Aw, forget it."

Rainey's grave tone caught Doc off guard. "You all right?"

"Good to go. So you got this here. I'm going back to see what Houston's crying about." With a heavy sigh, Rainey switched on the flashlight attached to his carbine and broke into a jog, steering himself back for the town but wishing he could jog home to Colorado to be with Kady and his son, if for only a few hours.

However, the commandant of the Marine Corps wanted Team Dogma in the Philippines, and he had called Rainey personally to make that request:

"Sergeant, there is no Force Reconnaissance team leader who comes more highly recommended than you. The situation down there in the Philippines is very tenuous, and I need my hardest men there to set things right. I know you will do me, the Corps, and your country proud. Are you up for it, Sergeant?"

"Sir, yes, sir!"

Consequently, Force Five had been loaned out to Bravo Company, 1st Battalion, Fifth Marines of the 31st MEU. Bravo, along with nearly six hundred more U.S. troops, was on Basilan for an annual two-week training exercise dubbed "Balikatan," a Tagalog word meaning "shouldering the load together." They would assist the armed forces of the Philippines in counterterrorism training and improve interoperability between forces. Other American units would also conduct multiple medical, dental, veterinary, and engineering projects. Of course, Rainey had expressed his full support of the mission, though he had his reservations about training men on an island home of terrorists.

Moreover, the team was still short one operator. Make no mistake, Rainey and his men were the Corps' varsity squad, the team everyone wanted to be on, but Rainey suspected that some men were unwilling to assume the cursed fifth position known as "Dogma Five." Every operator who had taken that slot had either been maimed or killed.

In fact, just two weeks prior to deployment, Rainey's old friend from boot, Sergeant Daniel Jones, a team leader in his own right, had been reassigned to Dogma to finish up his last two weeks with Force Reconnaissance after an absolutely awesome seven-year stint. Then, a few days before he was going to meet up with the team, he was involved in a helicopter accident in which he had broken both legs.

And there it was again, the curse of Dogma Five.

Groaning away the thought that he led a jinxed team, Rainey reached the town and had to push his way through a crowd of locals surrounding one of the largest NEPA huts, constructed of bamboo and thatch. He found Houston, carbine in hand, guarding the door, along with a trio of Filipinos from Team Crossbow, two of whom were holding back a screaming middle-aged woman. "Hey, Sarge, remember how I called this place Gilligan's Island?" asked the broad-shouldered Marine, his handsome beach-boy complexion hidden beneath his camouflage paint. "Well, I was wrong. Very, very wrong. The mayor's dead. Come take a look."

Rainey lifted his chin to the hysterical woman. "Who's she?"

"His wife. She found him. You have to see this."

"Takes a lot to surprise me. And hey, let's keep our radio transmissions professional. Demarzo's as anal as they come. Got it?"

"Sorry, Sarge. But I think he'll overlook my indiscretion when he sees this."

After slipping past the rickety door, Rainey looked up, froze, then muttered, "Those sick motherfuckers . . ."

Inside the meager hut lay a cot, a small wicker desk, and a number of crates used to store bananas, coconuts, tomatoes, and potatoes—but those items hardly commanded Rainey's attention. His gaze was riveted to a wooden pole jutting up out of the center of the hut's dirt floor. Atop the pole sat a bearded man's head, the eyes wide open, the jaw slack, the jet-black hair wet and matted. Flies buzzed the head as blood dripped from the slashed-up neck and painted candy cane lines down the pole.

"One guy outside was saying that Janjali and his gang had been threatening the mayor for about a month, but he ignored them."

"*We* won't ignore them." Rainey turned away. "All right. Don't touch anything."

Houston lifted his free hand. "Are you kidding, Sarge?"

Rainey grabbed the mike from Houston's 117 Foxtrot radio and rolled to the command frequency. "Yankee Thunder, this is Dogma One, over."

"Dogma One, this is Yankee Thunder, over," came

the radio operator's voice. She sat at her station back at
Camp Balikatan, a temporary HQ set up near the town
of Isabella on the northwest side of the island.

"Yankee Thunder, be advised we have captured two
bad guys and will confirm now that the mayor of Tipo-
Tipo is dead. We'll be handing this off to the local authorities and coordinate with AFP from there. At this
time request immediate extraction, over."

"Roger that, Dogma One. Wait, over."

Rainey lifted his chin at the disembodied head of the
mayor. "Find something to drape over that, okay?"

"But you said not to—"

"His wife is out there. Just do it!"

Houston nodded and went toward an old trunk sitting
near the food crates.

"Dogma One, this is Yankee Thunder. Be advised
Delta Eagles Ten and Eleven are en route your location.
ETA ten minutes, over."

"Roger that, Yankee Thunder. Dogma One, out."

Corporal Jimmy Vance pushed his lanky frame past
the door and slipped into the hut just as Houston was
laying an old flannel shirt over the mayor's head.
"Whoa, that's not the mayor, is it?"

"Want do you want, Corporal?" Rainey asked.

Vance collected himself. "Uh, Sergeant, the police
just got here."

"Good. Our helos are en route. We'll gather up our
prisoners and our Filipino team, then wait out in the
clearing."

Vance, the team's sniper and resident bass-fishing

junkie, gave a curt nod and exited. Oh, what Rainey wouldn't give to be under thirty again, like Houston and Vance. Couple of kids, really. Young men. But hard. As they should be. As he had taught them.

"Hello? You are the American sergeant?" called a Filipino policeman from the doorway.

"Yes, I am. Sergeant Mac Rainey, United States Marines." Rainey knew better than to extend his hand for a shake. Public displays of affection were often frowned upon by the Filipinos.

The cop introduced himself, and it would have been polite for Rainey to pay attention, but he didn't. He was leaving, anyway, and he didn't care to shoot the breeze while standing next to a human head on a pole.

"Oh, they are terrible, terrible men, these Abu Sayyaf terrorists," the cop went on. "They have no regard for human life."

"Most terrorists would shoot a baby as quickly as they'd shoot a man."

"But they are not most terrorists."

"These meatheads are all the same. We'll help you get rid of them. Trust me."

"You can try."

"United States Marines don't try. We *do*."

"It doesn't matter. The war here will not be solved by you or me, because we are walking among the enemy—and we don't even know it."

Later on, as Rainey climbed aboard his Huey for the ride back to Camp Balikatan, he paused to glimpse the still-gathering crowd of locals—fathers, mothers, sons, and daughters—some of whom stared wonderingly at him, some of who seemed melancholy, as though they were eyeing a man who was already dead.

CAMP NOVA

ARMED FORCES OF THE PHILIPPINES

SOUTHERN COMMAND HEADQUARTERS

ZAMBOANGA, PHILIPPINES

2350 HOURS LOCAL TIME

Charles Callahan sat alone in the borrowed office, reading the intelligence report glowing on his notebook computer's screen. His assigned CIA's Special Operations Group (SOG), one of many working under the auspices of the Directorate of Operations, did a remarkable job of keeping him abreast of all military operations occurring in the Philippines via a broad network of operatives plugged into an even broader network of wireless communications. Callahan had been working in the region for the past year, and he thought it ironic that he had left the Green Berets after ten years of distinguished service (and the loss of one full head of hair), had been recruited by the Agency to become a covert operative, and had wound up back in uniform. To those at Camp Nova, he was Lieutenant Colonel Charles Callahan, United States Marine Corps. He headed up an assessment committee charged with coordinating the Corps' efforts in the region. His real name, Markham James

Woods, was unknown to everyone except his superiors at the Agency.

All in all, being a spy was damned good. He made over 90K per year, all expenses paid. And, being a single man of forty-two who had never married, he could kite off at a moment's notice to see the world, meet interesting people, and sometimes (most times) kill them. Admittedly, Callahan was an adrenaline junkie whose six foot, five-inch, 275-pound frame was spanned by the scars of his addiction. No one missed the jagged line running from his sideburn to his sternum. And no woman had ever missed the flowery scars from gunshot wounds that riddled his abdomen and back. His legs bore a few scars he had earned at "Camp Swampy," aka "The Farm," the Agency's Camp Peary training center in the back woods of Williamsburg, Virginia. During his yearlong instruction, Callahan had learned how to communicate in code, retrieve messages from secret locations known as "dead drops," infiltrate a hostile country, and recruit foreign agents to spy for the United States. He had also spent some time at Delta Force's secret compound at Fort Bragg, where he could tell you what he had learned, but then he would have to . . . well, you know . . .

During his five-year tenure with the Agency, Callahan had been a member of many Special Operations Groups, and his missions had run the gamut from intelligence gathering to operative rescue to assisting rebel groups friendly to the United States. No matter the mission, his objectives had always been clear and conscionable. He affected lives positively, made a difference where and when he could, and his actions had always been in the best interests of the United States of America. Perhaps that self-assessment lacked humility and, as some colleagues put it, "a real-world perspective," but Callahan truly believed in himself and the work. Sure, he had heard rumors about other operatives who had been betrayed by the Agency itself, and he knew that the CIA could be as ruthless and cunning as any of its enemies, but thus far, Callahan had not glimpsed the truly dark side.

So it was that he read the intelligence report and accompanying orders in utter disbelief because the Agency was finally sending him to that part of hell reserved for men without conscience. Deep down, Callahan knew this day would come, but five years of living in denial had been awfully good to him. Perhaps he had been an idealistic fool, thinking he could join the Agency and not have to get his hands as dirty as some of the other operatives. Of course he had been a fool; the orders on his computer screen confirmed that.

What did they want from him?

It had started a year before. His first mission in the Philippines was to gather intelligence on one Senator Nelson Allaga, a man with reputed ties to the Abu Sayyaf terrorist group. The arrangement was simple: Abu Sayyaf guerrillas would attack tourist resorts and kidnap foreign nationals. Allaga would arrange for ransoms to be paid by European governments whose money would be funneled through Libya.

Of course, Allaga would receive his kickback from the terrorists, as would General Romeo Santiago of the Philippine Marine Corps, a fat pig and whoremonger who had become famous for having his troops literally "look the other way" as Abu Sayyaf guerrillas marched hostages through the jungle. The Agency's director felt certain that these men were the tip of a corrupt iceberg within the Philippine government and military. There was a lot of money to be made by getting in bed with the terrorists, and given the country's current economic state, making new bedfellows was a little more than tempting. Now, lo and behold and after a year's worth of investigation, Allaga and Santiago were about to go down. But why now?

Callahan knew. Both men were the most vocal opponents to the United States' plan to build a permanent military base on Basilan Island. Removing them before the next congressional session would put the United States in a much stronger position to negotiate for that base. And that was the real reason why the Agency wanted Allaga and Santiago out of the picture. Yes, they were aiding and abetting terrorists—and that was bad—but politicians all over the globe were aiding and abetting terrorists. Allaga and Santiago provided maximum bang for the Agency's minimum buck.

Now flash forward to Callahan's current orders. He would first target Allaga, and once the good senator was in custody, a deal would be struck so that Allaga would give up Santiago. Callahan agreed with that much of the plan. The general kept on the move and surrounded himself with assistants and personal bodyguards. Getting a routine meeting with him had already proven to be a one-month affair. So yes, Allaga was the natural first target. But the plan itself? That was another story.

In their infinite wisdom, the Agency's "thinkers" had decided that the two-week training exercise between U.S. forces and the armed forces of the Philippines presented a perfect opportunity in which to bait Senator Nelson Allaga. Callahan was supposed to meet with the Senator and, as an act of "good will," provide Allaga with the Marine Corps' plans for training exercises on the island. Times, dates, GPS coordinates, and even the exact exercises to take place would all be handed to Allaga on a silver platter in the hopes that he would, in turn, hand over that information to Ramzi Janjali, leader of the Abu Sayyaf Group. Janjali would then ambush the group of U.S. and Filipino forces and take some hostages. The key was proving that Allaga had, in fact, tipped off Janjali. Thus far, the Agency had been unable to do that.

On the surface, the plan seemed reasonable. The repeated use of phrases like "American forces" did a fine job of turning human beings into chess pieces. But further into the document, the specifics became painfully clear. The Agency had chosen a particular team to be used as the American bait, a group of Marine Force Reconnaissance soldiers nicknamed "Force Five."

Why Americans? And why that specific team? The logic was painfully clear. Americans presented a much bigger prize and more tempting bait to the ASG and the senator. Moreover, if the agency had to pick a U.S. team to take a fall, then why not pick the best of the best?

Why not pick a team with the best chance of surviving an ambush and/or hostage situation?

Why not have Callahan further entice the senator by mentioning that some of the United States' greatest Marines were training on Basilan?

Callahan wanted to puke. He was being asked to set up United States Marines, men he could easily call his brothers in arms. He was supposed to be okay with that. He was supposed to be a professional. He was supposed to recognize that sacrificing a few Americans was for the greater good of the United States of America.

Well, he did recognize that. In fact, he would sacrifice himself for his country. Indeed, as a former Beret, he had ordered good men to their deaths.

More important, he wondered if his superiors truly understood what they were doing. If they did not, then Callahan's mission was the kind of dirty work that soiled a man's soul.

"And the negotiations begin," he said under his breath as his fingers raced across the keyboard. He opened up a synchronous encrypted chat with his superior stationed in Manila:

OMEGA EAGLE: Be advised have read and received orders. Request alternate plan to exclude friendly bait.

METRO BASE: Negative on alternate plan. Order you to depart immediately for target destination and initiate plan at times specified per your route and CFA.

OMEGA EAGLE: Request permission to advise friendly bait of
    possible enemy contact once plan has been initiated.
METRO BASE: Negative. Execute plan as described immediately
    or face disciplinary action.
876452 END SYNCHRONOUS CHAT EXECUTED BY METRO BASE.

Callahan wrenched the notebook computer from his
desktop and hurled it across the room. Naturally, the
Agency had given him a computer that could survive an
earthquake, let alone an irate operative. The thing sat
upside down in the corner, glowing defiantly, as a
knock came at the door.

02

Located on the outskirts of Isabella, the island's capital and its most popular tourist destination, Camp Balikatan was little more than a jumble of thirty bamboo huts resting in the welcome shade of mahogany and coconut trees. Roosters crowed and goats grazed along rickety fences separating swaths of jungle from the living quarters proper. The ocean breeze swept into the camp, carrying a salty tang and keeping dozens of open cook fires well stoked. An infectious sense of calm gripped the place, making you want to kick off your boots and find a hammock. But, of course, there was never any rest for weary Marines.

As Sgt. Mac Rainey made his way to Lieutenant Colonel Demarzo's hut, he sensed that calm, but he also felt entirely out of place. He was a twenty-first-century warrior striding down a path beat by loin-clothed fisherman wearing necklaces of sharks' teeth.

Two days prior, Rainey and his men had been ferried from Zamboanga City to Isabella. They had passed through a kilometer-wide channel lined on both sides by densely packed mangroves and *Samal* houses built on stilts, the tide washing in beneath those ramshackle residences. The men had heard about the Karum Purnah mosque and Muslim village and the 400-meter-high Calvario Peak with its chapel of peace. They had seen a photograph of the great waterfall known as Kumalaray Falls, and Doc, resident tour guide and the only team member who ever read the field manuals from cover to cover, hoped that once the two weeks of training were over, he would be granted some time to explore Basilan, a place that reminded him of Martinique, the island home of his ancestors. Doc had been to the Philippines once before with his first Force Reconnaissance team, but he had never been as far south as the Sulu Archipelago. The corpsman was like a frustrated tourist trapped aboard a cruise liner during two weeks of bad weather.

Sniper Vance and radio operator Houston were far less impressed with the place. They kept harping on the fact that the Isabella Public Market was selling Coca-Cola in old-fashioned glass bottles with caps that did not screw off. Houston had said that you can judge a culture based on the way its people sell and distribute their Coca-Cola. Doc had taken issue with that conclusion, and those two had bickered while Vance had struck up a strained conversation with one of the local

fishermen, an old, sun-weathered man who drove a rattling pickup truck and who was fond of the phrases "big
fish" and "many fishes." He had taken Vance's hands in
his own, had examined the calluses, and had said,
"Fisherman, yes." Vance had gone on about his dream
to fish the Bassmasters Tournament Trail back in the
U.S., but the old timer's vacant smile said he understood little, if anything, regarding Vance's aspirations.

Rainey's overall impression of Basilan was less crit-
ical than Houston's or Vance's, but clearly he had not
fallen in love with the island the way Doc had. Basilan
(which meant "iron trail") was without question a place
of incredible beauty whose people, the Yakans, were
peace-loving growers of rice, corn, coconuts, and root
crops. Still, the island's trails did possess a certain
amount of "iron"—especially when they were lorded
over by terrorists lurking in the thickets.

Reaching the end of his own trail, Rainey turned and
crossed over to the lieutenant colonel's hut. A curt nod to
one of the sentries posted outside sent the kid off to alert
the colonel. Rainey had a pretty good idea why Demarzo
had asked for the early-morning meeting before training
day #3 commenced. It wasn't a debriefing; Rainey had
already made his report to Demarzo the night before in
the command and control center. The meeting was,
Rainey hoped, in regard to his repeated requests to temporarily fill that remaining slot on his team. He wasn't
asking for a world-class operator—just someone to help
them train the Filipinos for two weeks. After that, it
would be up to Lieutenant Colonel St. Andrew of Fifth

Force Reconnaissance Company to come up with another replacement. Still, if the temporary guy worked
out, Rainey could recommend him to St. Andrew—if the
temp survived his time as the cursed fifth member . . .

The sentry returned outside. "The lieutenant colonel
is waiting for you, Sergeant."

Rainey stifled a yawn, then ducked into the hut. He
found Demarzo seated behind a folding card table serving as a crude desk. Although the lieutenant colonel had
bad skin and white hair as fine as fishing line (Vance
would love the comparison), he had a body by Mattel:
action figure all the way. Some said he spent three hours
a day working out. Some said it was four. With biceps as
thick as some men's thighs, he had a hard time finding
uniforms. Rainey appreciated the colonel's field-worthy
appearance, which was to say that even if the guy
couldn't hack it in the jungle, he looked like he could
hack it, and sometimes appearances were enough to inspire mediocre operators to do extraordinary things.

Rainey stood at attention. "Sergeant Rainey report-
ing as ordered, sir."

"At ease, Sergeant. Take a load off on one of these
comfortable folding chairs our military has provided
for us to prevent back strain and chronic hemorrhoids."

Wincing a little over the strange remark, Rainey took
a seat and blinked hard, trying not to reveal how tired
he was.

"This is your first time inside my office, isn't it?"

"Yes, it is, sir."

"Well, how do you like it?" The colonel threw up his

hands. His expression said he was fishing for a compliment, but his tone had been unmistakably sarcastic.

Rainey glanced perfunctorily around the cluttered hut piled a meter high with footlockers containing who knew what. "Seems okay, sir."

"Do you believe 'okay' is good enough for a representative of the United States Marine Corps, part of the most powerful armed forces on this Earth?"

"No, sir, I do not. Which is why yesterday I requested that a fifth member be added to my team so that we can do more than an 'okay' job of training these Filipino Marines."

"They said you were all business, Sergeant. And in the short time I've known you, I have to say they were right."

"Just here to do the best job I can, sir. And while some team leaders prefer six or even eight operators, five is my magic number."

"Well, Sergeant, we put out the word. I didn't have time to discuss the matter with you last night, but while you were flying back from Tipo-Tipo, I interviewed our candidate."

Rainey frowned. "Only one candidate, sir?"

"Actually, there are five men within the company who meet the minimum qualifications, but only one responded positively to our invitation."

Glancing away, Rainey shook his head.

"What's the matter, Sergeant? Has your ego been bruised as badly as mine has by this hut and this card table for a desk I have? I mean this isn't about roughing it. I've been to some of the most hellish places on Earth. This is about respect."

"Yes, it is, sir."

"You haven't answered my question."

"Sir, my ego hasn't been bruised. I just didn't realize there would be a problem."

"And what is the problem? Superstition?"

Rainey clutched the edge of his folding chair. "Sir?"

"You and your men took out the world's most wanted terrorist in Pakistan and escaped from North Korea when no one thought you'd ever make it back. Force Recon has never had a team harder and sharper than yours." Demarzo rose. "But maybe pushing the envelope for so long, so hard, has dulled your blade. You're not as sharp as you used to be, and maybe some of our operators are beginning to realize that."

Rainey stood. "With all due respect, sir . . . I don't think so. I don't think so at all. Sir."

"And that's the answer I wanted to hear." Demarzo winked. "Fact is, there are a bunch of superstitious pussies out there, but like I said, we found one operator who thinks he's got the mean gene. He was part of first wave this year, been on the island three months already. Come on. I'll introduce you."

Rainey followed Demarzo out of the hut, and in silence they walked past a long stretch of lean-tos and NEPA huts constructed in the months prior as provisional billets for Bravo Company. At the end of the row lay an exercise yard where three shirtless Filipino Marines were squaring off with a muscular Hispanic man wearing a white T-shirt and standard-issue trousers. He couldn't have been more than five foot five or six, and sported a shaved head though he wasn't bald. A large tattoo of a playing card—the ace of spades— was emblazoned across his right bicep, along with two lines of indistinct writing.

"Is that him, sir?"

Before the lieutenant colonel could answer Rainey, the Hispanic man launched into a Tae Kwon Do side kick. His heel struck one of the Filipinos in the shoulder and leveled him.

As the short Marine came out of the first kick, he quite amazingly flew into another, a front kick aimed at his second attacker. The ball of his foot connected with the Filipino's abdomen and sent the guy flying backward as though he had been launched from a slingshot.

Then the guy turned, appearing as though he would use a wheel kick to bring down his final opponent. But he suddenly faced his opponent, grabbed the man's shoulders, then forced himself down to spin, leap, and deliver a back kick with his heel. The third Marine was already crumpling as the American came out of the move.

"Impressive, huh, Sergeant?" Demarzo asked.

"It would be, were he fighting U.S. Marines. Did you arrange this show?"

"No, he did." Demarzo waved to the group. "Lance Corporal? Front and center."

After helping his opponents to their feet, the young Marine hustled over to Rainey and Demarzo, then faced the latter and fired off a salute. "Sir!"

"At ease. Lance Corporal Ricardo Banks, this is Sergeant Mac Rainey."

"I already know who you are." Banks thrust out his hand.

Rainey took it, tightened his grip, then dragged Banks sideways so he could read the lettering beneath the kid's ace-of-spades tattoo: WOMEN WANT ME, DEATH FEARS ME. The skin beneath and surrounding the tattoo was still pink, still a little swollen. "You just got that art, didn't you?"

"Yes, Sergeant. The night your team got here, I heard you were looking for a replacement. I knew I was going to apply. And I knew I was going to get it."

"Is that right?" Rainey asked dubiously.

"Yes, it is. So I went out and celebrated. Local guy did it. Did a good job, too. Don't you think?"

Rainey released his grip and shoved Banks, just a little. "The work's good. But the words . . . I get the impression you haven't met my old enemy, Murphy."

"Murphy? He's wasn't on your team, was he?"

"Lance Corporal, the sergeant is talking about Murphy, the author of Murphy's Law," explained Demarzo.

Banks still didn't get it.

Snorting, Rainey asked, "So this is the best we got, sir?"

"Like I said the first time you made your request. Budgets have been cut and our forces have been spread so thinly throughout the world that no one's willing to give up an operator just for this exercise. I'm confident that Lance Corporal Banks is, in fact, the best operator for the job."

"Sir, you mean he's the best of the mediocre—and the only guy who wants the job."

Banks furrowed his brow, his clean-shaven face growing rigid. "Sergeant, you give me a chance, and I will prove myself. You saw what I did back there."

"Yeah, you took down three guys who barely fought back. And even if they did, I'm betting they don't know the Chung Do Kwan style we use. I might even bet that you paid each of them to take the fall. Truth is, I don't know what to believe, but your little show proved nothing."

Banks stood there, seething.

"How old are you, Lance Corporal?"

"Twenty-one, Sergeant."

"Yeah," Rainey said through a heavy sigh. They were always in their twenties, and he was always getting older. "Lance Corporal, you have a whole lot to learn."

"And I'm hoping you will teach me, Sergeant."

"And he will," Demarzo said. "Sergeant, Lance Corporal." With that, the lieutenant colonel issued a curt nod and started back for his hut. Then he stopped, turned back. "Sergeant, we'll be having company this morning. Senator Allaga, General Santiago, and a few others. Let's make sure we put on a good show for them—one that proves our presence here is most definitely warranted."

"Yes, sir."

Rainey waited until Demarzo was out of earshot, then

he grabbed Banks by the neck. "Listen you cocky motherfucker, this is a Mickey Mouse two-week training
mission, and you just happened to become the luckiest
dick in the world, getting assigned to me. But you are
not Force Five material. One look at you tells me that."

"What is it? A height thing? A Hispanic thing? Because if you—"

Squeezing the boy into silence, Rainey said, "I'm not
sure what you're trying to say, Lance Corporal Banks. I
cannot hear you. You sound as though you are choking.
You sound as though you are not honored to be *temporarily* assigned to my team. You sound as though you
do not recognize this as an incredible opportunity to
learn from the some of the hardest men in the Marine
Corps. You sound as though you got it all coming. But
now hear this: You do not. I only want three things from
my men: their hearts, their minds, and their souls. They
can do whatever the fuck they want with the rest. Do you
hear me, Lance Corporal?" Rainey loosened his grip.

"Yes, Sergeant," the kid managed. "Hearts, minds,
and souls. Just . . . give me . . . a chance."

"Oh, you'll get plenty of rope. My men will even
teach you how to tie a noose."

Banks nodded, rubbed his neck. "You won't be dis-
appointed."

"Oh, really?"

"Yeah, because I'm always right."

"Excuse me?"

"I'm not trying to be cocky. Ask the other guys in my
old unit. When it comes to doing this, when it comes to

being a Marine, this job . . . I am always right."

"You're a fucking piece of work, aren't you?"

"No, Sergeant. I'm just telling you the truth."

Rainey balled his hands into fists, wanting to beat the conceited idiot into a pulp. "Lance Corporal? Just get the fuck out of here. Go police up your shit and transfer it to our billet. I'll be calling roll in ten minutes."

Still rubbing his neck, Banks tore off, leaving three bewildered Filipino Marines in his wake.

The team's narrow hut reeked of warm mud, and Special Amphibious Recon Corpsman Glenroy "Doc" Leblanc tried to ignore the odor as he lay on his portable cot, reading *The Philippines Country Handbook*, issued to him before deployment. Similar to the handbook he had read about North Korea, the guide contained everything you never wanted to know about a country you would barely have time to see in two weeks. Doc hoped to squeeze a few days of downtime out of the Navy to tour a few of the places mentioned. He wanted to take some pictures and ship back some souvenirs to the wife and kids in Miami. That much he could cover. His boys always loved receiving "cool stuff from weird places." And his wife had managed to decorate their home with the eclectic collection he had amassed during his years of service as a corpsman. Yes, Doc had seen the world, although, as expected, many of the places he had visited had been war zones.

Doc made a face as he came across a disturbing fact about Basilan: while 71 percent of the population were

Muslims, Christians owned 75 percent of the land, and the ethnic Chinese controlled nearly 75 percent of the trade. No wonder the Muslims were pissed off. Still, that did not give them the right to set off bombs in public squares and kidnap tourists. Doc had no problem with Muslims; in fact, he had no problem with anyone's ethnicity or religion, so long as that group did not kill others in the name of their beliefs—which was what the Abu Sayyaf Group had been doing for over a decade. Analysts now argued that the group no longer committed acts of terrorism because they wanted an Islamic state in the Philippines. They said the group's leader, Ramzi Janjali, was just a bandit now, trying to extort money when and wherever he could. Abu Sayyaf was Basilan's answer to the Boy Scouts, a gun club for underprivileged young men who had traded in their dreams for grenades, mortars, and Kalashnikovs.

Doc looked over the top of his book. Vance was still snoring, and Houston rolled onto his side so that he might continue "expelling intestinal gas through his anus," as he had once read aloud from the definition of *fart* in the dictionary. Doc was about to yell at the radioman, when someone rapped on the bamboo door.

"Yeah?" Doc called.

"Lance Corporal Ricardo Banks," came a voice from outside. "I've been ordered to report to this billet."

Could it be? Was this Lance Corporal Banks going to become Dogma Five? No way. Doc sat up, listened to the old vertebrae crack, then padded his way to the door and swung it open.

"You must be the famous Doc Leblanc," said the short guy, cocking one eyebrow and shouldering a huge duffel.

"Yeah," Doc answered. "You're not our replacement, are you?"

"Bingo." Banks shoved himself between Doc and the doorjamb. As he moved into the billet, he inadvertently—or deliberately—smacked Doc in the gut with his duffel.

Still shaken from the blow, Doc staggered behind the guy and turned back into the billet.

"The blond over here is Vance, the fisherman," Banks continued. "And the surfer dude over here is Houston." Banks's nose crinkled. "Damn. Lance Corporal Houston, is that you?"

Houston flickered open his eyes, squinted at Banks, looked to Doc, then turned to Vance. "Who's this?"

Vance, who had pushed up on his elbows, yawned deeply. "New Guy. Dogma Five."

Houston smiled broadly at Banks. "Dude, you are fucked."

The lance corporal dropped his duffel on Rainey's cot—a definite no-no—then folded his arms over his chest, pecs tenting up his tank top. "If you gentlemen are talking about the curse, then you haven't read this." Banks turned, flexed his bicep, and showed off his tattoo. "Women want me, Death fears me. I'll say that again. Death *fears* me."

Vance rolled his eyes, fell back onto his cot. Doc made a face.

Undaunted, Banks went on. "Those other clowns you've worked with? They couldn't beat the curse because they never got in death's face the way I do. You don't beat death by playing it safe. You get right in the game, and you play hard, and you let death know that you are not someone to be fucked with. Do you read me?"

Houston sat up, burst out laughing. "Holy shit, dude. Are you for real?"

Banks widened his eyes like a voodoo priest. "I am the realest motherfucker you'll ever work with."

"Whoa, whoa, whoa. Hold on there," Doc said, raising his palms. "Lance Corporal Banks, I don't know what planet you're from, but there can't be a Marine Corps base there."

"That's right," Houston added. "Because you got no manners and no respect. No one walks in here and talks to people like us like that." The radio operator threw off his blanket.

"I'm not trying to insult anyone," Banks said, plopping down on Rainey's bunk. "Rumor has it that you guys are turning into the best of the has-beens. I figured that while I'm here, I'll raise the bar."

Vance draped an arm over his forehead. "Do we really have to work with this guy? Because if we do, then tell the sarge I've gone fishing."

"Don't worry. This guy won't last more than a day," assured Houston.

Banks gave a faint snort. "What's your problem, Houston? Little competition got you worried? Never had anyone really push you?"

Houston rose from the cot, crossed to Banks, leaned over the little guy. "Listen, buddy. Don't walk in here with your threats. Because you have no idea, man. You don't. And don't try to discredit the good men who served as Dogma Five. You didn't know them. They were both great operators."

"Bruno was a great operator?" Vance asked in disbelief, referring to Sergeant Anthony Bruno, a man who had tried to break Rainey's spirit during their mission to North Korea. Bruno had died during the HALO jump into the country, but Doc knew the man's ghost still haunted their team leader.

"Come on, Vance, I'm trying to make a point here," Houston spat. He regarded Banks. "The point is, you do not walk in here like you're the man who's going save our team. We don't need saving, and we don't need you."

Banks smirked. "Could have fooled me. I'm wondering why they sent you here instead of somewhere hotter."

"What are you talking about?" Houston asked incredulously. "This place is hotter than shit. Bro, you got some pair, walking in here like this. You will not survive."

"All right, Houston. Back off," Doc said.

The radio operator glowered a second more, then returned to his cot.

"So Banks, I take it you've been temporarily assigned to our team for two weeks, am I right?" Vance asked.

"That's correct. But when this is over, I'm positive

that Sergeant Rainey will recommend my permanent transfer to Lieutenant Colonel St. Andrew."

"Dude, you're talking some serious shit," Houston said. "And you'd better be ready to back it up."

"He can't. He's blowing smoke," said Vance.

"And guys like you, Banks, are a dime a dozen," Doc added. "All barrel-chested until the bullets start flying. Then you're shitting your pants, crawling into the nearest foxhole, and covering yourself with your buddy's corpse to hide from the enemy."

"Yeah, and another thing, Lance Corporal," Houston said. "We're Force Recon. We're the eyes and ears of our commander. Not his asshole!" Houston grinned at Vance, and they broke into laughter.

"Make fun all you want. Doubt me all you want. But none of you guys have been out there in the jungle, fighting against Abu Sayyaf. Do you know about the Tausug tribe?"

"Who?" Houston asked.

"Thought so."

"I know who they are," Doc said. "And I know why Janjali and his men recruit from that tribe. They're supposed to be the fiercest warriors in this part of the Philippines."

"They are."

"And you ought to know, right?" Houston said. "Now he's a fucking intelligence expert."

Banks leaned forward on the cot and steeled his voice. "Listen up. First month I'm here, we're out on patrol. Six on my team, and we're backing up two squads from the 1st Scout Rangers. We get ambushed, and you know what those fucking Filipino Rangers do? They run. So we hunker down until the crossfire stops. Every guy on my team's taken a hit. We gotta get back. But I'm not into falling back. I'm into payback. So I take off after these guys. I know they're Tausug, not only because they wear black bandannas—anybody can put one of them on—but because of the way they know the trails. It's like they can travel through the jungle with their eyes closed. But I'm *on* one, getting close. I shoot one bastard in the back, take out two more as they're running. Throw my K-bar at a third, catch him in the shoulder. But the last guy climbed a fucking palm tree. Believe that? He comes flying down on me like a fucking ape or something. And he's got a knife. He's going to punch it into my chest. I get two hands on his wrist and flip him around, but he won't let go of the knife. So I force him to stab himself. Do it three times. Then I throw him on the ground. And I'm just standing there, catching my breath, when this fucker gets back up and takes a swipe at me. I mean he's just been stabbed three times and is bleeding all over the place. He's fucking dying. But he doesn't care. Death fears him. And I don't get out of the way in time." Banks lifted his tank top, exposing a long, pink scar running straight down from his right nipple to his navel.

"Cut yourself shaving?" Houston asked, then he winked at Vance.

"Bullshit. This here? This is Tausug tribe. And they are Abu Sayyaf, not the fucking pussy Arabs you guys are used to fighting. These guys have spent their whole lives in the jungle. They know how to move quietly, how to spot tracks on the mountains. They know how to *smell* danger."

Something in Banks's tone struck Doc as honest. Cocky beyond belief, conceited beyond measure, and suffering from a severe case of diarrhea of the mouth made Banks lose nearly all credibility, but that tone, that convincing tone was just too hard to ignore. "You said that happened the first month. How long you been here?"

Banks lowered his shirt. "Nearly three months."

"Hey, Doc?" Houston called. "You believe this guy?"

Doc shrugged. "I'm just curious."

"What? About his scar?" Vance asked. "If he didn't cut himself shaving, then he got caught up in some thorns." The sniper narrowed his gaze on Banks. "Isn't that right, Lance Corporal?"

"You think a thorn did this?"

"I think you sound like old Chesty Puller on steroids."

"You'll all become believers once we're out there and you realize that everything I've been telling you is true. And then you'll realize, after you listen to me for a while, that I am always right."

Vance and Houston hooted and guffawed as Doc said, "Lance Corporal, I don't believe I've ever met a Marine like you, so lacking in humility. It's usually the loudest guys who die first. And all of this talk has really got me worried about you. It's going to be a very long two weeks."

"What did you guys expect? That I'd come in here and kiss your asses and worship you like gods? You're just Marines. Same as me. Maybe a little more worn out than me."

The door swung open, banged on the wall. In walked Rainey. His gaze found and locked onto Lance Corporal Banks. "Get yourself and your contaminated crap off my rack, Lance Corporal."

Banks grabbed his duffel. "I thought this one was mine."

"It is not."

"Then where's my cot, Sergeant?"

Rainey pointed to an empty spot on the dirt floor. "Right over there, between that pile of fire ants and that worm." The sergeant glanced at Doc, Vance, and Houston. "All right, gentlemen, we got company coming today. Colonel wants a good show. I'm going over to brief the Filipino teams. You're on the ready line by the time I get back with them."

"Aye-aye, Sergeant!" cried Vance, Doc, and Houston in unison.

Banks shook his head as Rainey trudged out. "He's way too old-school."

"There's only one school here," Doc said. "*His* school."

"Yeah, I get that. Completely." Banks opened his duffel, slid out a footlocker, then began digging through his clothes.

"Where are you from, Banks?" Doc asked while sliding into his own shirt.

"I was born in Puerto Rico but raised on Long Island, place called Lake Ronkonkoma in Suffolk County. Ever heard of it?"

"Can't say that I have."

Banks glanced over at Vance and Houston, who were whispering to each other as they dressed, then he said softly, "Doc, you believe me, don't you?"

"Thought you didn't care."

"You know what? You're right. I don't." The lance corporal turned his back on Doc, then began dressing in a fury. He reached into one of his breast pockets and withdrew a small note, muttering, "What the hell is this?" He quickly scanned the paper, then looked up at Doc. "One of you playing a joke?"

"Let me see that." Doc took the note and read it twice:

ASG has your training schedule and mission GPS coordinates. Be prepared for an ambush. Time and day unknown.

"What do you think, Doc?"

"I think we don't joke about stuff like this. Why don't you show this to the Sarge. See what he has to say."

Banks took the note, read it once again, his cocky expression turning to one of deep concern.

03

The metal folding chair squeaked as CIA operative Markham Woods, aka Lt. Col. Charles Callahan, stood before Lieutenant Colonel Demarzo's desk, holding a brown six-pocket folder containing all of the information he needed regarding Bravo Company's training schedule for the next two weeks. Demarzo had just turned over the information and he seemed a little antsy, so Callahan cut short their conversation. "Well, then, I guess it's time we go outside and wait for Senator Allaga and General Santiago to make their entrance."

"Yes, we should, Colonel. But before that, I'd like to discuss one more thing. I understand that your assessment team will be making recommendations to the Corps regarding every aspect of this mission, including equipment and supplies, numbers of troops, and the kinds of humanitarian and military operations we're conducting here."

"That's correct. All aspects of Balikatan will be included in our report. I'll also serve as a diplomatic liaison between the Philippine congress and the AFP. In fact, I plan on meeting briefly with the senator following this tour."

"Very good. But I'm wondering if I might make a small request."

Callahan smiled knowingly. "By all means, make your request. Whether I can honor it is, as we both know, another story."

Demarzo sighed deeply, stood, and seized the edges of his card-table desk, his knuckles growing white. "It seems my previous requests for adequate office furniture have somehow been ignored."

"I understand, Colonel."

"Look, I understand that I'm only here for two weeks, and I'm not complaining about the digs. It's more a matter of—"

"Say no more, Colonel. I'll have what you need delivered here by tomorrow morning. Just provide me with a detailed list of items. I can't guarantee they'll be standard issue, but I'm sure they will suffice."

Drawing his head back in surprise, Demarzo released his grip on the card table and proffered his hand. "Outstanding, Colonel. And to be honest, I wasn't aware you wielded that kind of power. I was just asking for the hell of it."

"Oh, it's petty power, Colonel. I've been in this part

of the world for a while now, and I've found a few more creative ways to navigate around the system and rely upon, shall we say, local sources."

What Demarzo did not know was that Callahan would use his Agency contacts to get that office furniture, sans the aforementioned delays and mountain of paperwork that would accompany such a request made through the Corps' chain of command. Callahan had heard about Demarzo's quirky nature, and now he would use that to turn Demarzo into an ally, even though Callahan was about to screw over some of the lieutenant colonel's own men.

Yes, Callahan had decided to go through with it.

Sort of.

He had spent the better part of the night imagining what form the CIA's "disciplinary action" would take, and he had repeatedly arrived at the same conclusion: If he didn't follow orders, they would do much more than simply remove him from the mission. He already knew too much. He was a security risk, a liability. He would meet his doom "accidentally" and abruptly. So he was going to send good men into an ambush.

But not without tipping them off. Upon arriving at Balikatan in the middle of the night, Callahan had planned to have a brief, unsigned note slipped into Sgt. Mac Rainey's uniform pocket, but Callahan's contact had been unable to get past the overzealous security team posted outside Bravo Company's billets.

However, that contact had informed Callahan that a new operator was being assigned to Team Dogma, a

Lance Cpl. Ricardo Banks. As fate would have it, Banks had yet to pick up his new utilities from a large cargo container serving as the supply office. The guards there were easily bribed, as was the supply officer, and Callahan's contact had been able to slip a note into the breast pocket of Banks's new shirt. The tip might give those men a fighting chance. It did make Callahan feel somewhat better about the mission, though the possibility that Team Dogma would ignore the warning still tugged heavily on his conscience. An anonymous tip did lack credibility, but it was the best Callahan could do.

"Lieutenant Colonel?" called one of Demarzo's men outside. "Senator Allaga and General Santiago have just arrived, sir."

"Very well. We're coming."

Callahan slipped the intelligence folder under his arm and left the hut, squinting against Basilan's pervasive morning sun. He and Demarzo shifted to the edge of a dirt road, where an old, black Grand Marquis idled noisily.

Senator Nelson Allaga, a short, bony man with thin, gray hair that might've been slicked back with motor oil instead of sweat, wiped his forehead with a handkerchief as he levered himself from the car. General Santiago emerged behind the senator, wearing his olive-drab uniform, his sagging breast covered in medals he hardly deserved, his thick moustache crying out to be trimmed. He puffed air and turned on a scrutinizing gaze, giving Callahan and Demarzo the once-over.

Ignoring the inspection, Demarzo approached their

guests. "Senator Allaga, I'm Lieutenant Colonel Demarzo, Bravo Company Commander. And this is Lieutenant Colonel Callahan, who is heading up the Corps' assessment committee for this year's Operation Balikatan."

In surprisingly good English, Allaga answered, "We can skip the pleasantries, Colonel. I want you to know from the start that it is my contention and the contention of many of my colleagues—including our defense secretary—that allowing U.S. troops to take part in combat violates the sovereignty and the constitution of the Philippines."

"Senator, we have no intention of allowing U.S. troops to serve in combat roles."

"That is what you say, but my office has received numerous reports indicating that the Visiting Forces Agreement is being violated. But whatever the case, we are entirely against this operation and your presence here."

"Perhaps we can change your minds."

"Of course, you may try. I will take your tour. But I am here as a critic."

"Very well, Senator. I appreciate your candor. And I'm certain that if you speak to some of your Marines— and ours—you'll find that these exercises are beneficial for all of us."

"And Senator, after the tour, I'd like a few moments of your time to give you a detailed briefing that will answer many of your questions and address many of your criticisms," said Callahan.

"I doubt that, but I will grant you thirty minutes of my time. No more."

"Thank you, Senator."

"General Santiago, I know that you have also been opposed to this operation," said Demarzo. "Perhaps this year we can address all of your concerns and allow you to become more familiar with our program."

Santiago cleared his throat, and when he spoke, his voice boomed and his accent had a hint of Arab ancestry, though Callahan knew that the man had been born and raised in the Philippines. Was the company he had been keeping rubbing off? "Colonel, your men come here to train us to fight with sleek guns and powerful stun grenades. You come with your night-flying helicopters, your night-vision scopes, and your bulletproof vests. You fly your spy planes day and night, but they cannot see through the trees and the rain. You bring your computers to the jungle because you believe this the way of the future. And you criticize my men because they carry weapons that were used in World War Two. But let me tell you something. My men do not need your computers or your night-vision scopes. They know this enemy. And they know the jungle. All they need is time, but your government is far too impatient to wait."

"With all due respect, General, it is not a matter of impatience."

"Then what is it? Your government's desire to have control over the Philippines?"

"Of course not. The Abu Sayyaf Group has confirmed ties to the Warriors of Mohammed, who are still

active—even after al-Zumar's death. The ASG is a
threat to the United States and to the Philippines. We're
here to create U.S.-trained counterterrorism units that
combine the best of both worlds: technology *and* those
natural instincts acquired through jungle warfare.
These units will help put an end to the ASG and literally
create a safer world."

Santiago smiled smugly, and Callahan wanted to
punch the man. In the heart. With a knife.

Over the years, Callahan had confronted and put
down at least a half dozen men who, like Santiago,
wore the same guise of loyalty and independence as
they turned their own men into unwitting participants in
corruption. General Romeo Santiago was a typical ser-
pent who smiled before he bit you.

"Colonel, your government has been telling us all
year that we are going to save not only Basilan but the
entire world. That is not true. While the ASG receives
outside assistance, there is no hard evidence that they
are linked to the Warriors of Mohammed. Really, Colonel, they are no more than a group of bandits, and the
Philippine Armed Forces could deal with them accord-
ingly. But enough of this. We could debate all day. Both
of our governments want this tour to happen, and we
will not disappoint." Santiago gestured toward the jungle trail.

Biting his lip, Demarzo nodded and led the group
forward. Two of Santiago's heavily armed bodyguards
kept close to the general, while Allaga's aide, a slight
Filipino woman who seemed consumed by the tiny,

glowing screen of her PDA, kept glued to his side and spoke quickly.

"Maybe we should make them buy breakfast," Callahan quipped softly.

Demarzo nodded. "In all honesty, Colonel, it's ridiculous for them to resent us—especially when we're doing so much."

"I agree."

"Consider all the humanitarian aid we're giving them in addition to reinforcing their military capabilities. You'd think a little gratitude would be in order."

"I do, Colonel. I do." Callahan lowered his voice. "I guess the general and the senator are not big fans of baseball and apple pie."

Demarzo sniggered. "Give me a baseball bat and a crate full of apples, and I'll turn them into believers . . ."

TEAM DOGMA

CAMP BALIKATAN

TOWN OF ISABELLA

BASILAN ISLAND, SOUTHERN PHILIPPINES

0930 HOURS LOCAL TIME

Sergeant Mac Rainey watched the Filipino Marines fire three-round bursts with the M16A2 rifles they had just been issued. The ten Filipinos lay in a broad row on their bellies, squinting through their weapons' attached scopes and sighting the paper targets that Vance, Houston, and Doc had pinned to the rows of palm trees across the field. A few of those dusky-skinned men with black hair and broad, often dopey smiles actually hit their marks. Rainey had not expected much from the mostly eighteen- and nineteen-year-old grunts, especially since they had never handled the M16 before, but they needed to get familiar with the rifles soon. Very soon. Like before his team went out with them on a "training patrol" (read actual, unofficial mission to hunt down Abu Sayyaf members. Shhh. Don't tell the Philippine government).

Unsurprisingly, the Filipino Marines were quite enamored with the M16, a weapon far superior to some of the antiques they had been using, and that excitement might inspire them to train harder. Rainey, on the other hand, preferred his trusty M4A1 carbine with its lighter weight (7.5 pounds compared to the M16's nearly 9 pounds), its ACOG Day Optical Sight or Mini Night Vision Sight, and its collapsible stock. The M4 was the preferred weapon of many Force Recon warriors like Rainey and Houston, though snipers like Vance packed the M40A3 Sniper Rifle with its McMillan A4 stock, and corpsmen like Doc generally carried the 15-pound M249 Squad Automatic Weapon, also known as the Para SAW, your basic bad-ass machine gun used for suppressing enemy fire and covering the movement of friendly forces.

For the moment, Doc, Houston, and Vance had shouldered or set down their weapons as they crouched down behind their students. During those occasional lapses in the booming, they gave pointers, helped adjust scopes, and corrected form.

Lance Corporal Banks, his carbine also shouldered,

his temper flaring, stood beside Rainey. After Demarzo and the company had come and gone, Rainey would allow Banks to join the Filipinos on the range to prove his marksmanship. Until then, the impetuous kid—and Rainey did mean *kid*—would stand there and do nothing, much to the lance corporal's chagrin.

During the walk over to the firing range, Banks had been chewing off Rainey's ear regarding the note he'd received, a warning about an ambush. Rainey had finally taken the note, read it, crumpled it up, and thrown it away. No doubt a guy with an attitude like Banks's made a lot of enemies, and no doubt some of his ex-teammates were having a little fun with the asshole. Yet Banks had taken the note quite seriously, which proved how naïve he still was. As a result, the Marine who was always right remained on the wrong side of Rainey.

"Sergeant, please. At least let me get on the line."

"Negative."

"I know you want to test me."

"Yeah, I do. Maybe this is the test."

"Come on, Sarge. Let me have my chance now."

Rainey put a finger to his lips and silenced the Marine with his gaze.

The thundering fire continued, and at times the pops and cracks grew so damned loud that Rainey suspected the rebels far off in the jungle were listening to it as well. Good. Maybe it would give them pause or at least a chill. Before the shooting commenced, some of the Filipinos had requested protective earphones or plugs. "Train as you fight," Rainey had told them. "Will you be wearing earplugs in the jungle?" The men did not like the answer, but they understood the importance of simulating a real combat environment.

One of the Filipinos, Sergeant Golez, a stout man of about thirty and Team Firelight's leader, rose from the line and came over to Rainey. "Sergeant, the rifles are very good. But we have been firing for a while now. Our hands are growing numb, and our ears are hurting."

"We'll take a break soon. That company I mentioned still hasn't arrived."

Golez pointed over Rainey's shoulder. "Is that them?"

A small group that included Lieutenant Colonel Demarzo, another lieutenant colonel Rainey did not know, and the civilian guests was headed toward the perimeter wire that fenced off the firing range. "Showtime," Rainey said under his breath, then quickly faced Golez. "Sergeant, if you and Sergeant Padua would order your men to hold their fire and get back on the line, I'll have a word with the company, then I'll give the order to commence firing."

"We are politicians now, instead of soldiers," Golez said with a nod. "And we are both not happy about that."

"Some soldiers have made great politicians."

"But you and I will not."

Rainey winked. "Not in this lifetime."

As Golez hustled off, Banks asked, "What do you want me to do, Sergeant?"

"Just go down to the line and stay out of trouble," Rainey answered quickly, then he headed toward the visitors.

"Aye-aye, Sergeant."

All right, you've played this game before. Don't say anything that will get you in trouble. Just keep your big trap shut. Okay. What do we got? Looks like some government type and his little assistant. Then we got the general and his two babysitter bodyguards. No problem.

"Sergeant Mac Rainey? This is Senator Nelson Allaga and General Romeo Santiago," Demarzo said as Rainey reached the fence line and came around the gate.

Rainey faked a smile and even accepted Allaga's handshake, an unexpected surprise. Santiago offered only a terse tip of the head, his babysitters wearing looks about as sour as his.

"And this is Lieutenant Colonel Callahan of the Corps' Balikatan assessment committee," Demarzo continued. "I'll be issuing all of our requests for personnel and equipment to him."

Callahan's vigorous handshake left Rainey wearing a frown. "Lieutenant Colonel," Rainey acknowledged.

"It's an honor, Sergeant. You have an outstanding team out there. It's good to know these Filipino Marines are being trained by the very best the Corps has to offer."

"There are some very hard men out there. First-class operators."

"Yes, they are, Sergeant." Callahan regarded the group. " 'Force Five Recon,' as they are called, is one of the most accomplished teams in all of the Marine Corps. They're routinely loaned out to other units, thus their missions have taken them around the globe."

Callahan kept staring at Rainey, his eyes a little glossy before he finally looked away.

"Thanks for the vote of confidence, sir. I know my team will work very well with these Filipino Marines. We already have a lot in common, namely a common enemy."

Demarzo stepped around the group and paused at Rainey's side. "Sergeant, if you would, go ahead and explain to the senator and the general what's happening today."

Song-and-dance time. Rainey cleared his voice and adopted a tour guide's tone. "Well, admittedly there has been some culture shock for both of our groups. I've heard some of the Filipino Marines talk about all the ammunition and even the bottled water we've brought along. They're pretty much blown away by our equipment and all of the preparation we do."

"But ammunition and bottled water do not win wars," the general quickly cut in.

"No, sir, they do not. But they do help. Ask any man who fought in Iraq. Anyway, during our two weeks here, we won't need to ration supplies—including water and ammo. With that in mind, those men out there have begun a two-hour-long firing exercise meant to familiarize them with their new M16A2 rifles. We'll fire as many rounds as necessary. And we'll work until every man is comfortable with his weapon. Later on, we'll do some scouting, and then at about dusk we'll launch a simulated attack on a rebel stronghold. The

Filipino Marines will teach us their jungle maneuvering tactics, and we'll teach them how to quickly clear rooms. It's going to be a very busy day for these men."

"Sergeant, I'm wondering if you can, from personal experience, address the rumors we've heard about U.S. Marines engaging in combat against Abu Sayyaf guerillas," the senator said.

"Sir, I am unaware of any such rumors. My orders are to train and assist the two Filipino teams over there, sir."

"We heard last night that an American team was dropped by helicopter into Tipo-Tipo," said General Santiago. "We have confirmed reports."

Rainey looked to Demarzo. No way was he taking on that one.

"General Santiago, first let me assure you that—"

"Let the sergeant answer the question," Allaga said, snapping at Demarzo.

"The sergeant will tell you the same thing, that—"

Full automatic gunfire rattled from the training field. A lone Marine stood among the grunts on their bellies. Elbows up, head tucked in, he fired at a single target tacked onto a palm tree.

"Is that Lance Corporal Banks?" Demarzo asked.

"I think so," Rainey said, his cheeks flushing. "Please excuse me." He took off running down the field as Banks lowered his rifle and a crowd of men charged up from their positions, heading for the target.

By the time Rainey reached the group, all ten Filipinos, as well as Doc, Houston, and Vance had gathered around the tree, while Banks pointed to the perfect score he had achieved. "It's all about accounting for the variables. The wind velocity and direction. The recoil. The stiffness of the trigger."

"I have never seen anyone shoot as well as you," Golez said, slapping a palm on Banks's shoulder.

"Lance Corporal Banks! What the hell are you doing?" Rainey cried, pushing his way through the group to get squarely in the kid's eyes.

"These guys looked so tired, Sergeant. Thought they needed a little morale booster." Banks wiggled his brows, raised his head toward the target—

Which Rainey ripped from the tree and tore up. "Okay, Marines. Show's over. Doc? Vance? Houston? None of you guys thought of stopping this idiot?"

Vance looked to his boots. Houston gave a silly shrug. Doc gave a wounded look, then said, "He was already firing by the time I saw him."

Rainey mimicked the corpsman, mouthing the man's lame excuse before he boomed, "Everyone back on the line. Everyone except you, Lance Corporal Banks." Rainey reached out, about to grab Banks's ear, but the entire group of visitors was heading down onto the range, an area restricted to only military personnel. It seemed that Demarzo had no problem with bending the rules for his VIPs; too bad his timing could not be any worse.

"Banks, just get back on the line."

"I will, Sergeant. But do you see that Lieutenant Colonel coming over here? Name's Callahan, heads up some assessment committee."

"No shit. I just met him."

"Yeah, well he's been here on and off for the past three months, poking around, asking questions, writing shit down."

"Why is that your business?"

"It's not. But I was talking to a few guys who met him, and they said they were discussing their training phase, and it was like he didn't know what they were talking about."

"Maybe your buddies didn't know what *they* were talking about."

"No way. I don't know . . . There's just something about that guy I don't like."

"Gee, thanks for sharing that, Lance Corporal," Rainey said, gritting his teeth. "Now get back on the fucking line."

"Sergeant, is there a problem?" Demarzo called, leading the group onto the field.

"No problem, sir. Lance Corporal Banks thought we were finished and was giving a firing demonstration. Sorry for the distraction."

"I'd like to talk with some of these Marines." Senator Allaga broke away from the group and walked toward the line.

"And I'd like to ask you something," General Santiago said to Rainey. "I know you, like Lieutenant Colonel Demarzo here, believe that it is your force that has more to share with our Marines."

Rainey's stomach churned—and not because he was hungry. "General, sir, that depends on the situation. I would think that your troops are far more familiar fighting in jungle terrain, and we have a lot to learn from them."

"You are right. The Philippine Marine Corps is acknowledged to be one of the best anti-guerrilla fighting forces in the world, and most of our fighting is done in the dense jungle."

"We've spent a lot of time training for urban combat, so this is a real break for us. I want my men to feel confident fighting anywhere, any time. Your men can help them accomplish that goal."

"And you will give us your new rifles and fancy Nintendo toys to combat the terrorists."

"Sir, I'm not a huge fan of technology myself. A piece of equipment is only as good as its operator. But there is some hardware that could give your men an edge. And sometimes just the thought of having the technology on your side gives you the confidence to fight harder and meaner. I think we'd both agree that the hardest Marines win battles."

"Sergeant, I don't want you or your men here. We don't need you. But you are quite eloquent for a fighting man. And I can see why your men and your commandant respect you."

From the corner of his eye, Rainey spotted Lance Corporal Banks engaged in a heated conversation with Senator Allaga as Doc, Vance, and Houston gathered behind their temporary teammate. Was it ever going to end?

"General, if you wouldn't mind?" Rainey did not wait for a reply. He sprinted down the field, leaving Santiago and a wide-eyed Demarzo behind. Callahan was already headed toward the group, and Rainey passed him en route.

"Like I said, Senator, I think it's really cool that you've dragged your butt down here to see what's happening. You're not just sitting in some office somewhere and complaining about everything. But I don't think you're being fair. We came here to help, and I can tell you just want to kick us out."

"Banks," Doc warned. "Not another word."

"Let him talk," the senator urged. "I'm here to get a sense of what the average U.S. Marine thinks of this operation. And by the way, the decision to kick you out is hardly mine."

"But you want us out," Banks said. "I can tell."

"And I can tell from you, Marine, that arrogance is alive and well in the United States."

Banks's eyes widened. "Whoa, I was just trying to make a point."

"Senator, I'm sorry if this Marine acted out of line. He's certainly not on the line, as ordered." Rainey looked darkness and death in Banks's direction.

"No, Sergeant. Do not apologize. I wanted to speak to him in particular."

"Of course you did." Rainey swung away and rubbed his temples.

"They don't pay you Force Recon guys enough for this," Callahan told Rainey as he headed for the senator. "All right then, Senator, we'd best let these men continue with their exercise. If you'll come with us now? We're heading over to the new hospital we're building."

Callahan placed himself between the senator and Lance Corporal Banks, who shrank away as Doc shouldered up to Rainey. "What are we going to do with that boy?"

Rainey took a deep breath, exhaled slowly. "Kill him before he causes an international incident?"

"What about that note?"

"It's bogus."

"What if it's not?"

"It doesn't matter, Doc. When we go out there, we're always ready."

"It's not us I'm worried about. It's those Filipinos. And Banks. I think we should take that note seriously."

"Okay, but the note means nothing, because it contained no specifics. The terrorists have been tipped off. No surprise there. Of course they know we're around. It's not like we've been very quiet here, right? Every time we set foot in that jungle, we should expect an ambush. Am I right?"

"Speaking of right, did Banks tell you how *he's* always right?"

"What's he overcompensating for? His height? His age?"

"I don't know. But what if he is always right?"

"Are you serious?"

Doc nodded gravely, held the look, then cracked a grin.

Rainey smirked, braced himself, then approached the group of visitors the way a condemned man approaches a guillotine.

Death by politics. What a way to go.

04

Ramzi Janjali emitted a faint cry as he reached orgasm and fell back nearly lifeless on the creaky bed.

The woman he had nicknamed "Garden" wiped off her mouth with a rag, got to her feet, then slid an errant strand of black hair over her ear. "Can I go now?" she asked, her voice deep and smoky.

Janjali looked at her, admiring her defiance as much as her beauty. She was an angelic schoolteacher who had been at the wrong place at the wrong time, now with him for almost a year. Her family had presumed her dead, and her old life had gone on without her. But Janjali could still not quiet her rebellious spirit or get her to fully surrender to him.

"Did you enjoy it?" he asked.

"There is no right answer to your question, Ramzi. If I

say I did, you will call me a whore. If I say I did not, you will make me do it again. Please, do as I ask. Just kill me."

"You are too pretty to kill, my Garden. Much too pretty." He dismissed her with the wave of his hand. She passed from the hut's cool shade into a harsh glare that melted her away.

I am not the young man I once was, Janjali thought as he zipped up his olive drab trousers. *I am almost forty. It is getting more difficult now. I've heard there is a drug that can help me. The tourists spoke of it once. What is the name? Niagara?*

Janjali pillowed his head in his hands and closed his eyes. No, he was not a young man anymore. Long gone were the days of studying in Saudi Arabia and Libya. Long gone were the days of going to discothèques and raping women in the bathrooms. He had been incredibly naïve back then. He had believed that he could return to the Philippines and fulfill the Muslim ideal of creating an Islamic state. He had believed that he could achieve that goal within a year's time. But over a decade had passed since then. And despite all of the bombings, the kidnappings, the shootings, and the beheadings, there was still no Islamic state.

More recently, one of their mentors, Mohammed al-Zumar, had taken his own life in Pakistan to avoid being captured. Al-Zumar's death was a tremendous blow to Janjali, who had been personally trained by the sheikh in Afghanistan and Pakistan. Since then, Janjali's determination to fight for an Islamic state had waned, and he had grown increasingly frustrated and bitter. *Abu Sayyaf* meant "Bearer of the Sword," but Janjali no longer wanted to fight. He had not even bothered to participate in last night's raid in Tipo-Tipo, and he almost always led his men into combat, in spite of the risks, because he had always thought of himself as a solider. Yes, he was growing older. Thoughts of securing his financial future seemed far more important now.

Just a year prior, a successful kidnapping and ransom gambit involving a group of European tourists had rewarded him and his men with nearly five million dollars. Janjali had used about two million dollars to procure arms (including rocket launchers and mortars); to purchase two speedboats, each equipped with five 250-horsepower Volvo engines; and to recruit members of the Tausug tribe.

Another million dollars had been divided between Senator Nelson Allaga and General Romeo Santiago, who had arranged for the ransom payment and for the release of the hostages—while still allowing Janjali's men to escape. Both Allaga and Santiago were underpaid, weak-willed men who were fattening their retirement funds thanks to Janjali's acts of murder and mayhem. Men in their positions were far too predictable, but useful nonetheless.

Finally, and most important, Janjali had taken the remaining two million dollars and invested it in American real estate. He owned waterfront property in Orlando, Florida, and two townhomes in Sedona, Arizona. Even his own brother, Hamsiraji, who had been fighting alongside Janjali since they had founded the group, was unaware of the investment. One more big ransom check would give Janjali the money he needed to abandon the foolish ideals of his youth and secretly retire in the land of the infidels. He saw himself lying by his pool, having a drink as his twenty-one-year-old girlfriend rubbed suntan lotion on his shoulders. He would live like a retired pop star without a care in the world.

"Ramzi, are you asleep? Wake up! Wake up!"

Janjali opened one eye and stared at his brother's rough melon of a face, scarred by acne and framed by a spotty beard turning gray. "Go away." He shut the eye, rolled over.

"Wake up, you fool!"

"You're the fool. I am already awake."

"Then roll over and open your eyes."

"Tell me what you want—or get out!"

"My man Charti found a new cave on the south side of the mountain. Inside he found Japanese markings on the walls. I think we are getting very close to finding it!"

"You are wasting your time."

"No, this is the closest we have come so far!"

For the past few years Hamsiraji had been obsessed with the buried Yamashita treasures. According to legend, General Tomoyuki Yamashita, known as the "Tiger of Malaya," stashed on Basilan literally tons of gold and other treasures the Japanese Imperial Army looted from countries in Southeast Asia during WWII. If Hamsiraji's obsession were not trouble enough, the idiot had recently spoken to a local journalist: "I know why the American military comes to Basilan with their tractors and bulldozers. They want to steal the gold from us. But they will get trouble if they come into the jungle."

The U.S. military was not on Basilan to steal Hamsiraji's precious gold, but in his warped mind it was all about that, and he repeatedly diverted many of their men away from their guard duties to search for the mythical treasure.

"How many this time?" Janjali demanded, propping himself on his elbows.

"Only twelve. Maybe fifteen."

"Fifteen? The Americans are here! You lost two men last night in Tipo-Tipo!"

"They will be questioned, but they will not betray us."

"Their capture is your fault."

Hamsiraji shook his head. "It is the mayor's fault. He should have paid the money as we asked. Then he would still be alive, and our men would not have gone to Tipo-Tipo."

"Brother, you weaken our defenses to chase gold. If there was any treasure here, it has long since been stolen."

"No, it hasn't. It's here. *We* can find it. And once we have it, we can build and finance a huge army. We can take over the entire island! Basilan will be our Islamic state!"

Janjali smiled bitterly. Hamsiraji in charge of a huge army? What a thought. His own men would kill him, and that might be a fitting destiny for the simple-minded buffoon. "You will not take another man to search for gold. Do you hear me, brother?"

"Have you heard me? They found a new cave! We're getting closer."

"I do not care."

"You must." Hamsiraji hunkered down next to the bed and seized Janjali's shoulders. "I love you, brother. But you are not the fighter you once were."

"That's right. I am twice the fighter."

"No, there is no more fire in your eyes. You stay here most of the day, eating, being with your woman. You do not train the men anymore."

"You can train them. The days have just grown very long now. Very long."

"What's wrong?"

Janjali hesitated, then suddenly answered, "Nothing. Now listen to me. We will speak with the mayor of Sabong. He will be more reasonable. We will get some money from him to buy more ammunition. And then we will plan another kidnapping. A big one. With many tourists."

Hamsiraji sprang upright and waved a fist. "Ah, yes. There is the fire!"

"But we should wait until after the Americans leave. Until then, we will not take any more risks like you took in Tipo-Tipo. I am your brother. Your older brother. I am the leader of Abu Sayyaf. And I say you will stop looking for this gold. Do you understand?"

Janjali's brother beat his fist into his palm, spun

around, spun back, then tugged nervously at his beard. "They found a new cave. And we have to do something!"

Forcing a calm into his voice, Janjali slowly answered, "No. We do not. And if you continue this search, it could be the last thing you do, dear brother."

"Do not threaten me, Ramzi."

"No, this is a promise."

Hamsiraji threw up his hands and stormed out of the hut, hollering for one of the men outside to bring him some of the bottled water they had stolen from an American supply truck.

Janjali whispered after the man, "Dear brother, you are going to get me killed before I can retire with the infidels."

One of Janjali's spies, whom he had assigned to Isabella, strode abruptly into the hut, dropped his heavy pack, and removed a damp, green bandanna from his forehead. Janjali liked this bright-eyed boy of eighteen or nineteen, though he could never remember his name. The boy usually brought good news from Senator Allaga—yet another reason to like him.

"The guard outside allowed me in. My apology if I have awakened you, but I did see your brother just leave."

Janjali grinned and dragged himself to the edge of the bed. "You've come all the way from Isabella today?"

"I left as soon as I could. Senator Allaga wanted you to have this." The boy reached into his pack and produced a brown, six-pocket folder.

"You have not opened this, have you?"

"The senator said it is for you alone."

Allaga opened the folder, took one look at the first stack of papers—

And his heart skipped a beat. Or at least it felt so.

"Go see my brother outside. Tell him to pay you double. Tell him I said so."

"Thank you! Thank you!" The boy raced out.

Janjali began pouring over the documents. Praise be to Allah. The senator, that greasy little man, had unearthed a *real* treasure, not some legendary gold looted half a century ago.

TEAM DOGMA

2.2 KILOMETERS SOUTHEAST OF ISABELLA

BASILAN ISLAND, SOUTHERN PHILIPPINES

1901 HOURS LOCAL TIME

The old Guns N' Roses song "Welcome to the Jungle" boomed from Cpl. Jimmy Vance's mental radio. He whispered the lyrics as he walked point, ducking beneath colossal fronds and keeping to the narrow path walled in by dense underbrush. A couple of huge snakes, a trio of those little spider monkeys you see at the zoo, and a few giant birds like the one from the cereal box would definitely complete the picture. Well, you could throw in a sexy Jane and leave Tarzan at home to wash the loincloths and tidy up the tree house. That would work out just fine, since, at the moment, Vance was a jungle boy without a jungle girl. Houston had tried to fix him up with a Japanese college student whom he had assured Vance was not a hooker, but Vance was a country boy looking for little country romance, not something so exotic. And it wasn't easy— even for a Force Recon Marine—to find a good ole country girl in a foreign city. Or in a jungle.

About five hundred yards ahead, teams Firelight and Crossbow led the way, and Vance wasn't thrilled about that. The Filipinos were sharp-eyed, all right, and it was their jungle, but Vance trusted his own skills. So why was he stuck where he was?

Politics, plain and simple.

There was some stupid rule about U.S. forces having to remain at least one hundred yards behind the local troops because U.S. Marines weren't supposed to engage in combat.

Caught in the middle, Rainey was trying his best to comply with the restriction, though Vance figured that the Filipino sergeants who had welcomed them with open arms weren't happy about having American firepower tucked safely away—and wasted—in the rear.

And you had best believe that if Vance and his buddies came under fire, not a politician in the world could stop the iron fist of the United States Marine Corps. Those terrorist assholes would die hard, because very hard men would kill them. No virgins for those varmints in paradise. Bye-bye . . .

Team Crossbow's leader, Sergeant Padua, a gaunt-faced Filipino of about thirty with a crooked nose, paused, then gave Vance a hand signal indicating that the trail would veer right.

Vance acknowledged with a signal, then continued on. All three teams were closing in on a well-known cluster of abandoned huts. Data from Eyes in the Sky spy satellites had revealed that the huts had once been part of an ASG camp. The huts would now be used to practice a night raid and to teach the Filipinos room-clearing tactics. This was where Team Dogma's training in urban warfare would come into play, quite ironically in the middle of the jungle.

"Dogma One, this is Firelight One, over," came Sergeant Golez's voice over the inter-team channel.

"Firelight One, this is Dogma One, over," Rainey responded.

"Be advised that our training ground is over the next hill. We should be there in about ten minutes, over."

"Roger that, Firelight One, out."

The Sarge's voice sounded cool and professional, though Vance knew Rainey was getting agita back there, having to babysit Banks, aka "Ricardo the Psycho." That boy was trouble, pure and simple. Vance had never met a Marine as pushy and conceited. What ever happened to the strong, silent type? The team did not need a short loudmouth. But that wasn't quite fair. You couldn't pick on the guy for his size. It's not the size of the fish in the fight but the size of the fight in the fish. Sometimes a two-pound bass could get to jumping and splashing a lot more than some of the five-pounders Vance had caught over the years. Still, largemouth bass were not egotistical know-it-alls, and they never made wiseass remarks after you pulled the hook from their mouths.

Vance shot a glance back, saw Houston falling in behind him, with Doc, Banks, and Rainey threading farther back. The sky was beginning to grow dark, and the shadows brought out the whites in the team's eyes. Everyone wore their bush covers, their face paint, and leaves and branches affixed to their rucksacks and shoulders. Game faces were on and senses were throttled up because the bad guys had no rules, had a keen sense of the terrain, and had a hard-on for killing Americans. Some routine training mission . . .

Vance sighed inwardly. They had been instructing the two teams for twelve hours already, and the day wasn't over. Even Houston's eyes cried, "Get me out of here!" and he'd been holding up pretty well lately. Vance raised his thumb at the radio operator. Houston mirrored the gesture, but his added smile was as sarcastic as they came.

Ignoring Houston's negativity, Vance faced forward, found where the path turned, then lowered his rifle and worked himself sideways to slip past some branches. He was back on the trail, hiking to the beat of Guns N' Roses, who were, unfortunately, supported by a chorus of buzzing and humming insects.

Lance Corporal Bradley Houston shuddered as he neared the super-sized bug. The dark brown abomination was shaped like a beetle and sitting atop a rubber plant leaf. As the thing began crawling across the leaf, Houston thought he felt it skitter across his face.

Yes, sir, he would take bullets over bugs any day.

And no, sir, he wasn't one of those Marines who could chew on a roach and smile as though it were a stick of Doublemint. He had seen guys eat all kinds of creepy-crawlies in idiotic attempts to demonstrate their survival skills. During his training, he had managed to avoid eating bugs while other operators did, though he had eaten raw snake meat, which tasted a little like chicken. He would even eat cats and dogs before eating a bug, but don't tell anyone that, especially his teammates. They would just laugh at him. Call him a pussy, what have you.

He focused once more on the trail, now just a thin clearing in the heavy brush that seemed to grow thinner. Reaching up, he tightened the chinstrap of his bush cover with the bullet hole in the rim. Back in Pakistan a round had cut through his ruck and had blown the cover clean off. Then, during their mission in North Korea, the cover had fallen off in the middle of a road and had nearly revealed their location. While the hat wasn't exactly a badge of honor and didn't exactly stick to his head, there was something about it that made Houston feel safe. Every operator had his rituals and good-luck charms. Funny thing was, most of the guys on Team Dogma were pretty secretive about them since, Houston guessed, they could be misinterpreted as signs of weakness.

In the past, Houston had known that former team-mate Terry McAllister had had a thing about packing his ruck. And one time before a big mission, Houston had caught Doc actually Scotch-taping a picture of his grandfather onto his chest, right over his heart. "What about your wife and kids?" Houston had asked. Doc had grabbed his bush cover, where inside he had taped more photos. "They will always be on my mind, and he will always be in my heart."

"That's fucking goofy, Doc. And it's a waste of perfectly good Scotch Tape."

"You're an asshole. Get the hell out of here!"

Houston carried around pictures of his mother, father, and sister in his wallet, but he wasn't about to tape them to his body. If he could find a photo of "Mr. Abu Sayyaf" himself, that mother of mothers Ramzi Janjali, Houston would tape the picture to his ass. Even the sarge would get a kick out of that.

And considering photos, Houston did spend a lot of time staring at his father's picture. All of the hatred was gone now. Yes, before dying, his father had come around, had approved of Houston's career as a Marine. And no matter how many wars Houston now fought, he would always have that inner peace.

But had that peace softened him? He had fought with a vengeance, with a desire to prove his father wrong. With that gone, what was left? Was he just a has-been, like Banks had said? Maybe guys like Banks were the true Recon warriors. They had a fire that wouldn't go out. Maybe Rainey would recognize that and eventually make Banks a permanent member. Maybe Banks would replace Houston. *Shit!*

Heaving a great sigh, Houston dug in his boots as the trail turned sharply up and the canopy suddenly turned to fluctuating black licorice dotted by small, moving things.

Family man Glenroy "Doc" Leblanc imagined himself back in Miami, having dinner with his wife and his two incredibly gifted sons. Deshawn had made flank steaks stuffed with portabella mushrooms, homemade mashed potatoes, and steamed baby carrots. The boys had refused to turn off the TV, and the sounds of some kid's game show echoed from the den and into the dining room.

Too bad Doc was really punching a clock in the jungle. There were no flank steaks, just Meals Ready to Eat. There was no TV, just a tactical radio with the voices of intense men crackling in his ear:

"Dogma One, this is Dogma Four, over," called Vance.

"Four, this is One, over," Rainey replied.

"Found something just off the trail. Don't know if the other teams missed it. Don't know how they could have. But you'd better have a look, over."

"Dogma Four, hold your position. Dogma Team, halt, out."

Rainey scampered up behind Doc, who was already on his haunches. "Keep an eye on Banks."

"Aye-aye." Hunched over, Doc veered around and rushed back to the lance corporal. "How we doing?"

Banks's eyes were like full moons, and he held his carbine the way little kids hold their blankies. Slowly, very slowly, he turned to regard Doc. His voice came low and edgy. "We're being set up."

Doc decided to play along. "Oh, yeah?"

"Yeah."

"Who's doing it?"

"Don't know. But the note was real."

"So why they setting us up?"

Banks glanced emphatically at Doc. "You don't know? C'mon, Doc."

"Because they hate us?"

"Of course they hate us. But it's for the money. It always is. And they're waiting for us out there."

Doc snickered. "Because you're always right."

"Later on, I won't have time to say 'I told you so.' A shit storm's going to hit."

"Dogma Two, this is Dogma One. Need you up here. Bring Five with you, out."

"Let's go," Doc said.

Banks held his index finger to his lips. "They're watching us. I know they are."

"Then let them watch you come with me. Right now, Marine."

Resignedly, Banks drew himself up and started on, moving far more warily than Doc. Hey, what did Doc have to worry about? Terrorists were out there, waiting to whack him and his teammates, and the new guy was going psycho paranoid.

Doc heard the buzz of flies before he saw them, and a sickly sweet odor wafted up as he elbowed past Vance and Houston, then crouched down near Rainey, who had pulled a flashlight from his ruck.

Sure, Doc knew death when he smelled it, but he wasn't prepared for the thing glistening in the beam of Rainey's light. It was lying on a bed of brown fronds, covered in flies, and decaying rapidly. It was . . . a human penis with attached scrotum.

Banks's mouth fell open. "They wanted us to see this."

"Shut up," Rainey barked at the lance corporal, then he lifted his brows at Doc. "This what we think it is? I mean is it human?"

Doc grimaced. "You don't need me to tell you what that is. And I'm not going anywhere near it, thank you."

"Those guys couldn't have missed this," Vance said. "Shit, I smelled it from back there. Heard the flies."

"Firelight One, this is Dogma One," Rainey said into his boom mike. "We need you here, approximately one hundred meters back, over."

"Dogma One, this is Firelight One, on my way, out."

Doc guessed from the incision marks that the penis and scrotum had been stretched taut and then hacked off. He shook as he imagined what that might have felt like for the victim. Damn. He had seen shit like this before, but this felt like real evil, and it assaulted his senses as much as his soul.

"So, can we stop dicking around?" Houston asked in a deadpan.

"This isn't funny!" Banks cried, then he shoved Houston. "This is a message from them, you asshole."

Houston shoved back so hard that he nearly knocked Banks down. "Do not touch me."

"Don't you get it? First they take away our power— our manhood—then they take away our lives."

"You don't got any manhood," Houston spat.

"Quiet," Rainey ordered, then faced Banks. "Another word and this will be your first and last day with Team Dogma. Do you hear me, Lance Corporal Banks?"

"Yes, Sergeant, I do."

No one spoke again until Sergeant Golez reached the group. The Filipino Marine barely glanced at the penis, then he said, "Abu Sayyaf."

"Did you see this?" Rainey asked.

"It is not an uncommon sight here, Sergeant. We saw it. And we ignored it. We give them no audience. And neither should you."

"All right. But do you want to collect this? The police might be able to use DNA to figure out whose this was."

"Sarge, I don't think they have a crime lab on the island," Doc said.

"He's right," said Golez. "But if you insist, Sergeant, I will have one of my men return for it."

"Please. I don't want to be accused of ignoring something like this, even though I agree with you about not giving the enemy an audience."

"I understand."

"And one more thing. Lance Corporal Banks here seems to believe that this is a message for us. Is it?"

Golez brought his lips together in thought, and Doc

figured that he wasn't deciding the answer to the question; he was deciding if he should share it.

"Is there a problem, Sergeant?" Rainey asked.

Finally, Golez said, "This is a message to anyone who dares to follow these trails into the mountains. Abu Sayyaf owns the heart of the island."

"Not for long," Rainey said.

"Sergeant, we want to learn as much as we can from you. And we want to teach you what we know. But to be honest, I did not want to come this far into the jungle. Your lieutenant colonel suggested this place, and so we go. But make no mistake. There is danger here."

"That's right, Sergeant. *We're* the danger."

Golez nodded and rushed off, muttering orders into his boom mike, while Doc slapped a palm on Rainey's shoulder. "Thanks."

"For what?"

"For making them deal with this."

"Hey, Doc, we're Force Recon Marines. We don't dick around. Isn't that right, Houston?"

The lance corporal grinned mildly. "You're damned right, Sergeant. You're damned right."

"This isn't funny," Banks said.

"Lance Corporal Banks, this time you're right," Rainey said, his tone growing serious. "This is just sad."

A few minutes later, after the Filipino Marines had collected the penis, Lance Corporal Banks ascended the next hill with the rest of his new team. He gritted his teeth and held his rifle against the tremors working into his hands. That damned note had scared the hell out of him. And he didn't scare easy. No way was it a practical joke. The other operators from Team Rattlesnake knew better than to mess with his head. True, they were probably glad to see him go, but that was only because he had pushed them harder than even the sarge had.

Banks had not joined the Marine Corps and had not worked his ass off to get on a Force Recon team to "make friends." Sure, he respected his fellow Marines, but in his estimation, the Corps did not always push them hard enough. He knew that every man on his old team—and every man on Team Dogma—was capable of much more than he showed. They were capable of being *great* men. Banks saw it as his mission to get each of those men to find his burning core, his animal, and get it out there, where it would totally annihilate the enemy. The problem was, other operators kept telling him that that wasn't his job. He was a lance corporal, now a Force Recon scout, not a team leader.

But how was he supposed get promoted and become a team leader if he didn't push himself harder and inspire others to do the same?

These guys have no clue what makes me tick. They think I'm all about ego. They think I'm all about attitude. They don't know me. They don't know my life, what I've been through.

Five years prior, Banks's mother had lost her battle with breast cancer. Her death had not been unexpected, but the years of watching her wither away had deeply saddened him. Once she had passed, Banks, an only child, had been raised for the next year by his father, a local mason who worked union jobs.

But then, a mere year after his mother's death, a long-standing feud between Banks's father and a fellow mason had come to a head. One night after work, the other mason retrieved a revolver from his truck's glove compartment and shot Banks's father in the head—right on the job site and in front of over a dozen witnesses.

Banks's aunts and uncles had tried to console the boy, but their words could not take away the pain of losing his father.

However, just a few days before the murder, Banks had sat down with his father and had confessed that he wanted to join the United States Marine Corps. His father's words were the ones that eventually helped Banks overcome the man's death. And they were the words that he whispered to himself every morning when he rose from his rack:

"If you're going to join the Marines, then all right. Try your best. Be a great man, Ricardo."

The United States Marine Corps had a reputation for producing great men. Banks had known he would be in good company. He had joined to become that great man that his father wanted him to be.

But nowadays many of his fellow Marines were driving him nuts. Some had grown lazy, complacent. And his own drive for greatness wouldn't allow him to tolerate their weaknesses. Sometimes he even thought that their laziness would rub off. He wished he could stop letting it all get to him. But he was just too hard core for that.

With all of his senses reaching out into the jungle ahead, he kept tightly to the trail as the team reached the summit of the next hill. From there they would head down into a clearing, where the abandoned huts stood in the shadows.

"Security Team Victor, this is Dogma One, over." Sergeant Rainey was calling the three Filipino Marines charged with guarding the huts for the training mission.

"Dogma One, this is Victor One, over."

"Victor One, be advised we are prepared to begin our exercise. Request you fall back to designated wait zone, over."

"Roger, Dogma One. Team Victor falling back to wait zone. Give us two minutes, out."

"Roger that, Victor One. Crossbow One and Firelight One, this is Dogma One. Assume Raid positions. Dogma Team will clear the first hut, then we'll clear the rest with you, over."

Banks listened to the responses come in as he and the others rushed up to the edge of the clearing and fanned out behind the gnarled brush. Rainey called for a radio check, and when his turn came, Banks answered, "Dogma One, this is Dogma Five, radio check, over."

"Dogma Five, this is Dogma One, good to go, over."

"Dogma One, this is Dogma Five. Good to go, out."

But was he? Really?

ASG has your training schedule and mission GPS coordinates. Be prepared for an ambush. Time and day unknown.

"Dogma One, this is Victor One. Security team in wait zone, over."

"Victor One, this is Dogma One. You are in wait zone, over."

"Dogma One, this is Victor One. You are clear to advance, out."

"All right, Dogma Team?" Rainey called. "Execute!"

Holding his breath, Banks dropped smoothly into the line of Marines. He was part of them now, a force of five moving swiftly, silently, and deadly toward the first hut.

05

With Teams Firelight and Crossbow watching them, Rainey and his men reached the first NEPA hut, a square structure about the size of a two-car garage and the largest of five arranged in a loose string across the clearing.

Vance slipped his portable mirror near the wide gap at the bottom of the hut's door. Despite knowing that no one was home, they needed to simulate everything for the Filipino Marines, right down to the smallest detail. Vance studied the mirror, searching for signs of movement, then he shook his head.

Rainey gave a nod, pointed—

Then Vance kicked in the door, and, flipping down his Night Vision Goggles, he passed into the darkness, making a sharp right turn into the hut. He would advance along the right wall to the far corner and would wait there.

Number-two man Houston entered, slipped left, and reached the nearest corner, where he would remain, his line of sight taking in the far left-hand corner and Vance's position.

Doc, clutching his big Para SAW, followed Vance's path, only he moved to the nearest corner, his line of sight now on the rear and left walls.

Finally, Banks, his lips tight, his movements impressively sharp, followed Houston's route, arriving beside the other lance corporal. Banks was in charge of securing the door should an enemy soldier be hiding, hoping to make a break.

Rainey maintained his position outside the hut as the reports of "clear" came in over the radio, his Marines working like four parts of one entity. He stared through his NVGs, sweeping the jungle perimeter until he spotted the three-man security team hunkered down beneath a stand of palm trees. Then he came upon the Filipino Marines, a few with binoculars in hand, studying him.

"Firelight One and Crossbow One, this is Dogma One. We have secured the first hut. Request Team Firelight secure second hut on my mark. Wait." Rainey switched off his radio and called his team inside. "All right, Marines. Everybody out. Team Firelight's taking the second hut, and we're going to show them how it's done."

Banks exited first. He flipped up his NVGs and asked, "How'd I do, Sarge?"

"You did all right."

"I thought I did excellent."

"You would."

"Sarge, where you want us?" Vance asked.

"We'll wait to play bad guys. I want to make sure they have the sweep down first. You, Doc, and Houston get inside the second hut and watch as they come in. Banks, you stay near the door. Let's move."

"Wait a minute, Sergeant," Banks said, his attention focused on the three-man security team beneath the palm trees. "Look at those guys out there."

"I already did," Rainey snapped.

"Uh, Sarge . . . I can't see their faces from this range. But they ain't moving. I mean not one bit."

Rainey smacked down his NVGs and zoomed in on the men, who were now seated in a row, leaning back against the trees. Though the image became blurry, he picked out one man's face and realized that the Filipino's eyes were closed. He activated his radio. "Victor One, this is Dogma One, over."

Before the security leader had a chance to reply, Banks screamed, "Ambush! Ambush! Get down! Get down!"

Gunfire exploded from Team Firelight's position, echoed immediately by more fire from Team Crossbow, located just twenty yards south.

"Dogma One, this is Victor One, over," acknowledged the security leader.

"Jesus Christ, are they firing?" cried Houston.

"Where are they?" Vance hollered as he hit the deck.

"Victor One, this is Dogma One. Report your situation, over." Rainey dropped and crawled back to the hut's wall, where Banks lay propped up on his elbows, squeezing off three-round bursts toward a patch of jungle near the security team's position.

"Lance Corporal! Hold your fire!"

"But I saw one, Sergeant! They're out there! They killed the security team! They're out there!"

"Hold your fire!"

Banks's rifle fell silent, but the booming was replaced by his whining. "Sergeant, I'm telling you. They're out there. I'm right, Sergeant! I'm right!"

"Shut the fuck up!" Rainey felt chilled by his sudden loss of control. "Firelight One, Crossbow One. This is Dogma One. Hold your fire! Repeat! Hold your fire!"

"Dogma One, this is Firelight One," came Sergeant Golez's voice. "Are we under attack?"

"Negative, Firelight One. Negative. We are not under attack! Hold your fire! Team Crossbow? Hold your fire! Dogma Three? Dogma Four? Move to designated wait zone. Report immediately from there, over."

"Dogma One, this is Dogma Three," Houston called. "Moving to designated wait zone with Dogma Four, out."

A final round thundered off across the mountains, then came nothing, save for the insects and Rainey's ragged breath. He shook his head unbelievingly at Banks. "What the hell were you thinking, Lance Corporal?"

Banks maintained his position on the ground, staring hard through his rifle's scope. "I was thinking I'd like to stay alive, Sergeant."

"And I was thinking you are no longer a member of Team Dogma. You are finished, Lance Corporal. Finished."

"Before you kick me out, try calling Victor One again. Listen to his voice. It ain't him. It's one of them!"

Hunched over, Doc came rushing up to Rainey. "Looks all clear out behind the huts, Sergeant. I also checked in with Padua. His team reports all clear from their position."

Rainey nodded. "Victor One, this is Dogma One, over."

"Dogma One, this is Victor One, over."

The voice did sound a little different. Banks couldn't be right. Could he? "Victor One, why haven't you reported your situation, over?"

"Dogma One, this is Victor One. We are clear here, over."

"Dogma One, this is Dogma Four, over," Vance called.

"Go four."

"Dogma One, be advised the security team is dead. They've been stabbed. I say again. The security team is dead, over."

Rainey placed a hand over his boom mike. "Aw, shit." He had been talking to one of the bad guys.

"We have to get out of here, Sergeant," Banks said. "There are only fifteen of us—and who knows how many of them. And these guys from the Tausug tribe are like animals. They're on to our scent. They're stalking us, baiting us, waiting to make their move. And we need to make ours."

Rainey looked to Doc, who was already nodding.

"We're not staying here, are we?" Houston asked Vance as they kept tightly behind the palm trees, the bodies of the security team splayed out before them. All three had been expertly gutted, as though they had been killed by Marines instead of terrorists.

"I don't know if we're staying," Vance said, his mouth dry, his neck tingling. "Dogma One, this is Dogma Four. Should we rally your position, over?"

"Dogma Four, this is One. Switch to encrypted channel Bravo-Zulu. Remain your location until I signal for you to rally mine, over."

"Roger that, One. Will switch channels and remain this location, over."

"Dogma Three, monitor inter-team channel and contact Yankee Thunder for immediate extraction, out."

Houston removed the microphone from his Foxtrot radio and dialed up the encrypted frequency. He and Vance both knew that the enemy had gotten their hands on one of the Filipino security guys' radios, but those units weren't capable of decrypting U.S. Marine Corps signals. The team had been communicating via the Filipino codes during the training, but now it was back to the good old U. S. of A. encrypted channels. "Yankee Thunder, this is Dogma Two, over." Houston waited, got his reply. "Yankee Thunder, request immediate hot extraction these GPS coordinates, over." He waited again. "Roger that, Yankee Thunder. Dogma Three, out."

"Hey, bro, I don't think this clearing is big enough for our helo," Vance pointed out in a whisper.

"They'll make it happen," Houston said, then pressed himself tighter against the tree, his rifle held high.

"Fuckin' Banks was right all along. This is an ambush," said Vance.

"Banks got lucky," Houston snapped. "That's all."

"Maybe these ASG assholes don't plan on attacking. Maybe they're still messing with our heads. Like leaving that . . . thing . . . back there. You know, kill a guy here and there, get us all paranoid, kind of like Banks."

"That asshole will get us killed."

Vance shrugged. "Maybe we should be more like him. He fought these guys."

Houston glanced at Vance as though the fisherman had gone insane. "Fuck that."

"Hey, I'm just saying—"

Houston raised an index finger, cutting Vance off.

A pair of fronds about ten yards out began to rustle.

Houston gave Vance a hand signal, and while Vance trained his weapon on that location, Houston knew better than to do the same. It was an old trick. Get your enemy focused on one target while you came at him from another position.

As Houston swung around and scanned the trees and rubber plants behind them, Rainey's voice came faintly over the inter-team channel: "Firelight One, Crossbow

One, this is Dogma One. Be advised the enemy is monitoring this channel. Maintain radio silence. Stand by for rally signal, out."

Houston continued to probe the branches and fronds and thick tree trunks, but nothing set off his alarms. He lifted his chin at Vance, who shook his head, then gave the hand signal for Houston to inspect the fronds that had first rustled. All was still and silent.

Then, about twenty yards to his left, something clicked.

Houston whirled, his trigger finger tensing.

Vance mouthed the word, "Wait."

They held tight, statues fixated on the jungle. And in his mind, Houston heard another click, then another. After nearly two minutes, he finally sighed and glanced up as thunder boomed and huge raindrops began smattering on them and the fronds.

Houston had not even realized the sky had clouded over and that huge thunderheads had rolled in. Good. The rain was on their side and could conceal their departure. But bad. The weather could pose a problem for their chopper, and even a mild storm could also conceal the enemy's movements.

How much longer would they have to wait for Rainey's signal? Who knew? For the uninitiated, that might be too much to bear, but they knew all about lying in wait like predators. They had once spent nearly twelve hours on a cold mountainside, waiting to get off a single shot. God, Houston hoped they wouldn't be sitting there that long.

As he diverted his attention to the first hut, a pair of faint flashes made him sigh with relief. It was time to rock 'n' roll. He gave Vance the high sign, then the sniper led them on a quick but guarded dash along the clearing's perimeter, their bush-covered heads low, their eyes and ears trying to collect data that might very well keep them alive.

They weren't halfway back to the hut when shots sent them lunging for the deck.

Three muzzle flashes from across the clearing told Rainey all he needed to know. Bad guys were targeting his men from that position. Time for bad guys to die.

But even as he lobbed a fragmentation grenade at the shooters, AK-47 fire went off from all around him, set into motion by his own movement. He hit the ground as clumps of dirt kicked up by incoming rounds blasted into his face. Shit. He was alone, lying outside the first NEPA hut. Bamboo and thatch shattered behind him, pieces flying all over the place as the rain came down even harder, the gunfire grew even heavier, and Rainey's grenade heaved a colossal bang, sending smoke billowing up through the palm trees.

A few minutes earlier he had signaled for Teams Crossbow and Firelight to rally on the huts, but for some reason they had not. Either they had misunderstood the signal or had simply chosen to ignore the order. In any event, Rainey had had to send Doc and Banks back to their position to get a heads up.

Now all three █████ as thirty or forty █

Off to his left, H████ through the mud. Ra█ with salvo after hellish ████ saw number on the trees few terrorist heads. He eve█ sure grenade with the 203QD tached to his carbine. The rou█ trees to smithereens, beneath wh████ three guerillas.

"Dogma Two, this is One. Sitrep, over."

"One, this is Two. Five and I are with Team Firelight, taking heavy fire from north of the huts. Be advised we already have two wounded, another KIA, over."

"Dogma One, this is Crossbow One," called Sergeant Padua, breaking radio silence over the inter-team channel. "My corpsman is dead. So is my radio operator. We cannot hold our position for much longer, over."

The only good news was that Houston and Vance reached Rainey's position, then all three swept around to the back of the first hut.

Vance and Houston raked the jungle perimeter with heavy fire, then dashed to the hut's bamboo wall.

Rainey squatted and cleared his throat. "Dogma Two, this is Dogma One, fall back to the second hut, over."

"Stand by, Dogma One," answered Doc. "I believe they've stopped firing. Wait."

With eyes hurting from staring so hard, Rainey lay

...re went silent once more.

...Rainey flashed a hand signal

...On the count of three they would

...c's location, ghosting their way from

...ming around the clearing.

—

...charged off, with Houston close behind.

...ey covered their rear, swinging his wet carbine toward the jungle perimeter. Pieces of thatch and bamboo
littered their path, and Rainey nearly took a nosedive
before they reached the last hut. There, Vance called a
halt and yanked out his Nightstars, picking apart the
now-glowing terrain with magnified vision. He turned
back, gave the signal that he had spotted Doc and
Banks.

Rainey withdrew the small clicker from his breast
pocket, gave a couple of squeezes on the signaling device, waited. Then he received the same cricketlike reply from Doc.

About forty yards stood between them and the corpsman's position, forty yards through fairly dense brush
lining the clearing. The rain drummed down with no
hint of letting up. The path looked innocent, ripe, ready
to be crossed. He stared through his carbine's scope,
giving the jungle a last sweep. Then he looked up, gave
a nod to Vance.

They bounded off and Rainey flinched, expecting to
hear gunfire blasting against the droning rain. But the
jungle had grown even quieter.

While still hunched over, Vance wove his way wildly between the shrubs and rubber plants, sliding almost effortlessly past them, careful not to strike any branches hard enough to shake them. He was the best point man Rainey had ever worked with, and when push came to shove, he was the man you wanted up front, the man you could count on to steer you through hell. All that time he had spent on the water had surely contributed to his skills as a Force Recon scout and sniper. Vance was tuned into nature, tuned into the Earth in a way city slickers did not understand. God bless him and his country-boy roots.

Even Lance Corporal Houston, admittedly a city boy, wasn't doing too badly. He knew how to shadow Vance, how to anticipate which way the sniper might turn, and how he might maneuver himself stealthily around the next obstacle. Houston did all of that while lugging along the team's long-range radio.

After a heart-pounding pair of minutes, they reached Doc's location. The corpsman was working feverishly on one of Team Firelight's scouts, a thin man of about twenty with mocha-colored skin and pleading eyes. The scout had received a gunshot wound to the chest.

Two more scouts lay dead behind him, while another pair of casualties from Team Crossbow were about five yards back. Across from them, two more wounded men were being treated by Team Firelight's corpsman—who was wearing a bloody bandage around his own neck.

Of the ten Filipinos, only three appeared uninjured: Golez, Padua, and one other man. Those three squatted in the bushes at the clearing's edge, covering Doc and the wounded.

Before Rainey could approach Doc, Houston answered a call on the Foxtrot radio, then handed the microphone to Rainey. "Yankee Thunder," the radio operator said. "Our helo's been delayed."

Rainey snatched up the microphone. "Yankee Thunder, this is Dogma One. We have wounded personnel. Need immediate extraction, over."

"Dogma One, this is Yankee Thunder. Repeat, Delta Eagle Ten has been grounded. Waiting on the weather, over."

"Yankee Thunder, just send that helo A-SAP! Dogma One, out." Rainey returned the mike to Houston and said, "Take up a position along that line back there. See how they can come in through there?"

"Yeah. Aye-aye, Sergeant."

"Doc, can you hold tight?" Rainey asked as he jogged back to the corpsman.

"We'll do it, Sarge." Doc took some trauma bandages from Lance Corporal Banks, who was assisting him.

The Filipino Marine was now lying very still, his eyes narrowing, his mouth twisting in agony, though he did not make a sound.

"He takes the pain like a man," Banks said softly.

"Our helo coming?" Doc asked as he removed the scout's blood-soaked bandages and replaced them with new ones.

"Delayed."

"Jesus, Sarge. But hey, with this rain, they won't engage again."

"What do you mean?"

"There's an unwritten rule. When it rains, no one fights. It's just understood."

"Used to be that way, Doc," said Banks. "Before Janjali started recruiting the Tausug tribe. Now they fight wherever and whenever they can. Rain means nothing."

"Then why did they stop firing?" asked Doc.

"They're regrouping. Probably moving up into the hills around us so they can fire down when we make our break."

Rainey agreed with that, but he wouldn't give Banks the satisfaction. He palmed Doc's shoulder. "Just do what you can here." He left Doc and stole through the bushes, toward Sergeant Golez's position. He came upon the man, who rested on one knee and gazed intently through his weapon's sight. "Sergeant, anything?"

"They are moving out there. I cannot see them. But when the wind pauses for a moment and stops blowing the rain, you can hear them. Sergeant, my men are . . . They . . ."

"I know," Rainey said. "I know. Now our chopper has been delayed. We can't wait for them. Can you take us back down the trail?"

"Yes, but what about our dead and wounded?"

"We'll carry the wounded. We'll have to leave the dead behind and come back during daylight."

"Janjali and his men will chop up the bodies. We cannot leave them here."

"Then we'll die trying to carry them out."

"Sergeant, we won't get very far either way. Somehow, Janjali knew we would be here. And because of that, we may die here."

Rainey cocked a brow. "Sergeant, I heard that the Filipino Marines were some of the hardest soldiers in the world. You guys have been fighting all of your lives, fighting more wars than we have. You know we can't stay. You know we can't give up. So we go—without the dead. I'd rather be a moving target than a sitting duck."

"All right, Sergeant. I will tell Sergeant Padua what we plan to do. I will wait for your signal."

"Outstanding. We'll get out of here. Believe that. And be ready. I'll be giving that signal very—"

The characteristic thump of mortar fire sent Rainey and Golez dropping to their bellies and covering their heads. The mortar struck with a sharp bang about thirty yards south, and the reverberation came up through the ground and into Rainey's arms and legs. Before the first blast subsided, a pair of fragmentation grenades went off, nearly in unison, and someone shrieked.

"Dogma Team? This is Dogma One! Grab the wounded and rally back on the original trail, over."

"Dogma One, this is Dogma Two," called Doc. "This guy won't make it. Dogma Five and I will assist Team Crossbow's medic to get his two men out, over."

"Roger that, Two. But be advised I need suppressing

fire first. Believe mortars are coming from the north hill overlooking the huts, over."

"Roger that, One. Setting up, out."

Golez was back on his knee, targeting muzzle flashes winking like fireflies across the clearing, out near the huts. Some of the guerillas had moved up while others had fallen back to the hills to set off their mortars. What Rainey found curious was how most of the bad guys near the huts directed their rounds into the treetops. And why had that mortar fire been so poorly placed? Curiosity turned to realization. The bad guys now wanted to get Rainey and his men on the run, surround them, and take hostages. They obviously didn't mind killing Filipinos, but they wanted to keep their prized Americans alive. Consequently, they would drive Team Dogma toward the best escape route: the original trail leading out of the clearing.

"Team Dogma? This is Dogma One. Cancel previous order. We are not rallying back to the original trail. Stand by for new orders, over." Rainey pushed himself up beside Golez. "Sergeant, is there another way out of here—without having to climb the hills?"

"I'm afraid not, Sergeant."

"Dogma One, this is Dogma Two. We're being overrun! Repeat, we are being overrun!"

As Rainey turned back in Doc's direction, the corpsman's Para SAW, which had been *rat-tat-tat*-ing, suddenly went dead.

A heartbeat later, Rainey saw them: four men wearing black bandannas and green fatigues, and clutching AK-47s. The guerillas charged the tree line, leaped over low-lying bushes, and opened fire, even as three more sprang from the huts and followed. Somewhere up on the mountainside, a submachine gun brought new thunder to the jungle.

Rainey fired four three-round volleys at the first wave of men, still visible between the tree trunks and fronds. He paused, tugged out a fragmentation grenade, lobbed it at the second wave of men, turned, saw two more guys coming directly at Sergeant Golez. He took one out with a quick burst, capped the second as the first dropped.

Then he whirled to find yet a third wave advancing on Doc's position.

But those four men dropped, one after another, two succumbing to Vance's Dragunov while the other pair got spoonfed their deaths by Houston and his M16.

Rainey glanced to the hill towering behind his sniper and radio operator. All alternate escape routes looked bad, so the hill was as "good" as any. "Dogma Team? Rally south, up the big hill, and regroup there. Dogma One, out."

While Doc heard Rainey's order through his earpiece, there wasn't much he could do about it. He and Banks had fled deeper into the jungle to avoid being overrun. Team Crossbow's medic had been shot and killed, along with the remaining wounded. There was nothing Doc or Banks could have done. Had they stayed, they

would've been captured and killed. So they had run—
and that wasn't something Marines did very often.

Banks had taken point because, frankly, he was just
faster than Doc. It seemed Banks wasn't blowing as
much smoke as Vance had thought. The guy moved
swiftly, authoritatively, owning the ground he covered,
wary of attack but never slowing.

After a two-minute burst of running, they reached a
shallow creek snaking along the base of a rocky hill that
seemed to go up for fifty, maybe one hundred feet.
Jagged outcroppings studded the hillside, with chutes
of rainwater pouring from them and diffused by the
trees.

"We can climb it, Doc. Let's fucking move," Banks
grunted. "See those trees and rocks up there? We get up
there, and we can look down and pick off these guys as
they approach."

The shuffle of leaves off in the jungle, followed by a
shout, sent a chill down Doc's spine. "We won't make it
in time! I can hear them coming."

Banks began ascending the hill, his boots finding
minimum purchase on the mud and rocks. One boot
gave way, and he flopped onto his gut.

"Forget it! We'll follow the creek! Come on!" Doc
waved and jogged by the lance corporal, then he turned
back, saw the man following.

On the run, heavily outnumbered, and paired with a
temporary teammate, Glenroy "Doc" Leblanc wasn't
particularly thrilled with being a Special Amphibious
Recon corpsman. Nights like this made that alternate

career as a civilian paramedic look pretty damned good. You still had your adrenaline rush over saving a patient. And nine times out of ten you didn't worry about saving your own ass.

"Where you going?" Banks called.

"We can take this creek to the south, rally back on that hill with the sarge."

"You don't know where this fucking creek goes."

"I think it runs south. Just shut up and run."

They traced the muddy creekbank, and Doc couldn't help but grow more paranoid. Every shadow beneath every frond could hold a terrorist who would spring up, level his weapon, rob a beautiful woman of her husband, and two handsome young boys of their father.

But he knew he couldn't think about that. He shouldn't. Now matter how scared he was, he and Banks would reach the rally point. There was no one in the world who could stop them.

Lance Corporal Banks saw the terrorist before Doc did. The corpsman ran right on by the guerilla just as the bad guy swung around from behind a tree, lifted his rifle, and prepared to shoot Doc in the leg.

Banks fired first, and all three of his rounds punched the bad guy in the head. Doc dropped to the creekbank as Banks turned toward a flickering shadow at his right—

And fired again, catching another bandanna boy in the chest as—

An arm slid around his neck, cut off his air.

They were trying to take him alive.

They wouldn't.

His hand shot down for the K-bar sheathed at his hip. Gasping, he withdrew the blade, reached around, stabbed his assailant in the side, felt the man's arm go slack—

Then Banks pulled free, spun, kneed his opponent in the groin, then punched the blade into the terrorist's heart. He never saw the man's face. And he didn't look back as he broke into a sprint, with Doc leaping up to join him.

"They want hostages," Doc said, fighting for breath.

"We don't."

"Damn straight."

"Come on, old man. Keep up!"

Houston knew that he and Vance would be first up the hill, so it was their job to find and cover the sarge and the rest of the team. Utilizing a tree for cover, Houston stood there, rain spattering on his bush cover as he surveyed the clearing and jungle perimeter through his night-vision scope. Vance stood a few trees down, dividing his gaze between his scope and the hill behind them. You couldn't assume the hill was clear, although as of yet no fire had come from up there. They had only ascended about halfway—and who knew? A hundred bad guys could be waiting for them on the summit.

"I got the sarge, Golez, and Padua," Vance said.

Houston panned around with his rifle, studied the grainy images displayed through his scope, and found the three men dashing up the hill. He widened the view and counted six guerillas in pursuit, just forty or so yards back. "Got trouble behind them."

"I see."

"On your mark?"

"My mark. Take three on the right. Just like on the range, bro. We can do this."

Between the wind, the rain, and the dense cover, it would be a small miracle if Houston could hit a single man. Vance would work his surgical magic, but Houston . . . damn. He would fire. Miss. Prove he had become soft. Prove Banks right. Lose his spot on the team.

Bullshit. Fuck you, Banks. Fuck you!

Houston was all about the rifle, the scope, and the men who wanted to kill his team leader. He was all about the moment, waiting for the word from Vance, keeping the first guy in his sights while anticipating where the next guy would be. He had to fire three bursts, had to hit his mark, had to execute perfectly. One shot could kill Sergeant Rainey. One shot from a man Houston was supposed to kill.

The deadliest weapon in the world is a United States Marine and his rifle. My weapon is clean and ready. My killer instincts are clean and ready.

"Okay, Houston. Steady. Steady. Execute!"

Vance's sniper rifle cracked a millisecond before the three rounds exploded from the muzzle of Houston's rifle. As his first target fell, Houston moved the rifle a fraction of an inch, saw his second target dropping down for cover, sent the second burst off. He didn't wait to confirm that kill. On to the next guy, who was crawling toward a tree—then, *bang-bang-bang*—he crawled no more. A quick pan again confirmed that his number-two man had been blasted onto his back and lay inert.

"Houston, you are the *man*," Vance said softly. "Out-fucking-standing . . ."

"I am on a roll," Houston said, pumped over the feat. In his mind's eye he saw Banks's grin fade. "So are you." Of course the sniper's three targets had been neutralized by three precisely timed, precisely aimed rounds.

Vance worked his clicker, and Sergeant Rainey came slogging up the steep grade, the two Filipino sergeants just behind.

Houston offered his canteen to the sergeant, who took a tremendous pull and then shoved it back. "Doc? Banks?"

"Don't know where they are."

"Vance, you see them?"

"No, Sergeant."

"Sarge, are these the only two Filipinos left?" Houston asked.

Rainey nodded, took a deep breath, pushed his boom mike up to his lips. "Dogma Two, this is Dogma One, over?"

Doc's heart sank as he and Banks reached the base of another hill that stood between them and the rally point. The creek had, indeed, taken them south, but Doc had failed to anticipate the second hill. What was worse, the rain was sending huge torrents of mud down one rocky slope and could easily begin doing the same on their side. Flashbacks of a mudslide in North Korea, one that had sent him plummeting down a mountainside and had nearly killed him, had Doc thinking twice about playing mud park victim again.

"Dogma Two, this is Dogma One, over?" Rainey called for the second time.

"Dogma One, this is Two. En route your location, over."

"Reading your GPS coordinates. See that hill between us. Your ETA, over?"

"Dogma One, this is Two, our ETA is"—Doc glanced up the hill, sized it up, issued his guesstimate—"five minutes, over."

"Roger that, Two. We're heading to the summit. Will transmit GPS coordinates from there. Dogma One, out."

Banks had started his climb, his gaze fixed on the rocky path above him. Had he been looking behind, he would have seen the bad guy who had exploited a sudden burst of rain to move up on Doc and jab a pistol into the back of Doc's neck.

Doc jolted, spun, came face to face with a bearded man with coal black eyes, a long nose, and round, puffy cheeks. "No," the man said firmly, lifting the gun to Doc's head as a dozen or more bandanna-wearing terrorists materialized from the trees.

With a suddenly dry mouth, Doc answered, "Okay."

He took his hands off the Para SAW hanging from his shoulder and raised them over his head. "Banks?"

With that, a dozen rifles trained on the lance corporal, who took one look back and dropped his jaw. "Aw, fucking shit!"

Laughter spread through the group of dusky-skinned men as some mimicked Banks.

"Come down here," said the bearded man who had captured Doc, his accent unmistakably Arab. "You won't find any gold up there . . ."

06

While Vance, Houston, Golez, and Padua had paired up
and shifted off to the flanks to run reconnaissance on the
valley, Rainey had chosen to move a few yards down the
hill to a cluster of rubber plants. He lay on his belly, concealed amid the fronds, his Nightstars pressed firmly
against his eyes, as though holding them closer—holding them tighter—might bring Doc and Banks closer to
him. They should be coming over the hill. Where the hell
were they?

"Dogma One, this is Dogma Three. Banks just activated his beacon, over," Houston reported.

Team Dogma's MBITR radios included a personal
survival feature that broadcast the operator's GPS coordinates to both the team's Foxtrot and the command center when the mike was keyed. The beacons were most

often employed when the operator was incapacitated or being captured.

Since Banks was apparently in trouble, Rainey immediately called Doc. "Dogma Two, this is Dogma One, over." After a few seconds of dead air, he repeated the call. Still nothing.

"Dogma One, this is Dogma Three," came Houston's voice again. "Be advised I have Dogma Five's GPS coordinates, over."

"Uh, Dogma Leader, this is Abu Sayyaf! We have two of your men. And we have hundreds of fighters looking for you. You should not have come to Basilan. You will not escape our jungle."

"Dogma One, this is Dogma Three," Houston said, his voice more terse. "Be advised that last transmission came from Dogma Two's radio—and I've just lost Dogma Five's beacon, over."

Golez dashed down the hill, came up next to Rainey. "We must go now, Sergeant."

"Not without my men."

"They will not kill your men. At least not yet."

"But they will when they realize that the United States does not bargain with terrorists."

"You are naïve, Sergeant. Or maybe just uninformed. But trust me. Your men are worth more alive. And your government will secretly bargain for them because Janjali's fortress is deep in the jungle, near one of the highest mountains. It is impenetrable."

"Sergeant, are we going back for Doc and Banks?"

Houston asked. "I have their GPS coordinates."

"Dogma One, this is Dogma Four," Vance called. "Be advised I count ten, maybe twelve bad guys en route our location. Maybe another dozen behind them. First wave's ETA just four, five minutes tops, over."

Rainey glanced at the grim-faced Sergeant Golez, then turned to Houston, whose face-paint barely hid his anguish. "C'mon, Sarge. We can't leave them. Doc's down there. Our Doc, man. Our Doc!"

Bolting to his feet, Rainey brought up his Nightstars, saw the bad guys Vance had spotted, then turned a stony expression on Houston. "We're getting out of here."

"We're leaving them behind? Sarge—"

"You heard me." Rainey hated the order, hated his tone, but Houston and the rest needed clear, unequivocal direction.

"I don't believe this."

"Believe it. Now get back up there and get ready to move out."

Houston's gaze fell to the mud. "Aye-aye, Sergeant." He jogged off.

"Dogma Four, this is Dogma One. Take point. We'll see if we can push south, run parallel to our original trail, then pick it up about half a klick up, over."

"Roger that, One. Good to go, over."

For a second, Rainey closed his eyes, heard Houston say again, *We're leaving them behind?*

No one gets left behind.

Doc? Banks? We're coming back for you.

"Dogma One, this is Dogma Four," Vance signaled. "First wave is ascending the hill, over."

"All right," Rainey boomed. "Let's go! Let's go!"

OPERATIVE OMEGA EAGLE

COMMAND HUT YANKEE THUNDER

CAMP BALIKATAN

BASILAN ISLAND, SOUTHERN PHILIPPINES

2020 HOURS LOCAL TIME

Charles Callahan had sat next to Lieutenant Colonel Demarzo and had listened to the entire ambush unfold over the radio. The strain in Mac Rainey's voice was, at times, almost too much to bear. Now the Abu Sayyaf Group had captured two Marines, one of them being L. Cpl. Ricardo Banks, the very soldier Callahan had tried to warn.

"They must have been tracking our teams," Demarzo said, rubbing his temples in frustration. "They must have followed them to the training ground." Demarzo rose, crossed over to the radio operator, and began making demands regarding the liftoff of the team's evac chopper. He was interrupted by one of three Philippine Marine Corps colonels who were also monitoring the situation. The stocky man with a shaven head appeared even more uptight than Demarzo.

Exploiting the opportunity for privacy, Callahan retreated to the back of the hut, where he powered up his notebook computer, logged on to the network, and clicked on an encrypted message that had been waiting for him. For the past several months, one of his paid informants had been providing intelligence on a courier who worked for Senator Allaga. At the moment, the courier with the green bandanna was being detained by one of Callahan's fellow operatives, and he had confessed that Senator Allaga had given him the six-pocket folder of information to deliver to Ramzi Janjali. The boy could not say precisely where Janjali's stronghold was located, but he knew the trail by heart.

As Callahan finished reading the message, yet another one came in from Metro Base in Manila. The message contained one sentence, a sentence Callahan had been waiting over a year to read. Hallelujah.

He slammed shut the computer, sprang to his feet, and crossed the hut to Demarzo. "Lieutenant Colonel, I need a small security team—five or six men—to accompany me into town."

Demarzo glanced back from the radio operator's terminal. "For what purpose?"

"I'm afraid this one's classified, compartmentalized, Colonel. I would appreciate your full support."

"Does this have anything to do with my men out there?"

"I wish I could say, Colonel. I just need that team. And I need them A-SAP."

"They told me to work with you, give you what you want. You give me a couple of minutes. I'll have a team meet you at the gate."

"Thank you, Colonel." Callahan went to leave, turned

back. "Oh, and by the way, Colonel, your furniture is on its way."

"Outstanding," Demarzo said through a sigh. "But that's the last thing on my mind."

Within ten minutes Callahan was riding back into town aboard an HMMWV with a security team of five heavily armed Marines. Senator Allaga had checked into the Green Tree Hotel, where he planned to stay for the night. In the morning he would catch a ferry back to Zamboanga.

Unfortunately for the senator, that ferry was going to leave without him.

One of the Marines, a sergeant named Madison, shoved his thick-rimmed glasses up the bridge of his nose and asked, "Sir, if you don't mind my asking now, what's the mission?"

Callahan, who had been less than forthcoming at the gate, faced the group of hard-faced men seated in the crew compartment. "All right, Marines, listen up. We're going to detain a man. He's staying at the Green Tree Hotel, room 305, located in the back of the building. He'll have one, maybe two bodyguards posted outside his door. This needs to go down quick and quiet. No shots. No one hurt. Understood?"

The team voiced their acknowledgments, then Madison added, "Sir, do you want to direct the men?"

"Negative. It's your show, Sergeant. Just bring me this man." Callahan reached into his breast pocket, produced a small photograph of Allaga, then passed it to the Marine seated to his right.

Once the photo made it back to Madison, the sergeant took a second look and said, "I know who he is."

"Then you know we can't afford mistakes."

"We'll get the job done, sir. Quickly and quietly, as you ask, sir."

"I know you will."

Barely five minutes later they reached the hotel. The Marines burst from the assault vehicle and charged across a muddy road toward the main entrance, where two heavy wood doors hung propped open by a pair of cracked flower pots. The hotel was a five-story affair with stained white stucco chipping off and shutters buttoned down against the rainstorm. Despite its stage of decay, the place was considered one of the better establishments in Isabella, worthy of a senator's stay.

Callahan was the last man out, and while he considered drawing his sidearm, he thought better of it. Instead, he wiped the rain from his eyes, dropped in behind the last Marine, and followed the man up the staircase. On the third-floor landing, he heard hushed voices coming from the hallway beyond.

By the time Callahan crossed the hall and reached room 305, Allaga's two bodyguards were being escorted away at gunpoint by a pair of Madison's Marines. "Good work, Sergeant," Callahan said.

Madison nodded curtly, then regarded his other two Marines, who took up positions on either side of the door. Madison was about to knock—

But just then Allaga's door opened, and the senator, wearing only a pair of hastily donned boxer shorts, stepped out. Behind him, past the crack in the door, Callahan saw the senator's lithe assistant lying on the bed and pulling the sheets up to her neck.

"What is this?" Allaga demanded. "Where are my men?"

Callahan ignored the question. "Senator, I've been ordered by the United States government to detain you for questioning."

"You have been what?"

"Ordered to detain you, sir."

"Detain me? I will not be detained by anyone." The senator's assistant called for him in her little girl's voice. He snapped at her in Tagalog, then said, "You've taken my men, haven't you?"

"That's correct, sir." Callahan shoved his way past Allaga and into the hotel room, where the assistant scowled at him. Madison and his Marines blocked the senator, forcing him back inside. "Sir, we can do this quietly," Callahan said. "Please, get dressed."

"I'm not going anywhere! I demand to know what this is about."

Callahan drew closer to the man and spoke through his teeth. "Sir, this is about the release of classified military information to the Abu Sayyaf Group. This is about kickbacks received from ransom monies paid to that group."

"Get out! Get out of my room right now! And release my men. I am a senator! And you have no jurisdiction here!"

Allaga started for the phone on the nightstand, but Callahan reached it first, put his hand over the receiver. "Senator, you'll be coming with us."

"Remove your hand! I'm going to call the American consulate right now. By the time I am finished, you will be court-martialed, Colonel. Do you hear me? Court-martialed."

Callahan glanced at the doorway. "Sergeant Madison? I'm afraid the senator does not want to play nice."

"Yes, sir." Madison nodded to his Marines, who immediately seized Allaga by the arms, while Madison handcuffed the senator.

"You are making the biggest mistake of your life."

"Not me, Senator. But today you did. I provided you with classified documents as a gesture of good faith."

"No, you set me up! You did it! You're not a Marine! Who do you work for?"

Callahan rolled his eyes, looked at Madison. "Take him downstairs."

"Yes, sir."

As the Marines dragged Allaga out of the room, he barked orders at his assistant, who immediately reached for her purse and produced a cell phone.

Callahan was about to leave, but a familiar voice from the TV screen turned his attention there, where reporter Rick Navarro of Wolf News stood outside Camp Nova. He wore fatigues as though he were an embedded reporter, but Callahan had heard that he had been thrown off the base for disclosing classified information about Balikatan.

"Marty, I'm outside Camp Nova in Zamboanga, the Philippines, and the atmosphere here is quite tense. This year's Balikatan training exercise with the armed forces of the Philippines kicked off just a few days ago, and already we're receiving unconfirmed reports of heavy shooting from Basilan, the island just south of us and the reputed stronghold of the Abu Sayyaf Group. Already troops are preparing to ship over hundreds of crates of supplies and ammunition in preparation for what could be an all-out war with these terrorist thugs. It's well known that their leader, Ramzi Janjali, was personally trained by Mohammed al-Zumar, once the world's most wanted man. Of course, Marty, I couldn't stay home for this one, and tomorrow, I plan to ferry across to Basilan to bring our viewers coverage from the front lines."

By the time Callahan turned his head away from the TV, Allaga's assistant had risen from the bed and was padding to the bathroom, completely naked and still squeaking away on her cell phone. She looked at him, stopped talking, started to cover her breasts, then her gaze turned a little salacious as she lowered her arm.

Callahan smirked, shook his head, and ambled toward the door. "Sorry, honey. I know your game—same as I know his . . ."

"Hey, soldier," she called.

He paused, glanced over his shoulder, saw that she now covered herself. "Yeah?"

"Fuck you."

Callahan winked. "Okay."

As he made his way down the stairs, he was feeling a

little better about the plan. So far not a single American
had been killed, and now they even had a witness who
would help indict Allaga. Once that threat became real,
Mr. Nelson Allaga would give up General Santiago in a
heartbeat. Callahan's one-two punch would be complete.

But there were still two American Marines to consider, and Callahan wondered if there might be a "creative" way to get them back.

55TH INFANTRY COMMAND CENTER
ARMED FORCES OF THE PHILIPPINES
BASILAN ISLAND, SOUTHERN PHILIPPINES
2105 HOURS LOCAL TIME

General Romeo Santiago enjoyed his private guest quarters with the 55th infantry so much that he had spent the
better part of the evening eating, drinking heavily, and
singing and dancing with two female companions (local
girls who needed "charitable donations"). Once he had
sent them home, he had fallen back on his bunk, had listened to the falling rain, and was about to drift off into a
wonderfully long and peaceful sleep—

When one of his bodyguards rushed into the room
with the news that Senator Allaga had been detained by
United States Marines.

And it all hit the general at once: The fool had gone
through with the plan—even after Santiago had warned
him that it could be a trap.

Santiago had received unconfirmed intelligence reports that U.S. government operatives were working on the island and that he and Allaga were under surveillance.

When Allaga had called to say that he had information that might prove very profitable for all concerned, Santiago had said that the Americans were as cunning as Ramzi Janjali himself. He had told Allaga that this Lieutenant Colonel Callahan was laying a trap.

But Allaga had obviously been too money hungry, and he had probably used the same damned courier for the job. His greed had blinded him.

And now he was being questioned by American interrogators who would grant him immunity from prosecution if he named names. His mouth would open, and the first name to escape his lips would be Santiago's.

The general fumbled with his clothes. His thoughts raced as he worked through an escape plan. He could surround himself with troops, make his way to the port, and board a patrol boat while several squads of men warded off the Americans. That could work, but a hasty departure would still make him appear guilty, and, of course, the Americans would have more people waiting for him in Zamboanga.

Then again, he might not get that far. A clash at the port could become violent. And it did not matter which nearby port he chose: the Americans already had men stationed in Lantawan and Pangasang, as well as troops in Maluso.

And then it came to him. The plan wasn't pretty. It wasn't brilliant. But it could very well work. He buttoned his shirt, took a deep breath, and spoke calmly to his bodyguard. "Tell our two special friends that the senator's time is now up. Then I want you to report to AFP Command that Abu Sayyaf bandits attacked this camp and took me hostage. Do you understand?"

His bodyguard nodded and without a word left the room.

Santiago smiled inwardly. Ramzi Janjali did not know it yet, but he was about to entertain a distinguished visitor whom he would smuggle off of the island.

TEAM DOGMA
EN ROUTE TO CAMP BALIKATAN
BASILAN ISLAND, SOUTHERN PHILIPPINES
2207 HOURS LOCAL TIME

Team Dogma was on the run, and Cpl. Jimmy Vance had overheard one of the Filipino sergeants say that it was highly unusually for Janjali's men to continue their pursuit. They had, at least for the evening, abandoned their hit-and-run tactics and gone asymmetric. It was hard to tell if they wanted to capture Vance and the rest or just kill them. Sometimes their fire came very close; other times the salvos fell remarkably wide, as though they were trying to drive the team in one direction or another.

As Vance raced on, he thought he heard something to his left, where broken walls of thorny shrubs thinned out near the original trail. He stole a glance there, probed the darkness, the windswept undergrowth, then squinted toward the mahogany trees beyond.

A figure darted from one tree to the next.

"They're right here!" Vance shouted as he raised his rifle, sighted the bastard, squeezed the trigger. The figure's arms went up as he toppled onto his back.

Good. But Vance's shot also released a torrent of full automatic fire that sent him to the mud, crawling forward as the canopy of tall grass and leaves hissed and split.

Being under fire knocked his senses into high gear. He could tell that the machine gun was about twenty yards off, heard one, two, three more AKs popping about fifteen yards back, noted that they were north of the machine gun's position. He listened a second more, realized that a lone bandit was up ahead, sending fire down the trail.

"Oh, I get you now," he whispered.

Basically, the enemy was coming at their line from one flank, with a single guy positioned in a frontal assault. Of course, the first group who had been chasing them was still back there and may have radioed up to these guys.

Whatever the case, Vance and the others needed to get moving, otherwise they would get pinned down. If that happened, more guerillas would advance and surround them. This group was trying to buy time for the others.

"Dogma One, this is Dogma Four," Vance called to Rainey. "Incoming from the east, with one shooter dead ahead. I can take him out, over."

"Roger that, Four. Take him out! Keep us moving."

"Call it clear on my mark, out," Vance responded.

Rainey had once told Vance that the remedy for chaos is confidence. Sure, "the fog of war" was a very real thing, but you didn't need to contribute to it by panicking or by thinking about the buddies you had just lost. There would be time for that later. Way too much time. You cut through the fog by remaining in your zone, by remaining confident.

But they got Doc. Good old Doc. What the hell are they going to do to him? Shit!

With burning eyes, Vance shot from his mark and charged directly ahead, the incoming fire a few meters off to his right, snipping through branches and leaves.

With a firm grip on his sniper's rifle, he shouldered through the underbrush, picturing himself a human machete sharpened by the Corps and by his confidence. More chutes of rain struck hard, as though pouring from broken gutters. Trees turned into soldiers, lifted their rifles, wanting to shoot him . . .

And the popping fire spattered on, growing so close he could reach out and touch it. But he didn't stop.

Running directly at an attacker letting loose with an AK could be considered an act of suicide for anyone other than a United States Marine. Vance had already realized that his opponent wasn't paying enough attention to his environment. He was leaning too heavily on his trigger and would fail to hear Vance's approach.

Time to clear the path. Where was he, that shooter, that scumbag who thought he would take on Force Recon?

Vance spotted his muzzle flash, alighted on one knee as gracefully as a bird, sighted the man through his powerful, AN-PVS-10 night optic, and exacted payback, imagining that this was the guy who had personally captured Doc and Banks. This was the guy who needed serious killing. And he got it. In spades. One shot. One kill. Down he went.

"Clear ahead!" Vance announced over the radio, then he hustled on, leaping over the corpse as the gunfire behind him turned sporadic.

He came through a curtainlike row of intersecting branches—

And nearly smashed directly into another guerilla who had been waiting there. He locked gazes with the guy—

No, the kid. Maybe sixteen. He whimpered. Dropped his rifle. Raised his hands. "No shoot."

The muzzle of Vance's weapon hung about two inches from the kid's forehead.

Houston suddenly burst through the bushes, and in the second that it took for Vance to turn his head, the kid took off.

But Houston, who had not gotten a good look at the boy, cried, "There!" and opened fire.

Vance cried, "No!" over the shot.

The kid slumped beneath a palm tree.

"He was just a kid," Vance gasped. "He didn't want to shoot."

"Fuck him. They're all gonna die," Houston said, panting through his teeth.

"Dude, what's the matter with you?"

Rainey came blasting through the underbrush, slowed, took one look at the fallen boy, then simply said, "Move!"

Vance didn't need to be told twice. Houston didn't, either. Later on, the sarge would undoubtedly tell Vance that he should not have hesitated, that the kid had made his decision to join the terrorists, that hesitating could have cost Vance his life. And the sarge would also tell Houston not to feel guilty about killing a kid. Happened all the time. Part of the business of war. But it seemed Houston would have no remorse.

Drawing closer to the trail, Vance wondered how much longer Janjali's thugs would keep coming. They had to break off soon. They had to assume that the Filipino Marines and Army would send in a counterforce. But for the moment, they seemed entirely unaware of that. Shots continued resounding behind him. The only good news was that the brush had become more navigable. The scratches on Vance's face and on the backs of his hands were already screaming for relief, as were his legs. Thorns had stuck to his pants and were repeatedly digging in. But it would all be over soon. If he just kept on. Point man. Eyes on the course. Never stop.

Rainey drifted back, telling Golez and Padua to go on ahead. He hunkered down in the shrubs, waiting until he saw the first pair of guerillas zigzagging from tree to tree like wraiths defying gravity. He lobbed a grenade at them, and as it hurled through the air, he opened up, intent on emptying a full mag.

But as the frag exploded, logic kicked in, told him to get the hell out of there. He turned, ran.

And it felt far too comfortable to run away. It was the safe way to go. If he were single and not a father, would he have made the same decision to leave Doc and

Banks behind? Or would he have gone straight into hell to bring those men back?

"Dogma One, this is Dogma Three," said Houston, his voice shaky as he spoke and ran. "I have Yankee Thunder on the Foxtrot, over."

"Dogma Three, this is One. Tell them to wait, over."

"Roger that, out."

"Dogma One, this is Four. Reaching the second clearing. Looks big enough for Delta Eagle Ten LZ, over."

"Roger that, Four. Make your way around the back side, scout for obstructions, and hold there, out."

Rainey stopped dead, crouched, heard the team shuffling off, listened to the jungle behind them. The firing had ceased. Were the thugs still pursuing? He strained to hear above his breathing and the rain thumping on the leaves.

"Go home," he muttered. "You got your two."

He slipped off, rejoining the men on the far side of the clearing, where they had taken up defensive positions beneath the rubber plants. Vance had been right. The Huey's main rotor would easily clear the tree line, and there were no apparent obstructions to prevent the chopper from landing. The real question was, could they hold out long enough? Maybe. Rainey thought he heard the Huey's rotors thumping in the distance. With his hope sparked by the sound, he took the Foxtrot's mike from Houston's pack, called Yankee Thunder, got an immediate reply:

"Dogma One, be advised we have received your GPS coordinates and have been related to Delta Eagle Ten.

Your helo is off the ground and en route. ETA five minutes, over."

"Roger that, Yankee Thunder. Transferring to Delta Eagle Ten's frequency, out."

Thank God the front had finally moved through and the rain was quickly turning to drizzle. Five minutes wasn't bad at all. They could stick it out that long, no problem. Right?

Rainey blinked hard against sore eyes, tried to steady his breathing. "Delta Eagle Ten, this is Dogma One, over."

"Dogma One, this is Delta Eagle Ten, over."

"Ten, we are Tango Mary, standing by in LZ clearing, over."

"Roger, One. Our ETA approximately three minutes to your GPS coordinates, the clearing to our starboard side, over."

"We'll be on east side. Turn ninety degrees and approach. Look for our smoke and strobe, over."

"Roger, One. Delta Eagle Ten, out."

"Now we pray there isn't some maniac sitting in a tree with an RPG on his shoulder," Houston said. "Fuckin' flashback to Pakistan, when our slick went down."

Rainey snickered. "You had to remind me?"

"No, but I think Murphy's got us by the balls this time. Right by the balls. Goddamn politics. We should have had a lot more support for this exercise. And now they should be dropping in two full companies to whack these bastards."

"All right, Houston, that's enough."

"They got Doc! We have to go back in there and kill all those motherfuckers! Come on!"

"I said, that's enough." Rainey shifted quietly along the bushes, coming up behind Golez and Padua. "Sergeants, we'll be out of here in a minute."

"I hear the helicopter," said Golez. "So does Abu Sayyaf."

"No, they have broken off the attack," Padua argued. "They have what they wanted. They are going home."

"You still wait for my order to get on board. Good to go?"

"Good to go," they answered in turn.

As Rainey left them and took up a new position between Vance and Houston, he called the former. "Dogma Four, this is Dogma One. Pop our smoke and activate your strobe, over."

"Roger that," Vance said. "Popping smoke and switching on strobe, out."

Vance tossed the M-27 grenade into the clearing, and thick yellow smoke poured from the canister. He then switched on his portable strobe light, which sent a bright flash up from the jungle into the rainy night. The smoke was supposed to both mark the LZ and help camouflage the team's approach to the chopper, while the strobe would allow the pilot to mark at least one side of the LZ and keep his main rotor clear.

"There he is," Rainey muttered aloud as the Huey came chugging overhead, its silhouette clearly and painfully superimposed over the night sky.

As the Huey turned ninety degrees on its final approach, an enemy flare shot up from the opposite side of the clearing, burst brilliantly in a crimson glow, and exposed the Huey's dull green fuselage.

"Firelight One? Crossbow One? Dogma Team? Direct fire across the clearing!" Rainey ordered.

Just as Houston, Vance, Golez, and Padua commenced firing, Houston's forewarned RPG arrowed up from the treetops, a Roman candle jetting toward the chopper.

Rainey couldn't look. He maintained his gaze on the clearing and the men who lurked near its opposite edge. He fired with the others, rounds belching from his carbine.

Where was the explosion?

He turned his head a fraction of an inch, saw the rocket arcing over the mountains. Whew, the wind had altered its course, and Delta Eagle 10's pilot owed his life to the RPG's most common weakness.

"Dogma One, this is Delta Eagle Ten. LZ is Tango Mary negative. Too hot. Repeat. Too hot. Am bugging out. Sorry guys. Sorry. Delta Eagle Ten, out."

The Huey's engines roared as the pilot increased throttle, tipped his nose down, and thumped off.

Rainey held his fire. Maybe running away wasn't so easy after all.

Damn, it would have been nice if he could call in some real air support, say three heavily armed Cobras whose 20 mm turreted cannons would tear up the tree line. However, Balikatan was supposed to be a low-profile training mission with nothing but positive outcomes. Big guns would call way too much attention to themselves. Worse, they would signal that a real problem had occurred and suggest an American failure. No big deal. Lack of air support was nothing new to Rainey and his men.

"All right, Marines! Vance on point. We're humping it back to camp. We can do it! Come on, come on, come on! Run it out! Run it out!"

07

Lance Corporal Bradley Houston mused that if the team were running back to camp in a straight line, the journey would take them a half hour, forty-five minutes max.

However, the jungle is a place of bends and curves and switchbacks. Moreover, going up and down the hills, trying to find paths that weren't full of thorns, and trying (at least he did) to avoid walking face-first into spider webs strung between many of the plants slowed you down in a big way.

And then . . . a small miracle, a tension reliever of a kind nearly all strung-out Marines could appreciate. Yankee Thunder had called in to the sarge and said that a platoon of Filipino Marines was on the ground and heading their way.

But the joke was, by the time Houston and the rest

linked up with those fresh combatants, the guerillas had long since broken off their attack. In fact, Houston believed that once they had left the clearing, the terrorists had not followed.

So he and the others dragged their whipped asses into camp and were taken directly to the field hospital for the requisite post-mission exam. He had no problem taking off his soaked utilities in front of strange doctors. He just wanted to get clean and forget that his friend had been captured.

As ointment was applied to his scratches, he leaned over to Vance, who was seated beside him on the gurney. "Look at the sarge over there. Fucking stone-faced motherfucker."

Vance gave him a sharp look. "Shut up."

"We leave Doc behind, and it's like he doesn't care. If Banks gets whacked, all right. No biggie."

"Why do you hate the guy so much?"

"Because he's an asshole."

"You used to be an asshole just like him. But I gave you a chance."

"But we ain't talking about me. We're talking about the sarge. Look at him. Doc out's there. Jesus . . ."

"Come on, you know he cares. He's blaming himself. But he won't show it. He doesn't want to come across as weak."

"Kind of hard now, after we just got our asses fucking kicked!"

"Shhh. Demarzo's coming in. See?" Vance lifted his head toward the door.

* * *

It took a moment for Rainey to meet the lieutenant colonel's gaze. When he did, he realized he was staring into a mirror. They shared about as much anger and frustration as men in their positions could bear.

"Sergeant, I've already put in a request to form a tactical rescue team, essentially a small commando force not unlike a SEAL team. We're going back in there, and we're bringing back our people alive."

"This shouldn't have happened."

"They must've tagged you early on, followed you to the training huts."

"No, they were already there, waiting for us. They kept the security team alive until the last minute."

"Hold on now. You're saying they were already there? What did they do? Keep a team at the huts day and night to wait for you guys to show up?"

"No. They knew exactly when we were going to be there."

Demarzo's gaze went distant. "Then we have a mole."

"Sir, Lance Corporal Banks received a message before we left. He said he found it in his pocket. The message indicated that the ASG had our training schedule and that we were going to be ambushed. Unfortunately, sir, I dismissed the note as a prank. Lance Corporal Banks is the kind of Marine who warrants such things. I guess this was one time he cried wolf and I should've listened."

"Maybe we have a mole with a guilty conscience."

"Sir, I think we're walking among the enemy—and we don't even know it."

"Then we had best wise up and open our eyes."

Rainey breathed a deep sigh. "Sir, has the ASG announced their demands?"

"Not yet. But it's too soon. I'm sure in the next few hours we'll hear something."

"Sir, that rescue team you mentioned? I'll be leading it. And I'd like to take Vance, Houston, Golez, and Padua with me. I'll need a corpsman as well."

"You know what they'll say if I—"

"They don't have to know."

"They do, Sergeant. And I have my own reservations."

"Sir, permission to speak freely?"

"Go ahead."

"Sir, while others sit on their hands, Marines take action. Those are my men out there. I'm responsible for them. I need to bring them home. That's my job. No one else's."

"That's not good enough, Sergeant."

"Then tell me something, Colonel, if you had to hang your career on a Force Recon sergeant, who would you pick?"

Demarzo scrutinized Rainey a moment more, then slowly nodded. "Sergeant, I will show you the respect that they should have shown me."

"Thank you, sir."

"Very well, then. Go get some sleep. If you can. We'll do a full debriefing in the morning, followed by a mission brief and warning order review."

"Good. And colonel? I'm wondering if we can't get General Santiago's support on this. A lot of his men died out there tonight. I'm sure he'd be willing to commit troops."

"Of course, he would. And I'd speak to him if I could, but we just received word that bandits raided the Fifty-fifth Infantry headquarters and kidnapped the general."

"Damn, this gets better all the time."

"He's probably being smuggled to the Abu Sayyaf stronghold right now."

"So I'll add him to the list of hostages. Guess we'll make a party of it."

"In truth, Sergeant, General Santiago is not one of my most favorite people in the world, but he doesn't deserve that kind of death."

"Yes, sir."

Two hours after leaving the hospital, Cpl. Jimmy Vance lay on his portable cot, staring at the hut's thatch roof. Doc's bed lay empty, as did the spot on the dirt floor where Banks would have slept. Houston, who lay to Vance's right, had his fingers laced behind his head, his eyes wide open. Beyond him, Rainey had collapsed on his bunk and had fallen into a troubled sleep. Every few minutes he tossed and turned.

"You awake?" Houston asked softly.

"Just too pumped up. Can't fall asleep."

"You ever been a POW or a hostage?"

"Just when we did those exercises. Remember them?"

"Yeah, they really sucked. You ever know anybody who was captured?"

"Not until now."

Houston rolled over to face Vance, his face still red from scrubbing off the face paint, his expression as gloomy as ever. "They're going to torture him. You know that."

"Maybe not. They can't damage the merchandise."

"They can rough it up a little."

Vance closed his eyes, saw Doc's little boys, his smiling wife, his nice house in an upscale suburban neighborhood—and Vance knew the corpsman would fight as hard as ever to get back home. "Doc is all about the pain. Taking it and treating it. He'll be all right."

"And if he's not?"

"I just don't want to hear it."

"You know what the real kicker will be? He dies, and Banks lives. How much would that suck?"

"Are you listening to me?"

"Doc's not like us. He's got a family that needs him."

"Yeah, they do. And now the sarge has a family, too. And someday, you and I will be there."

"Yeah. But do you think it's fair, putting a wife and kids through this shit? Is it really fair?"

"I don't know. But we're Marines. It's hard to change that, you know? Doc's wife knew what she was getting into, and so did Kady. They learn how to deal with it."

"I don't know if I'd want to do that to someone. I mean, look at what's happening now. Maybe Doc won't come back. And his boys will grow up without him."

"But they'll know that their father died for his country. He died a hero."

"No, he'll die like a dog. And they'll put his head on a fucking pole—just like that mayor."

"All right, I don't want to hear any more."

"I'll tell you what? If Doc doesn't come back, my mind's made up. As long as I'm a Marine, I will not get married and settle down. I won't have kids worrying about me coming home. No fucking way."

"But you'll still have your mom and your sister worrying."

"That's different."

"No, it's not. And even if you had no family at all, you still got your brothers here in the Corps who will worry about you—the same way we're worrying about Doc."

"Shit. There's no way out of this, is there . . . ?"

Vance closed his eyes and muttered, "*Semper Fi*, brother. *Semper Fi*."

TEAM DOGMA HOSTAGES
NEARING ABU SAYYAF STRONGHOLD
SOMEWHERE IN THE CENTRAL MOUNTAINS
BASILAN ISLAND, SOUTHERN PHILIPPINES
0623 HOURS LOCAL TIME

Stripped of all gear (they had even removed his bush cover), Doc staggered down the damp jungle path, his eyes barely open, his knees so sore that his legs threatened to give out. His hands were bound behind his back by a pair of old but functional handcuffs, and the thugs had tied a thin cord around his neck and had attached it to the cuffs' chain, forcing Doc to keep his bound wrists high behind his back. If he lowered his arms, he would choke himself. Banks had been similarly bound and shuffled to Doc's right, his gait a bit more purposeful.

They had been hiking through the jungle all night and had stopped only twice for water. Their escorts, a small party of about ten Abu Sayyaf fighters whom Banks had said were definitely former members of the Tausug tribe, kept unusually silent and simply gestured with their AKs if they wanted Doc to speed up or slow down. They didn't mind if Doc and Banks talked. Which was bad. Very bad. Doc didn't know which had worn him out more: the hump through the jungle and up into the mountains or having to listen to Banks drone on with escape plan after escape plan.

In fact, the lance corporal was in the middle of yet another ploy when the group's leader, the bearded guy whom the others called Hamsiraji, suddenly turned back and said, "Marine, do you ever shut up! All night I listen to you mumble and whisper! You drive me crazy!"

"It's your fault. If I were taking me prisoner, I would have taped my mouth. I would have blindfolded me. And I would have kept me away from the other prisoner so we couldn't talk about escape plans. Shit, I thought you guys were professional scumbags."

Doc furrowed his brow. "Banks, shut up!"

Hamsiraji wrenched back, locked thick fingers

around Banks's shoulders, and said, "I do you a favor by not gagging you. And a blindfold is pointless. You could never remember all of these trails. Now if you do not shut up, I will cut you, and you will bleed! Do you understand!"

"Yeah, I get that," Banks spat.

"Good, you get that. So you don't get dead. Yet." He shoved Banks, knocking the lance corporal back into one of the guerillas, who managed to break Banks's fall.

After Hamsiraji shouted something in either Arabic or Tagalog, Doc wasn't sure, the party moved out, heading up some of the steepest ground they had covered.

The trail soon ran along a cliff wall, the jungle some five or six hundred feet below. Despite being a thoroughly exhausted hostage, Doc had to admire the landscape, the emerald green tree tops blanketed by a loose layer of morning mist. Several small waterfalls streamed down from a mountain adjacent to theirs, and farther back, several more peaks were veiled by postcard-perfect clouds. The sound of running water, the calls of exotic birds, and the scent of something rich and earthy saddened Doc. It was hard to accept that criminals controlled such a beautiful land.

Whew, he was tired. He wasn't even sure what he was doing anymore, walking along, admiring the view, when he should be worried about staying alive and getting back home. But he had spent most of the night doing that, and his nerves had drained him, really drained him. He had never been a prisoner before, and he tried to remember what he had been taught. He tried to remember the articles of the *Code of Conduct*, but everything was a complete blur.

"Doc, know what I'm thinking?" Banks asked.

"I don't care. I'm thinking you'd better shut up."

"I'm thinking we should make a break for it now, before we get to their camp or wherever it is they're taking us. We have a better chance to escape now."

"Just shut up. We'll talk later—if we can."

Two guerillas took Doc by the arms and helped him as the trail turned to a sixty-degree climb but with plenty of footholds. They steered him up the mound and onto more level ground, where they looked up at the mountain before them—

And Doc lost his breath.

He counted no less than ten machine-gun nests, though an untrained eye could easily overlook them. Doc knew that the patches of dense brush had been man-made, and if you strained your gaze, you could see the thin metal muzzles jutting out. And as he gazed longer at the mountainside, the snipers came into view, their green fatigues slowly materializing from the trees. How many did he count? Seven, eight, nine, the count would go on. About twenty meters to the right lay a dark seam framed by pieces of brown rock sticking out from the mud like crumbling teeth. Was that a cave entrance? It might be.

Hamsiraji issued a series of short whistles, two low

pitched, one much higher, and a single whistle answered him. They started up the mountain. Within ten
minutes, after they had passed the first line of
machine-gun nests, they reached a second line, then a
third, with most manned by a pair of guerillas, though
a few had three. While Doc had spotted some snipers
in the trees, dozens more stood in rows of bunkers
about a meter wide and several meters long. The
trenches had obviously been there for a very long time
and been fortified with camouflage netting, wooden
beams, and the occasional steel crossbars and metal
flaps raised to redirect running water around them.
Doc's heart sank even farther as they reached a barb-
wire fence some seven feet tall that ringed off a broad
area of flatter, heavily wooded land, as though nature
had dug a great chip out of the mountain. Barely visible beyond the trees lay dozens of NEPA huts, their
roofs camouflaged by thick layers of brush tied directly to the thatch.

"Look at this fucking place," Banks muttered.
"They've moved so much shit up here."

"And we haven't seen the half of it," groaned Doc.

"We'll never get out of here."

"This from the guy with all the escape plans."

"I give, man. I give."

"You got a will, Banks?"

"Yeah."

"That's good. I got one, too. And I'm heavily insured."

Two guards smiled broadly and opened a small gate,
allowing the group through.

"These motherfuckers see money," Banks said, leering at the guards.

"And I see even more defenses up there in the high ground." Doc sighed in despair as he picked out another half dozen machine-gun nests overlooking the terrorist village.

For the next five minutes, they trekked down a forest trail, then reached the first group of huts, standing near an open yard where a few dogs and a half dozen chickens roamed free. Farther up, six or seven children played with sticks and a small ball.

"Kids, here?" Banks asked.

"Hostages, more likely. Janjali's taken a lot of schoolkids over the years. I bet most of them have been presumed dead. But here they are."

"Why's he keeping them? As shields?"

"Maybe."

"This is so fucked up, man. This guy has his own little utopia here, and he's the king."

Hamsiraji began yelling, the words now definitely Arabic, and a man appeared in the doorway of one hut and came striding over. As the man got closer, Doc remembered the photographs of Ramzi Janjali he had studied before deployment. Captions had indicated that the photos were nearly a year old. Still, the man had not changed much. His black hair was wired with strands of gray, his face clean shaven and with a pronounced jaw line, and his eyes were deep brown, narrow, and intense. Sporting the green fatigues of his men and topping off his uniform with the seemingly requisite black bandanna, Janjali sucked in his paunch as he neared Banks. He loomed over the lance corporal by nearly six inches and gave Banks the once-over, while the lance corporal had K-bars in his eyes and murder in his heart.

"You are Hispanic," Janjali observed.

"That a problem?"

Janjali smiled cryptically. "Where are you from?"

"New York."

"New York? I thought maybe California."

"I was born in Puerto Rico."

"Ah, yes, but you moved to New York because like the song says, it's a helluva town."

Although Janjali's men did not know English, they took their cue from Hamsiraji and chuckled loud enough to suit their leader.

Satisfied with the group's response and with his inspection of Banks, Janjali approached Doc, lifting his chin to find Doc's stoic gaze. Something sour came on the terrorist leader's breath, and it was all Doc could do not to gag.

"And you," rasped Janjali. "You look like a fat Michael Jordan."

Again, Janjali's men laughed heartily.

"Do we get to say who you look like?" Banks asked.

"Lance Corporal," warned Doc.

Janjali cocked a thumb at Banks. "He will be trouble." Then he stared hard at Doc. "But you look soft. Maybe it doesn't bother you when they call you 'nigger,' huh? You are so soft now, you don't care."

Doc opened his mouth. His reply was about to contain enough four-letter words to make even the most filthy-mouthed Marine cringe, but his damned sense of logic and reason, his damned levelheadedness, kept him still and silent.

Abruptly Janjali spun away, took a few steps back, then faced them. "Gentlemen, you know who I am. And by now you know that I, too, have been looking for a few good men."

Banks snickered. "What do you got? Satellite TV?"

"We understand this is a game of politics," Doc said. "And we'll play along—for the sake of our families."

"You speak for him?" Janjali asked, glancing at Banks.

"Yes, I—"

"No, he doesn't," Banks said. "I am a United States Marine. I will continue to resist you by all means available. I will make every effort to escape and assist others to escape. I will do this because I trust in the Corps, in God, and in the United States of America."

"Why don't you believe that?" Janjali asked Doc.

"I do. But I'm not willing to die for a game. Only for my country."

"I do not believe either of you. I believe that inside you are both cowards. You are both scared. One wants to make a deal because maybe he has a family or he is too scared to die. The other believes he can hide his fear behind his big chest and his Marine Corps."

"What are you hoping to prove?" Doc asked. "That you can create an independent Islamic state in the Philippines? Is that what you really want?"

"What are you? A politician?"

"I've read a lot about you and your group. You've failed to create that state. Why not just stand down? Or just disappear? You can't win here. You won't."

Hamsiraji barked his outrage in Arabic, and Janjali shot something back, then said, "We owe you nothing. Someone will pay for your release . . . or you will die." He switched his gaze to his men, boomed an order, and suddenly Doc and Banks were being ushered away.

As he watched the prisoners being whisked off to their cages, Ramzi Janjali felt a sudden surge of adrenaline course through his veins. He had not felt so powerful in a very long time. "Brother, we have finally struck gold."

"This is not the true gold," Hamsiraji answered.

"It is. And if I go down to the caves, I will not find any of our men digging for gold. Will I, brother?"

"No, you will not."

"I hear a lie. We lost many men last night. Do you even know how many? I do."

"We're fools if we abandon the search."

"I won't hear any more of this. Go. Make sure the prisoners are locked up properly while I prepare our message for the Americans."

Hamsiraji moped off as Janjali shook his head, then returned to his hut. He sat down to begin writing his message, which would be hand delivered to the American base camp in Isabella while his spies attempted to get a copy of it out to the media. He had written all of ten words when one of his guards called from outside.

Annoyed by the interruption, Janjali bolted out of the hut and stopped short in surprise.

General Romeo Santiago stood beside a group of six Filipino Marines. Santiago's uniform was soaked in sweat, his cheeks unshaven. His men appeared equally ragged. "Ramzi, we have a big problem."

"We do now," Janjali said, ripping a pistol from the holster on his belt and pointing it at the general's head. "I told you never to come here. Never!"

At once, the general's men brandished their rifles, as did Janjali's guards.

"You shoot, and everyone dies," the general said.

"Maybe we're already dead," Janjali growled. "Maybe you killed us."

"There was nothing I could do. They set up Allaga and used their own people as bait. They have him now. And he will talk."

"So you came here?"

"Listen to me. I ordered Allaga's death, but I don't know if my men have finished the job. Before I left, I sent word that I had been captured by rebels."

"You fool."

"I need you to get me off Basilan. And you will do it. You owe me your life."

"I owe you nothing. And it is true. You have been captured by rebels. The only way you will get off Basilan is in the hands of the government. Or in the hands of the Americans."

"Don't play with me, Ramzi!"

"I'm not. The game is over for you. You shouldn't

have come here. Now I will ransom you as well. I always knew you were a fool, but I never knew *how* foolish." Janjali lowered his pistol.

"You can't do this."

"It's already done. Where can you go now?"

"I will kill you!"

Janjali turned his back on the general and on the rifles pointed at his head. He walked slowly toward his hut. "If you want to die here and now, that is all right." Janjali hesitated, glanced over his shoulder. "Otherwise, you can live, although I'm not sure they will pay very much for you if Allaga has already told them the truth. Maybe they will say, 'Let him rot out there. We don't want him back.' "

"You're making a big mistake, Ramzi! We can still help each other. I still control the Marines here! If the Americans come in force, I can help you escape!"

Janjali held up a hand. "I don't need your help. Now tell your men to surrender, otherwise by the time I reach that door, you will all be dead." He continued on to the hut.

"Ramzi, listen to reason. You have to join me."

Janjali came to within a meter of the hut's door.

"Ramzi!"

He swung around—just as the general's men lowered their weapons.

08

Long nights were par for the course in Charles Callahan's chosen profession; but the prior night had been one of the longest of his life. He and his fellow operatives had interrogated Senator Nelson Allaga, who would not talk and who had threatened to turn his detainment into an international incident. But then Callahan had surprised Mr. Allaga by producing the boy—the courier who would confess that Allaga had given him the documents to deliver to Ramzi Janjali. The boy's confession had cost Callahan only one hundred American dollars. You had to love that. However, Allaga would still not take the deal, saying one boy's confession meant nothing. Then Callahan had produced a videotape made by one of his colleagues, a tape that showed Allaga handing over the documents to the boy. Still, the senator would not deal. By 2 A.M., word had come in that one of Callahan's colleagues would escort the senator back to Zamboanga, where agents of the Philippine government would be waiting for him. A helicopter was being sent.

As Callahan had stood on the edge of the makeshift helipad, watching the senator's transfer to the chopper, automatic weapons fire erupted from the nearby jungle. Callahan hit the deck, drawing his sidearm. By the time he was ready to return fire, the shooting had ceased.

Senator Allaga lay on the tarmac, blood pooling around him. Callahan rushed over. Too late. *Shit!*

Callahan's colleague had been struck and killed as well, and after more than an hour of questioning with local authorities, Callahan had flown to Zamboanga.

There he had met with another superior who ordered him back to Basilan to pursue their only target now: General Romeo Santiago, who had purportedly been captured by rebels (though the Agency felt certain that he had fled into the jungle to seek Ramzi Janjali's help). The Agency had planted false intelligence with the Philippine Marines to throw them off Santiago's trail. Thus, with shredded nerves, Callahan had boarded the return chopper and dozed off a few minutes after liftoff, only to awaken when the chopper touched down.

Now, as he reached Lieutenant Colonel Demarzo's hut, Callahan could barely keep his eyes open. He even dropped the envelope he was to deliver to Demarzo, and one of the colonel's sentries fetched it for him as he announced Callahan's arrival.

"Good morning, Lieutenant Colonel," Callahan said as he entered the hut.

Demarzo pored over documents spread across his desk. "If you can call it that." He glanced up.

"The senator would've been a great help, if we could've swayed him to our side, sir. It's too bad."

"You have to wonder, though, if the rebels really did it, or if somebody on our side wanted to see him gone." Demarzo lifted his brows.

"Who knows, sir? Anyway, this is for you."

The lieutenant colonel reluctantly accepted the envelope. "What now?"

"You'd best read it yourself, sir."

Demarzo tore open the envelope and quickly scanned the enclosed document. "Are you kidding me?"

"No, sir."

"How do you go from heading up an assessment committee to being an observer in the field?"

Callahan hardened his tone. "We have our orders, sir."

"They don't trust me, do they? That's what this is about: trust."

"And respect."

Demarzo rapped his fist on the desk. "You're damn right it is! They want their own eyes and ears on my recovery team. Because they neither trust nor respect me."

"I won't interfere in any way."

"When's the last time you were in the field?"

Callahan shrank at the question. If Demarzo only knew . . . "Sir, I won't be a problem. Have you chosen a team yet?"

"In fact I have. Sergeant Mac Rainey, Corporal Jimmy Vance, Lance Corporal Bradley Houston, and Sergeants Golez and Padua of the Philippine Marines. I'm still working on getting them a corpsman."

"Sir, do you believe that roster will be approved, given the fact that—"

"Colonel, I got Rainey and his men assigned to this mission not only because they're the best we got, but because they're highly motivated to succeed. No one will fight harder to bring those men back. And they're going with the Corps' full support and acknowledgment."

"That's outstanding, sir."

"But now I know why they sent you: to pull rank and keep everybody honest."

"No, sir. Sergeant Rainey will have full command. As I said, and as my orders indicate, I am only an observer."

"An armed one, to be sure."

"Yes."

Demarzo came around his desk, folded his arms behind his back, and leaned toward Callahan. "I've been at this a long time, Callahan. You may be an observer, but you will act if the team jeopardizes our relationship with the Filipinos."

"No, sir. I have no authorization to do that. I'm supposed to report what goes on. That's it."

"Bet you're a good poker player, huh, Callahan?"

"Never played the game."

"Right . . ."

Demarzo's sentry called from outside. "Sir, Sergeant Rainey here to see you, sir."

"Send him in."

"Speak of the devil," Callahan muttered, though he was glad for the intrusion.

"Actually I was expecting the sergeant," Demarzo said. "You're the devil today, Colonel."

"It would seem so."

Mac Rainey snapped to, saluted.

"At ease, Sergeant. Take a load off on one of these comfortable folding chairs our military has provided for us to prevent back strain and chronic hemorrhoids."

Rainey smiled tightly as Callahan assured Demarzo, "You'll be getting rid of these chairs today."

Demarzo shrugged. "We'll see."

In the minute that followed, the lieutenant colonel dropped the bomb on Rainey, who listened coolly to the news, eyed Callahan, then closed his eyes and said, "I understand that we have our orders. But this op is way too dangerous to have an observer along."

"Sergeant, the warning order includes your name and the names of your men. I got the boys back in Fifth to officially endorse you. They gave. So now we have to."

"But sir—"

"If I go back and argue to remove Callahan from the team, they could turn around and change the entire roster. I don't want that to happen. *You* don't want that to happen. You go, he goes."

Callahan softened his tone. "Sergeant, as the lieutenant colonel indicated, you'll maintain full command of the team. I have no intention of interfering with your mission in any way."

"Sir, it's the unintentional I'm worried about."

"Don't be."

"Sir, with all due respect, I'm taking seasoned combat veterans into an unfamiliar jungle to rescue hostages. We'll be heavily outgunned and outnumbered. We're doing what Force Recon does best: going in swift, silent, and deadly."

"I appreciate that, Sergeant," said Callahan.

"Yes, sir, but even with your scars there, I'm unsure if you're any of those things. And to be honest, we both know that when a lieutenant colonel is assigned to a recon team as an observer, he's really there as a spy for the brass. He's there to make sure the boys in the field do it by the book."

"Sergeant Rainey, you're walking the fence of insubordination," Demarzo warned.

Callahan swore to himself and groped for a way to tell Rainey that he was experienced and that he didn't care if Rainey broke the rules. "Sergeant, suffice it to say that I may be less rusty than you believe. And I appreciate your reservations. I would be surprised if you didn't have any. I don't expect you to endorse me, only to respect me. If you consider me a spy, that's your choice. But we're on the same side here. We both want to do our duty and rescue those men. Are we clear?"

"Yes, sir. Crystal clear."

"Sergeant, I know your preparations are already underway," said Demarzo. "Take the lieutenant colonel back to your hut and bring him up to speed."

"Aye-aye, sir. And sir, any word yet from Janjali?"

"Nothing yet. The Filipinos tell us he'll most likely deliver a message here, and he'll try to go public via another courier. He's usually careful not to use radios or cell phones, but sometimes he'll take a chance with either or. We know he has contacts with the media, but we're doing everything we can to secure the island and misdirect the news people."

"Very good, sir." Rainey stood.

"You're dismissed, Sergeant."

Rainey regarded Callahan. "Lieutenant Colonel?"

Callahan rose, rubbed the corners of his eyes, and went outside with the sergeant, who was already marching away.

"Hey . . ."

Rainey stopped, slowly turned around. "Yes, sir?"

"I know how much those Marines mean to you."

"No, you don't."

"Look, I just want to say it's your show. I wasn't just saying that for Demarzo, and I won't be looking over your shoulder."

"Sir, permission to speak candidly?"

"You're asking a little late, aren't you? But it's granted."

"Two of my men are out there. We're going to do whatever it takes to get them back. *Whatever it takes.* You want to go back and tell them everything I did, you'll probably end my career, because out there the gloves are off and the rules of engagement mean nothing. These meatheads think they're tough, but they'll learn just like the Germans did in World War I.

We're the devil dogs, and they're going to die."

"I understand."

Callahan could tell that Rainey was trying to stare right through him. "Do you really?"

"Yeah, I do. Because if I were in your shoes, Sergeant, I'd be telling me the exact same thing."

"I hope so, sir. Ready?"

They shuffled down the trail, and after a moment, Rainey said, "Don't take it personal, colonel, if my men, well, if they hate you."

"What about you, Sergeant?"

"Hate you? Nah. Trust you? No way."

"Fair enough, Sergeant."

"Yes, it is. When we get in the field, the truth will come out. It always does."

Callahan took in a long, hard breath and trailed Rainey toward the billets.

TEAM DOGMA
CAMP BALIKATAN
TOWN OF ISABELLA
BASILAN ISLAND, SOUTHERN PHILIPPINES
0950 HOURS LOCAL TIME

During the mission briefing, the announcement came that the Filipinos were sending out two commando teams of their own in search of General Santiago. Their intelligence indicated that the general might have been taken to the northeast end of the island, so they would concentrate their efforts there. Demarzo thought the Filipinos were just plain wrong in their assessment, but he wasn't telling them that. Rainey knew the lieutenant colonel was far more concerned with the American effort.

"Let's be clear here, gentlemen," Demarzo said, standing tall before his critics in the command hut. "For our Marines, this is not a combat operation. It is a recovery mission, and since it is a joint operation, we might even classify it as a training opportunity."

Houston and Vance laughed bitterly under their breaths. Their definition of military diplomacy was a bullet between the eyes. Rainey silenced them with a sharp look.

"Sergeant Rainey, if you'll come up now?" Demarzo asked.

Rainey rose and crossed the room to the map of Basilan hanging on the back wall. "While we can't be certain, we believe that Janjali has taken Lance Corporal Banks, Recon Corpsman Glenroy Leblanc, and possibly General Romeo Santiago back to a central command base he has been constructing for the past year. Our intell indicates that the base is well hidden in the central mountains; however, recent reconnaissance photographs from one of our drones have revealed small numbers of troops moving near Mohajid Mountain. Therefore, we'll be focusing our operations in that region." Rainey crossed to a chair, from where he picked up some nondescript green utilities and a black bandanna. "To keep the enemy confused and maintain security, our commando team will don his clothes and carry some of his weapons, although we'll supplement with infrared and thermal capabilities, including NVGs and the SOPHIE, which is our lightweight thermal imager and a very capable unit. We'll be moving at night, heading southeast, directly into the central mountains." Rainey traced their path on the map. "While this is not the easiest approach, intell indicates that we can move parallel to a few of the trails and take advantage of some very good cover."

"What if your intelligence is wrong, as we already believe it is?" asked one of the Filipino Marine Corps colonels.

"Colonel, Sergeant Rainey and his team are prepared to improvise as necessary, should our intelligence prove false," Demarzo answered. "That's what we Marines do, Colonel. We improvise."

Rainey sighed inwardly. For him, this was the mission of his career, the pinnacle, the one that counted the most, because his brothers would die if he failed. Improvise? Damn. Rainey was already ten steps ahead of these pogues. And the briefing was already giving him a headache.

Thankfully, Demarzo took the reins back and discussed the three most likely extraction scenarios. Rainey took a seat and let his eyes glaze over. He would bet everything he had that if they managed to get Doc, Banks, and the general out, the extraction would be far different from anything the pogues could anticipate at this early stage.

When the briefing was finished, Rainey and the others said their good-byes to the Filipino brass, who eyed them with that same look the villagers had given Rainey back in Tipo-Tipo: *So sorry that you are going to die.*

Outside the command hut, Callahan caught Rainey's attention and said, "You did well in there."

"I'd rather do well out there." He glanced back at the jungle.

"You will. And I'm looking forward to seeing that."

"Oh, really?"

"We can plan this forever like we always do, but if it's going according to plan, then it must be an ambush. So as far as I'm concerned, most of this is just for the Filipinos."

Rainey drew back in surprise. "That's sounds weird, coming from you."

"I'm not a pogue, Sergeant. I just play one."

"How well do you play Recon Marine?"

"You'll find out."

Houston and Vance had all of their equipment spread out on the ground near their hut. They usually inspected and took inventory of their own gear, but given the importance of the mission, they had decided to play devil's advocate with each other and question the other guy's choices.

"What's this paper here?" Houston said, picking up the last letter Vance had received from his mom back home in Florida.

"Don't touch that."

"You don't need this." Houston tossed the note over his shoulder. "We're merciless here, cutting the load down to the bare essentials."

"And what about your letter, the one from your dad you carry around? You're not taking that?"

"Nope. Too valuable. Leaving it in my duffel back here."

"Don't you want to have it with you? You know, in case—"

"No, man. It stays here, which means I have to come back and get it. So get rid of that letter from your mommy."

"How do you know that it's . . . wait a minute. You went through my stuff and read it?"

Houston turned his head and smiled guiltily.

Vance crossed around the pile of equipment to deliver a solid punch to Houston's bicep. "You asshole."

Houston returned the punch, then glanced over at Callahan, who hadn't spoken to them since they had left the briefing. He sat alone across the trail, banging keys on a notebook computer that seemed grenadeproof. "Look at our boy over there. He's on a mission. We're taking into him into the jungle so he can take some pictures for the pogues."

Vance shrugged. "Something's up with him, for sure. Observer, my ass. You'd best watch it. He could be gunning for us, who knows?"

"How come the sarge isn't bitching about this?"

"Oh, he's trying to keep morale up. Which is pretty hard, considering. Or maybe he knows something we don't. Maybe Callahan's our secret weapon."

"You know, he sounds like a pogue, but he looks like he's been there, done that, you know? Hard core, I bet.

He's downplaying it." Houston switched his gaze to Vance's equipment. "Whoa, buddy. Just what in God's name is this?" Houston reached down and picked up one of Vance's favorite bass fishing lures, a Lucky Craft Pointer 78 Minnow that he had bought in Japan.

"Don't touch my fishing shit, man."

"Why are you taking this?"

"I got some line and a little travel rod, too."

"Doc's out there! Maybe he's being tortured, and you're thinking about fishing!"

"I'm not thinking about it."

"Then why are you bringing this?"

"I don't know. I just want to."

"Maybe we should ask the lieutenant colonel what he thinks about this."

"No way."

Houston wiggled his brows. "Let's go talk to him— not about your stupid fishing shit. Let's see if we can feel him out. Maybe he'll slip up, tell us he's really a spook or something. I'm going lay some stuff on him that Doc told me. Come on."

"Don't think that's a good idea. The sarge said to lay low."

"Lieutenant Colonel, sir?" Houston called as he ambled over to the man, who was still in his computer trance.

"What is it, Lance Corporal?"

"Sir, we were just wondering if we could check our email, sir."

"Sir, don't listen to him, sir," Vance said quickly. "He hasn't been feeling well since last night, you know?"

Houston shoved Vance. "I'm fine, good to go."

"Gentlemen, if you really want to check your mail—"

"We don't, sir," Vance said.

"You sure?"

Vance gave Houston a menacing look. "Yes, sir."

Callahan slapped the lid on his notebook computer, shoved it back into his ruck. He got to his feet. "See the door on our hut?" he asked. "Keep looking."

Something flashed in the corner of Vance's eye, and when he looked once more, a K-bar was jutting from the door.

"Jesus Christ, sir," Houston gasped as he ran and fetched the knife. "That was fast!"

"Yeah, pretty fast."

Even Vance had to force a grin. "Sir, we're sorry we bothered you."

"You didn't. The waiting's the hardest part, right? We all want to go running out there and bring back those men. But we just can't. Not yet. You boys scared?"

Houston looked to Vance, who raised his brows, unsure how to answer that.

"You don't have to say," Callahan said. "But I'll tell you this, if you're not, then there's something wrong."

"What about you, sir?" asked Houston, returning Callahan's blade.

"I wouldn't call it fear. More like anxiety." Callahan glanced to his right as Sergeants Golez and Padua came walking over, both burdened by heavy duffels.

"We sleep today," said Golez. "And we sleep together, in your hut. A team, no?"

"That's right," said Vance. "We sleep by day, and we hunt by night." Vance lifted his hand, and Golez gave him a high five.

"Sir, just one more thing," Houston said to Callahan. "I figured I'd ask you this, because for a colonel, sir, you seem pretty approachable."

"I'll take that as a compliment."

"Sir, our corpsman was telling me about a rumor he'd heard. We know the Corps and the other services want to build a permanent base here on Basilan, but the Philippine government has thrown up a bunch of roadblocks."

"That's no rumor, Lance Corporal; it's a fact."

"But we like you here," said Padua. "They are politicians. We are Marines."

"Yeah, that's right," Houston said, then he returned his gaze to Callahan. "But Doc heard that if the ASG is put down, then the U.S. has a weaker argument to build a base here."

"That's probably true."

"Doc also heard that maybe the ASG is being supported by the CIA because we need Janjali and his crew to keep raising hell to justify our presence here."

Callahan grinned dubiously. "So you're saying the Agency is supporting terrorists?"

"I'm not saying that. Just a rumor, really."

"Sounds pretty far-fetched to me."

"Just wondering if you heard anything, because this has me thinking that if the CIA is involved, then maybe we can go through them to get our guys back."

"Houston, if the CIA was supporting Janjali, then why would he want to take American hostages?"

"I don't know. Maybe they're putting on a show or something?"

"Give me a break. If the Agency were involved, deals would've already been struck. We wouldn't be going out there, and maybe our hostages would already be on their way home. And to be honest, Lance Corporal, if I knew something, do you think I'd be authorized to share it with you?"

"No, sir. You wouldn't."

"And to answer your question, sir," Vance said, butting in, "Houston is definitely scared. He wants to give the CIA a call so he can get out of fighting."

Houston's expression went sour. "You know what I'd tell you if the colonel wasn't here?"

"Gentlemen, I suggest we all hit the hay," said Callahan.

"Yes, sir." Vance nodded, wrapped a hand around the back of Houston's neck, and led him away from the lieutenant colonel. "What the hell was all that about?"

"Dude, did you see the look on his face when I said CIA?"

"He's no spook, just a spy for the brass."

"I don't know . . ."

"Come on, now you're getting really paranoid."

"That guy could turn out to be the boogeyman."

"If he does, he won't last long. The sarge will make sure of that."

"And so will we."

09

Ramzi Janjali was so excited about the news from the gate that he went down to the fence line himself to greet the informant, a young man of no more than twenty who had spent most of the day traveling through the jungle to reach the camp. Janjali took the man by the shoulders. "What do you have for me?"

"An American news crew in Lantawan."

"Perfect. We can get word to them."

"Yes, but they may not trust me."

"We have no dog tags to give them because these American Marines don't wear them during their covert missions, but we do have some photographs that they carried. And Hamsiraji has a digital camera he stole from a tourist. You will photograph me with the prisoners and give them the camera. When they see all of that evidence, they will believe you."

"I will do you as you ask. But it is much more difficult to move, and I must bribe the police at every checkpoint. I need more money. And I need some now."

"When all the world knows that Abu Sayyaf has taken American hostages, then—and only then—will you collect your fee. Understood?"

"I will get word to the Americans."

"Good. Now come up to my hut. We will eat and get you what you need to take back." Janjali slung his arm around the young man's shoulder and escorted him up the trail.

As they rounded a bend, Hamsiraji came lumbering down toward them, waving his hand. "Ramzi, all of the men are in place, but the general keeps calling for you."

"Let him call until his voice is gone. How are the Americans?"

"In their cages. One is very quiet. The other keeps asking for water."

"His suffering has only just begun." Janjali squeezed the informant's shoulder. "But good news now, brother. We will have direct contact with an American news crew."

Hamsiraji looked confused. "I thought you sent the courier to Isabella."

"I did. He should be arriving by now. But the military will try to keep this a secret to save them from embarrassment. So . . . we will let the world know."

"And awaken a sleeping giant? Ramzi, this is insane! The public will put pressure on the U.S. military to attack us."

"But they won't—because the Philippine government will not allow it."

"Do you think they will respect the government?"

"Yes, I do."

"Then you are mad."

"Probably. But you are naïve. The Philippines are very important to the Americans. They will not jeopardize their relationship for two Marines. But they will send a rescue team, and that team will head out tonight. If the team fails, then the military will do as they always do—send the Scout Rangers and the Special Forces after us. And we will do what we always do. Hit, run, then vanish into the brush."

"But now that Allaga is dead and the general is here, who will arrange for the ransom payment?"

"Brother, do you think Allaga and Santiago were the only men I've dealt with? Let's just say that a cabinet secretary very close to the president of the Philippines is a dear friend of mine."

Hamsiraji crossed in front of Janjali and blocked the path. "Why didn't you share this with me? Why the secrets?"

"I've left you in charge of our army. That is enough responsibility for you. And now that you have abandoned your search for the gold, you and the men will be more than ready when the Americans come for their hostages."

"Of course, brother. But I wish to be informed of everything—from now on."

"I hope that is not a threat."

"Maybe it is." Janjali's brother kept walking but veered away from Janjali and the informant. Hamsiraji's ego had been bruised, and Janjali should do something to calm the man.

"Hamsiraji, as a token of good will, I will give you one night with my woman."

"Two nights."

Janjali sighed loudly. "Two nights."

When the terrorists had first brought Doc and Banks to the cages, Doc had been caught off guard. He had expected to be locked inside a hut, but apparently Janjali and his crew had stolen a collection of four shark cages from some marine biologists or other such group, and bamboo had been fastened across the rectangular slots used to take pictures or prod the big sharks. The makeshift prisons stood about a meter apart beneath a cluster of palm trees, and they had been there for months, perhaps a year. Weeds had grown up through and alongside the bars, and the twine that held the bamboo stalks in place was already beginning to fray. Had the cuffs and rope around their necks been removed before they had been placed inside, Doc and Banks might have had a fighting chance to escape. Now they could do little more than sit there, warding off ants and watching the children play across the clearing.

Behind the cages paced four guards who had been ignoring Banks's pleas for water. The lance corporal even gestured with his mouth that he was thirsty, but the men just looked at him, and occasionally one would shout something that Doc translated for himself as "Shut the fuck up, you ugly American."

At the moment, Banks was getting ready to ask them again, and Doc said, "Forget it."

"Doc, man, I can't take this shit anymore. I thought we were the big prize. I haven't had a drink since yesterday. My throat is so dry."

"You told me you were a hard operator."

"I am. This is different."

"Just hang in there, man. If this is the worst it gets, we got it made."

"Oh, it's going to get worse, Doc. They'll keep us alive, barely. All we need is a pulse to be worth something."

"And I should remember, once again, that you are always right."

"Yeah, they're going to do something to us. If there's a way out, we have to find it. We're not going to let these motherfuckers touch us. We're going to get out." Banks got up, crossed to the edge of his cage, turned around. He began rubbing the twine attached to his neck and wrists on one of the cage's bars.

The act, of course, drew the attention of a guard, a skinny young man who jammed his rifle's muzzle into Banks's shoulder and shoved him across the cage. Banks slammed into the opposite wall, cursed, then eyed the guard. "Come here," he said softly, tipping his head. "Come close."

"Don't do it, Banks," Doc warned as the guard edged toward the cage.

"That's right. Come right here," Banks cooed. Then he hocked the requisite loogie and scored a perfect hit to the guard's eye.

As Doc shook his head, the insulted guard shouldered his weapon, violently opened the lock on the jerry-rigged door Janjali's men had cut into the cage, pulled Banks out, and screamed something in Tagalog. Banks spit again, and the guard kicked him, driving him down onto his side.

The other three guards crossed behind the first, chuckling and goading their comrade with their AKs.

Feeling the pressure to continue, the skinny guard reared back, about to deliver a kick to Banks's head—

But Banks rolled, got back to his feet, and then, before the guard knew what was happening, Banks delivered a wheel kick that flattened the skinny guy in the bat of an eyelash. The guard did not get up.

"Holy shit," Doc whispered.

One of the other guards raised his weapon, about to fire.

"Banks!" cried Doc—

As another guard shouted and knocked the shooter's rifle away—just as it discharged, sending rounds hammering into the trees.

The kids in the clearing screamed and fled, while Banks dropped to the ground, got his legs around the shooter's, tripping the guy.

As the shooter fell, Banks slid sideways, rolled back, swung up his legs, and delivered a boot into the jaw of yet another guard. The man staggered back, while the last guard was about to drop to his knees and drive his rifle into Banks's head.

But Janjali beat the man to it. He had jogged over and now shoved the guard aside. He placed his boot on Banks's neck and applied pressure. "If I had a thousand of you, there would be an Islamic state in the Philippines."

"A thousand of me will be coming. Maybe more," Banks muttered.

"I don't think so." Janjali removed his boot, then snapped at the guards, who cowered and scampered back to their posts behind the cages. One guard hesitated, pointed to the man who had opened the cage, and said something.

Janjali's face darkened as he eyed the skinny guard, who began stepping away. Suddenly, Janjali yelled at the young man, who ripped off his bandanna and bolted for the trees.

Another shout from Janjali sent all three guards dashing after the man, one of them reaching for a large knife sheathed at his waist.

The guards disappeared into the jungle as Janjali shouted to two men posted outside a nearby hut from where Doc had heard the cries of another man. As the guards hustled over, a strangled cry from the skinny guard rose in the distance.

"The Tausug tribe will be upset with you," Banks told Janjali.

"They already are," said Janjali. "I have stolen all of their best fighters—except for that one."

"Treat them like that, and they'll turn on you."

"You know nothing." Janjali ordered the new guards to get Banks to his feet. During the struggle, Banks's shirt had been yanked down, over his bicep, revealing his tattoo, and as he finally stood, Janjali noticed the art. "What is this?"

"It's the ace of spades," Banks said.

"I know what it is," spat Janjali. "The writing interests me. The writing . . ." Janjali suddenly popped open the cover on his own sheath, withdrew and unfolded a six-inch blade.

Doc's gaze darted about the cell. Trembling, he reared back, booted his cage door. Booted it again and again until he knocked the entire cage onto its side. He tumbled down with it, rolled to face the terrorist. "Janjali, you need us! Remember that! You need us to collect the money!"

Banks started pulling away from the guards, but they held him fast. "Aw, man. Don't fucking do it, man!"

"So . . . death fears you? Some have called *me* death." Janjali drew up on Banks, the blade sticking from his fist. "And I do not fear you. I do not fear you at all." The man's hand flashed, and suddenly a bloody line opened across Banks's bicep.

With another swipe of his arm, Janjali finished the *X* across the tattoo as Banks's face twisted in pain—but he did not make a sound.

"Janjali!" Doc called. "Let me treat him."

The terrorist leader glanced incredulously at Doc. "I already have."

"I'm all right, Doc." Banks lifted his head at Janjali. "But you're going to pay for that, buddy. My friends will make sure."

Janjali smacked Banks's wound, his hand coming up bloody, then he wiped the blood on Banks's cheek and seized the lance corporal's jaw. "Death, young man, fears no one . . ."

TEAM DOGMA

CAMP BALIKATAN

TOWN OF ISABELLA

BASILAN ISLAND, SOUTHERN PHILIPPINES

2030 HOURS LOCAL TIME

While Houston, Vance, Callahan, Golez, and Padua slept away the afternoon, Rainey had tried to get some shut-eye, but it was just impossible. He was so wired that even while sitting he had to push up on the balls of his feet and shake his legs.

Consequently, he spent some of his time going over the maps, going over every step his team would take, and anticipating the kinds of defenses Janjali and his crew would have established around their base camp. In reality, it didn't matter if the terrorist had an entire mechanized division up there. Team Dogma would get in and get out without engaging the enemy, without firing a single shot. Call that a best-case scenario.

However, old Murphy had a way of taking best-case scenarios and ramming them straight up your . . .

Which was to say that no plan ever survived the first enemy contact. Murphy had Rainey's name. He had Rainey's number. And he really hated Marines with a passion. When it came to operating under Murphy's scrutiny, the easy way was always mined, and anything you did—including nothing—could get you shot. The list of his damned laws of combat went on and on.

Yes, sir, Rainey had psyched himself up to expect the worst. And if things actually went for the better, he would allow himself a few seconds of self-congratulatory relief, during which time he would flip Murphy the bird, then move on to the next screw-up.

And while he expected the worst, he would remain confident that he could meet the challenges. He figured that out there, it wasn't about bullets and brawn; it was about brains, about creativity—and that's where he excelled.

When he had finished mulling over his mission plans, he shifted mental gears to complete a final task before grabbing his ruck and leaving the hut: He wrote letters to Kady and to his son. While brief, they had been two of the most difficult pieces of writing he had ever attempted. How could he put into words how much he loved that woman? And how could he leave something that would some day help his boy become a man? He had realized as he started the letters that he had put too much pressure on himself. He then simply gave Kady the usual update (he didn't want to worry her), didn't mention anything about Doc's capture, and said he loved her and would talk to her soon. Something inside said that was the right thing to do. If he had written something out of the ordinary, he might have jinxed himself and the team.

In the second letter, he had told his son about the things he hoped they could do together when the boy grew up. Rainey hoped that if he did not return from the mission, in the years to come his son would read the words and know how much his father had cared for him.

Yet, teaching the boy to be a man was Rainey's job, and no one was going to take that away from him. He would go out there, get his men, and get back to his family.

"All right, gentlemen," Rainey said as the men gathered around him. They had donned their nondescript utilities, black bandannas, and Filipino Marine Corps boots (the ones Janjali's men were fond of stealing). Kalashnikovs and RPG-7 Rocket-Propelled Grenade launchers hung from Padua's, Houston's, and Callahan's shoulders, while Golez toted a 5.4 mm RPK-74 light Machine Gun, and Vance, despite his mild protests, carried the Russian Dragunov Sniper Rifle, which was, according to the fisherman, "like trying to catch bass with a broomstick." The rifle was only half as sexy as Vance's M40A3, was fed from a ten-round magazine, and was only reliable out to eight hundred meters, but it was the sniper rifle most often employed by Janjali's men. So Vance would have to "suffer."

"Everyone looks good to go," Rainey continued. "Now, the lieutenant colonel has found us a corpsman, and he's going to meet us at the southeast gate."

"Damn, this is getting better by the minute," Houston groaned. "Now we got a last-minute guy . . ."

"I'm sure you won't have any complaints—should you require his services, Lance Corporal. His name is Mindano, and he comes highly recommended. Sergeant Golez has worked with him before."

"Yes, I have," Golez said. "And don't let his age fool you. He is, as you say, a hard operator. I saw him save two men after we were attacked by the rebels last year."

Houston glanced at Vance and made a face. Rainey understood their misgivings, and they probably assumed Mindano was another typical Filipino kid. He couldn't wait until they met the man.

"All right, you've all had a chance to speak to the chaplain, and he's asked to give a blessing once we reach the gate."

"Can I say something?" Sergeant Padua asked.

"Go ahead, Sergeant."

"Last night I lost many good men." The dark-skinned Filipino began to choke up, and that made Rainey begin to fidget. "Yes, I wanted to go myself to bring them back, but I knew this was more important. You are all brave men, and I am very proud to be here." The sergeant gritted his teeth. "Now let's go kill Ramzi Janjali and bring the others home."

"Outstanding, Sergeant. Let's do it."

Rainey led them down the trail, and Vance hustled up beside him, his voice a near whisper. "Sergeant, we were hoping for, well, a U.S. Navy Corpsman."

"So was I," Rainey admitted. "But I heard this guy is the best they have. So let's see."

"All right, Sarge."

Within ten minutes they had reached the southeast gate. Demarzo was there, along with Corpsman Mindano, the company chaplain, and two of the Filipino colonels who had towed a ten-man security team.

Vance and Houston were, as expected, taken aback by Mindano's slight paunch, gray hair, and the thick glasses attached to his head by a tight lanyard.

"Marines, before you depart, some news," began Demarzo. "Earlier this evening we received a message from Janjali. He's demanding twenty-five million dollars for the release of the hostages. He's given us twenty-four hours to have the money deposited into his Swiss bank account, otherwise he will kill the men. Make no mistake, the United States does not bargain with terrorists. However, several independent Arab financiers are prepared to pay the ransom as an act of good will, should your mission fail."

Rainy knew all too well how that game worked. Those independent financiers (who had secret ties to the Warriors of Mohammed), would funnel money through legitimate sources, most notably the Philippine government. But that was no act of good will; it was simply terrorists funding each other under the guise of a ransom payment that would also grease Filipino palms and make those Arabs appear to be American sympathizers, when they were anything but.

And that was only the half of it. Rainey bet that arms and supplies would also accompany the money.

"Sir," Rainey said. "We don't intend to fail."

"Hoo-rah!" Vance and Houston shouted.

"That's right," Demarzo continued. "These cowards are holding a Filipino general and two United States Marines. And while we've yet to confirm it, they are probably responsible for the murder of Senator Allaga. We don't play by their rules—we play by ours. Now then. Filipino support teams Indigo Alpha and Indigo Bravo from the two battalions in Maluso are standing by. Check-in and extraction points have been marked. Saddle up, Marines!"

The chaplain stepped up and gave his blessing, and the gung ho atmosphere quickly turned somber. Rainey closed his eyes

Dear God, protect me and these good men.

With the blessing over and Demarzo leading off the group of pogues, Golez took a moment to introduce Mindano to the others.

"Most Americans say my English is excellent," said Mindano. "I spent over twenty years in Los Angeles before returning to my country. That probably helped, right, dude?" he asked Houston.

The California native smiled. "You know it, *dude*."

"And don't worry. I've seen and treated many, many wounds, the worst ones imaginable. The burns. The amputations. And I've tried to save many young men from the bullets of Janjali, but too many of them have died. So we go to change things."

"You're damn right," said Houston. "But do me a favor?" He cocked a thumb over his shoulder. "If Vance and I both get shot, you treat me first, right?"

"No, he treats the most seriously wounded first," Vance retorted.

"You're both wrong," Mindano said. "The man who treats me the best gets treated first." The corpsman winked, then chuckled under his breath.

"What should we call you?" Rainey asked. "We use the term 'Doc' for our corpsman, but the name has to be earned. I'm not sure if you guys do the same thing, but if you do, I'd feel a little weird calling you 'Doc,' since our own corpsman is still out there."

Mindano nodded. "I understand, of course. Just call me 'Mindano.' Or 'dude.' Or just scream at the top of your lungs. I am familiar with the sound of pain."

"Very well. Marines, we have about twenty-five kilometers to cover. I've given us just two hours to reach the first checkpoint. Vance is up first, followed by Golez, Padua, Houston, Mindano, Callahan, then me. Good to go?"

"Good to go," the men echoed.

In turn they slipped past the gate and sprinted off, crossing a narrow clearing to where shoots of bamboo, wandering vines, and long rows of reddish-brown mahogany trees separated the known from the unknown.

IO

Charles Callahan's orders were to bring back General Romeo Santiago alive. He was to accomplish the mission at all costs. The Filipino and American Marines were expendable tools, a means to an end, nothing more. Operatives were not supposed to have guilty consciences, and in the past, Callahan had been able to effectively shut down his emotions to get the job done. He would do so again. He had to.

But Rainey and the others . . . They weren't tools. They were men. Americans. Like him. They should know the truth, and keeping it bottled up inside was slowly killing Callahan. He kept reminding himself that while those men might die because of his actions, they would be sacrificed for the greater good. Callahan was doing his job. His duty.

So, he wouldn't say anything to the Marines. And

maybe they would make it easy. Santiago was a hostage
to them, and they would try to save the general. Their
mission was not at odds with his—not yet, anyway.
Callahan hoped to God he wouldn't have to chose between the lives of those men and accomplishing his
mission.

Damn it, he was thinking too much. He concentrated
on the path ahead, ducked to avoid a clump of
branches, and cursed himself as he misjudged the
height and caused the branch to rustle. He admitted he
was rusty, but it felt damned good to be back in the
field as a combatant. The AK-47 fit comfortably in his
hands. The small earpiece and attached boom mike fit
snugly to his head. He didn't mind the tugging of his
ruck or the Night Vision Goggles poised over his eyes.

"Dogma Team, this is Dogma One. Radio check,
over."

For the sake of clarity and in deference to the men
who had been captured and the men who had died,
Golez and Padua maintained their radio call signs of
Firelight One and Crossbow One, respectively. Mindano was given the call sign Papa Two, which fit the
older man quite well. When his turn came, Callahan acknowledged Rainey with his call sign, Eagle Six, which
bore an uncanny resemblance to his Agency call sign,
Omega Eagle. Dogma Two and Dogma Five would "remain open," as Rainey had delicately put it.

Disparate though they were, the call signs drew seven
men together for a common purpose, and Callahan had
actually felt a chill up his neck as he sounded off. For a

moment, he forgot he was a covert operative on a mission. He was a Green Beret again, humping through the bush, eating MREs and wiping his ass with leaves when the paper ran out. He was running a black side mission, and if he was captured, no one would ever know what had happened to him. Scary? Hell, no. He loved it.

The hand signal to hold traveled down the line, and Callahan shrank to his haunches and raised his arm.

"Dogma One, this is Dogma Four, over."

"Dogma Four, this is One," Rainey answered, the irritation in his voice hard to miss. They were only a few minutes into the first leg of their journey, and a delay was the last thing they needed.

"One, be advised we have troop movement ahead. Appears to be a team of Scout Rangers. Range approximately one hundred meters. They have crossed our path and are continuing southwest, over."

"Roger that, Dogma Four. Hold position until they're out of range, over."

"Holding position until they are out of range. Dogma Four, out."

Sergeant Rainey slinked through a patch of tall grass and came up next to Callahan. "So much for clearing our route," he said. "Those colonels assured us that the only troops in this area would be the checkpoint personnel along the main trails—or was I hallucinating when they said that?"

"No, Sergeant, I heard that, too."

"Then those guys out there—"

"Are either Scout Rangers," Callahan finished, "or Janjali's men. Do you appreciate the irony here, Sergeant?" Callahan tugged on his "enemy" utilities.

"I'd appreciate it if we could get moving. We got a lot of ground to cover before sunrise." Rainey adjusted his boom mike. "Dogma Four, this is Dogma One. Be advised 'Scout Rangers' could be guerillas. Search for today's band color. Confirm color is blue, over."

"Roger that, One. Searching."

"Dogma One, this is Papa Two," called Mindano. "Be advised I have identified the band color of blue. Confirm Scout Rangers wearing today's blue band, over."

Some Filipino units wore colored armbands that they changed daily to be positively identified in the jungle. They had marveled over the U.S.'s use of luminescent tape, along with thermal and infrared devices that allowed troops to be positively identified from great distances, as well as from the air. Boy Scout armbands just didn't cut it anymore, but they were all these soldiers had. When it came time for Team Dogma's extraction, they would apply luminescent tape to their arms. Callahan would wear his tape, label himself a good guy, and wonder . . .

"What do you think?" Rainey suddenly asked Callahan.

"I think those armbands don't mean anything. Janjali has informants in the military. They could have fed him today's color. Better yet, he could have paid off a team of real Scout Rangers to veer off their normal patrol route."

"I just keep loving this place more and more. So everyone is the enemy—except Doc and Banks."

"And General Santiago."

"Now there's a man I'd like to save, just so he can eat crow and admit that his forces need help."

"I thought he liked you."

"Yeah, because I took off my shoes before I stepped on his ego."

"Dogma One, this is Dogma Four. Be advised we are clear of Rangers and good to go, over," Vance reported.

"Roger that, Dogma Four. Good to go, out." Rainey turned to Callahan. "Keep a little tighter to Mindano."

"You got it."

"And hey, sir, you obviously have some field experience. When we get back, maybe you can buy me a beer and tell me all about it."

"I'll buy you two," Callahan said with a mild grin. "The stories are pretty long."

"I hear that."

As Rainey shuffled back, Callahan looked for Mindano's hand signal, then he adjusted his ruck's straps and trotted off.

When he came to the next low-lying branch, he was sure to duck and cleared it by several inches. Good. Slowly but surely he was finding his zone, and once he found it, there would be no distinguishing him from the other Marines, warriors to the core, for the Corps.

ABU SAYYAF STRONGHOLD
SOMEWHERE IN THE CENTRAL MOUNTAINS
BASILAN ISLAND, SOUTHERN PHILIPPINES
2105 HOURS LOCAL TIME

The dark-haired woman who had brought General Santiago his rice and pork sat across from him in the hut. Even without makeup, without combing her hair, and without the fashionable clothes worn by the women in Manila, she was a strikingly beautiful woman. As he ate, Santiago could not take his eyes off of her. "Why do you stay?" he asked, speaking softly so that the guards outside could not hear them.

"Because Janjali is busy at the gate, inspecting the machine-gun nests. And because I can."

"You are his woman, aren't you?"

She nodded slowly. "He has put too much trust in me." She glanced to the doorway. "And out there? Those men? Most are afraid of me. Janjali will kill the man who hurts me. Two have already tried. Their heads are still out there, in the jungle."

"Janjali is a brutal man."

"I know."

"You are here for something?"

"Maybe."

"I am always willing to bargain with a beautiful woman."

"That is good. Because I can help you."

"How?"

She edged toward him, lowered her voice even more. "I've heard that some who work for Ramzi used to work for you."

"Yes, there are some here who were once Marines. Now they are criminals."

"And you are an angel?"

Santiago's lip quivered. "We are not talking about me."

"No, but your men know what you've done. And they wanted some of the money you were receiving from Janjali. They couldn't get it from you, so they joined him."

"Fools."

"Maybe. And right now, not everyone is happy with him or his brother. Some who work for Hamsiraji, trying to find the gold, would like to leave the mountain, but they know Janjali would kill them. Some would speak with you, if they could."

"What are you saying, woman?"

"I am saying that there may be a way to escape. A few at the gate are with us. I can arrange it for you—"

"If I take you along."

She lowered her gaze to the dirt floor. The candle burning nearby cast her in a saintly glow. "The others will not have me. They are too afraid. But maybe you could persuade them. I have been here a long, long time. Please . . ."

"What is your name?"

"They know me as 'Garden.' That is enough for you."

"All right, Garden. Tell those men that if they want to escape, I will lead them. Janjali is no friend of ours anymore."

"You will persuade them to take me?"

"No. I will tell them you are coming." Santiago smiled weakly. "But can you trust me?"

"Yes, I can. Because all I have to do is tell Janjali that I will give him certain favors if he does certain favors for me, like kill you and deliver your head to the Marines. Do you understand?"

"Of course."

Garden rose slowly to her feet.

"Before you go, how about a favor for me?"

"Don't be a dog . . ."

"I didn't mean *that*. Earlier, I heard a commotion outside. I thought I heard voices, American voices."

"You did. Janjali has captured two Marines."

Santiago glanced away, chuckling under his breath. So the madman had won a prize with Allaga's help. Well, then, if Janjali would not help him escape from the island, then Santiago might have to fall back into the hands of the Americans. If they took along those captured Marines, when the Americans found them, Santiago could say that he had helped them escape—which would be true. Even if Allaga had ratted him out before Santiago's men had finished him, Santiago could deny the accusations and his actions might speak much louder than Allaga's words.

"Garden, tell these men that when we go, we will take the Americans with us."

She frowned, opened her mouth.

"Trust me, woman. I know what I am doing." Santiago rubbed his jaw, his thoughts charging forward. "I need to know what has happened to the men who came with me, including my bodyguards. We were separated after they surrendered to Janjali's men. They will come with us as well. We will need a plan. A very, very good one. Go now. Tell those men what you've heard, then come back to me with a plan for my approval."

"First I need to bring food to the Americans. I will tell them what you said."

"All right. Tell them to be ready. I want to leave before morning."

"General, I know what you've done. I know the kind of man you are. But for once in your life, do the right thing now."

As she left the hut, Santiago considered her words. He had always done the right thing—for himself. He was much too old to change his ways.

With his arms, wrists, and neck aching from being bound for so long, Lance Cpl. Ricardo Banks tried for the nth time to get comfortable inside the shark cage. He sat crossed-legged and rocked himself back and forth, flinching as the mosquitoes buzzed past his ears and occasionally landed on his cheeks. He tried to blow them off. Sometimes he won. The cuts on his arm had stopped bleeding, though he feared they might become infected and would leave scars across his once beautiful tattoo.

During his "POW 101" training course, Banks had been told that if he wanted to, he should hold firmly to his religious beliefs. Lots of guys in 'Nam, and more recently in Iraq, got through the experience by believing in God. Despite his foul mouth and lustful ways, Banks was a practicing Catholic and a professional sinner, and if Jesus was looking down on him at the moment, He was saying, "Ricardo, Ricardo, Ricardo. If you only would have walked in my footsteps, you wouldn't be sitting in a cage. You reap what you sow."

Maybe believing in God was a crutch, but Banks needed to hold himself up and keep a positive attitude.

"If you're going to join the Marines, then all right. Try your best. Be a great man, Ricardo."

"I will be, Dad. I will be . . ."

About an hour prior, the guards had finally brought him some water, and he had downed an entire bottle while one greasy bastard held it to his lips. But Banks's stomach still growled ceaselessly, and he wondered if they had any plans to feed him and Doc. He glanced over at the corpsman, who sat against the back of his cage, eyes closed.

"Doc? I'm starving."

"Save your energy. Who knows when they'll feed us—if they'll feed us."

"They're going to feed us. Soon. I am always right."

"Yes, you are. But that smell doesn't mean the food is for us."

"Yes, it does. They're cooking something. They have to feed us."

"They've been cooking for the past hour, man. It's driving me nuts."

"They can't leave us here to starve."

"Banks, listen to me. We have to cooperate with

these idiots. If we just lay low, we'll be all right. If we try anything, maybe they won't kill us, but they'll bring us pretty close. We've been lucky so far."

"You call what he did to me lucky?"

"Some day I'll have to introduce you to an old timer I know. He spent three years as a POW in Cambodia. They started with his toes. Then they moved on to his fingers . . ."

"I don't want to talk about it."

A woman suddenly drew up to the cages. She carried a large tray with two bowls and two cups. Beneath her somewhat ragged appearance lay real beauty, and Banks quickly pushed himself up to his feet. The woman muttered something to the guards, and one came forward to open Banks's cage.

"I have pork, rice, and some water," she said with a slight accent. Then she called back in her native tongue to the guard, who moved into the cage and began unfastening Banks's handcuffs.

"These Tausug don't understand much English," she whispered to him. "When the cuffs come off, don't try anything."

The woman had great timing. Banks had already envisioned himself spinning to seize the guard's weapon. He would crack him in the head with the stock, then turn and shoot the other guards, one, two, three down! As the first guard would get up, Banks would shoot him point-blank, get the keys, and go to Doc's cell. They would make a mad dash for the trees.

But Banks pushed away the vision and obeyed the

woman. Something in her tone was so powerful and al-
luring that it made him trust her.

Once the cuffs were off, Banks quickly untied the
thin cord around his neck and rubbed the flaming skin.
The guard barked angrily at him while gesturing with
his rifle. "Yeah, I get it, asshole. Fuck off, okay?"

The guard's eyes narrowed as he backed out of the
cage, then paused in the doorway as the woman set
down the meal. Banks snatched up the bowl and
reached for a piece of pork with his right hand.

"Use your left," the woman told him. "It is a custom
among the men. The right hand is used only for . . ."

"Right," Banks said, switching hands to satisfy her.

Before she backed out of the cage, she muttered,
"General Santiago has a message for you. He and some
others are planning an escape. They are going to come
for you. Be ready."

Before Banks could respond, she rushed out of the
cage and started for Doc. The guard slammed the door
and worked the lock, then turned a salacious gaze on
the woman.

As Banks wolfed down the food, he could hardly believe what he had just heard. General Santiago . . . That
was the pogue who had visited them during rifle training.
Yeah. He had been captured, too? Why would she lie
about that? No, she wouldn't. And now the good general
was planning a little escape party. Banks's RSVP was already signed and sealed. He glanced over at Doc, who
was just being uncuffed and groaning in pain. The woman
spoke quickly to him, and Doc shook his head forcefully.

Shit. He didn't want to go? What the hell was the matter with him? Was he worried about his wife and kids? Worried about doing something? Jesus Christ, getting captured meant that you had only one purpose in life:

Escape.

The woman flitted off toward the opposite huts, their windows outlined by flickering candlelight. Banks wondered who she was and how she had come by such important information. The answers to those questions would come in time.

Damn, the pork tasted sweet, the rice was cooked to perfection, the cuffs were off, and they were going to be rescued. Talk about a morale booster . . .

"Hey, Doc," he called. "How's your dinner?"

"It's good."

"Nice lady."

"Yeah."

Banks devoured another piece of pork, then said, "You up for it or what?"

"I'm not sure."

"Get sure."

"Hey, man. Eat slowly. Soon as you're done, they'll come in, put the cuffs and noose back on. Ride this out as long as you can."

"Don't worry, Doc. I'm done with the cuffs. And the noose."

"Banks . . ."

"What do we got out there now? Four guys? I can take them."

* * *

Doc did not want Banks to see the tears in his eyes as he ate the pork and rice. He kept telling himself that he was a U.S. Marine, much stronger than this. And he was. He wasn't crying for himself but for his family.

During Doc's first hour at the camp, a feeling had come over him. He had sensed that if he did anything to resist, he would not leave the place alive. That feeling was wreaking havoc with the rest of his emotions. He just wanted to stay in the cell until help arrived, even though he knew that his job was to escape, no matter the danger. Banks was right. The asshole was right. They had to escape—even if it killed Doc.

And then, a minor epiphany. He was crying for his family because he imagined himself already dead. He saw them at his funeral, saw his wife sobbing over his embalmed body, saw his two sons in their little suits, trying to be brave for their mommy. The feeling was making him believe that there was no way out, that he was dead, and that he should accept that now.

No.

He was still alive, damn it. And now he had a fighting chance. Fuck the tears!

"You know what, Banks? Don't let them cuff you. They open that door, you fight those motherfuckers till the end. You grab one and choke that motherfucker until he's fuckin' dead." Doc sprang to his feet. "DO YOU HEAR ME, YOU MOTHERFUCKERS! THE MARINES ARE COMING FOR YOU! AND YOU'RE ALL GONNA DIE HARD, VERY HARD!"

The guard nearest Doc's cell shouted something back.

Banks rose, came to the edge of his cage. "Doc, take it easy, man. I thought you didn't want us to try anything."

"I'm done feeling sorry for myself. I'm fucking done, man. We are going to get out of here. We are!"

"Yeah, man. But like you said, let's not do anything stupid. Maybe we'll lay low, like you said. Our time will come."

"Yes, it will." Doc took a deep breath, lifted his hand. He was trembling in anger.

"Doc, you all right?"

"Yeah . . . yeah . . ."

"Just chill, okay? And hey, when we get back, will you put in a good word for me with Colonel St. Andrew?"

The question caught Doc off guard. "What're you talking about?"

"How 'bout a rec from you, man. You know, to get me on the team."

"Assuming we live."

"Don't assume. *Believe*."

"Okay, believing we live, if that makes sense. You want me to give you a recommendation?"

"Come on, Doc."

"You need Rainey's blessing, not mine."

"Yours wouldn't hurt."

"Look, why are you asking me now?"

"Because I might forget."

Doc snorted. "I doubt that."

"Doc, you're the man . . . Come on . . ."

"For God's sake, Banks, what am I going to say? He made a fine POW. He resisted the enemy. He sought ways to escape. That won't get you on the team."

"Then I'll tell you what—and I'm making a promise to you right now—I'm going to prove myself. Rainey wants a hard operator? He's going to get one. You'll have stories for him and St. Andrew."

"I was going to say that 'I hope you're right,' but I know better now . . ."

TEAM DOGMA
JUNGLE SOUTHWEST OF ISABELLA
BASILAN ISLAND, SOUTHERN PHILIPPINES
2250 HOURS LOCAL TIME

Corporal Jimmy Vance lay on his belly, staring through his Nightstars. He didn't like what he saw. No, he didn't like it at all.

Vance had led the team on a course running about ten meters north of a trail frequently used by the Abu Sayyaf Group. They had been steadily climbing the first in a long, lazy chain of heavily wooded mountains stretching back toward the target area. Vance had kept close to the trees, until something ahead had caught his attention. Pushing himself up higher on his elbows, he took a second look.

There it was. About ten yards ahead. An empty plastic bottle with a familiar label. Were it not for the light of a waxing crescent moon, he might have missed it.

"Dogma Four, this is Dogma One, sitrep, over."

"Dogma One, this is Four, wait, over." Vance rose to his hands and knees, then shifted furtively toward the bottle. He reached it, picked up, then a faint glimmer to his right had him craning his neck. "What the fuck?" he muttered, then pressed the Nightstars to his eyes.

A small ring of NEPA huts lay ahead, with dim light shining from a few windows.

"Dogma One, this is Four. Be advised I have found an empty bottle of water in our path. Label indicates it is one of ours. Also be advised I have spotted a dozen or so huts lying dead ahead, range about ninety meters, over."

Sergeant Golez came shooting up behind Vance, flipped up his NVGs and replaced them with his own Nightstars. "I thought we were traveling away from the known villages."

"So did I. Somebody just build them, or what?"

"I don't think so."

"Dogma Four, this is One. On my mark you will bring us down around those huts, over."

"Roger that, One. But we're going to lose some time, over."

"Understood, wait, over."

"Why does he want us to wait?" Golez asked.

Vance grinned slightly as he imagined Rainey's face growing as crimson and shiny as a beefsteak tomato. "He's probably calling Demarzo right now because we should have known this village was here. Intelligence screwed up big time, and the sarge has no tolerance for that."

* * *

Lance Corporal Bradley Houston handed over the Foxtrot's microphone, and the sarge spoke tersely. "Yankee Thunder, this is Dogma One. We have encountered a small village just south our GPS coordinates, over."

"Dogma One, this is Yankee Thunder," the radio operator answered. "Wait, over."

"More surprises, huh, Sarge?" Houston asked.

"Scout Rangers, an empty water bottle, a village. I thought we were off the beaten path. This is a joke."

"Dogma One, this is Yankee Thunder, be advised that village is, in fact, your first checkpoint, over."

"Yankee Thunder, this is Dogma One. I was given GPS coordinates for first checkpoint. Why was I not told it was a village? Over."

"Dogma One, this is Yankee Thunder. Stand by."

Houston loved it when the sarge played hardball with the pogues back in the command center. He hoped that when he became a team leader he would have the courage to do the same—but he had to get back that recon fire first. "Being in the dark is one thing, being kept in the dark is another, eh, Sarge?"

"Houston? Shut up."

"Sorry, Sarge. This just sucks, you know? We're trying to get up there and get Doc back. And we have to deal with this stupid bullshit."

"Dogma One, this is Yankee Thunder. Unknown at this time why checkpoint is a village. Proceed with caution, over."

"Roger that, Yankee Thunder. Dogma One, out."

"We're not stopping there, are we?" Houston asked.

"No, we're not."

"Yes, we are," said Lieutenant Colonel Callahan.

"No, sir, we're not," Rainey corrected. "My team, my show."

"The people there are friendlies. There's a priest, an informant. Name's Father Nacoda. I need to speak with him. I'll be no more than two minutes."

Rainey held up a palm. "Whoa."

"Yeah, whoa," Houston added, drawing a sharp stare from the sergeant.

"Who established the checkpoint coordinates? You, sir?" Rainey asked Callahan.

"As a matter of fact, I did. Father Nacoda may have information that can help us."

"Why wasn't I informed of this?" the sergeant asked.

"I'm afraid that's classified," said Callahan.

"An observer, huh?" Rainey said, bearing his teeth. "Tell you what. You'll get your two minutes. But you're going in alone."

"That's fine with me, Sergeant."

"Dogma Four, this is Dogma One. On my signal, take us around that village. When we are approximately fifty meters southwest, call halt, over."

"Roger that. On your signal, taking us around, fifty meters to call halt, out."

Houston looked over his shoulder as Rainey and Callahan resumed their positions. He swore as he considered what other "classified" surprises the boogeyman had in store for them.

* * *

Rainey waited until he and Callahan were far enough away from Mindano so that the corpsman could not see what was happening. Then Rainey gestured for Callahan to come behind a nearby tree—

And that's when Rainey slipped behind Callahan, wrapped his arm around the lieutenant colonel's throat, then pressed his K-bar against the man's chest, right over his heart. "They'll never know," Rainey breathed into Callahan's ear. "They'll have to take my word for it. You were jumped by a rebel who got away. By the time I found you, you had bled out."

"You want the truth?" Callahan gasped, dropping his weapon and using both hands to work on Rainey's arm.

"I'm not leaving here without it."

"Let me go."

Rainey loosened his grip enough so that Callahan could speak. "Talk to me."

"I'm an observer, but I'm also gathering intelligence."

"No shit. What's your mission?"

"Just that. Intell has provided me with the names and locations of several informants. I'm making contact with them—it's all meant to help the mission, not hinder it."

"Then what's the problem? Why is your mission classified, compartmentalized? Why haven't I been informed?"

"Even I don't know that."

"You must have some idea."

"Just speculation."

"Then speculate. Your life depends on it."

"We're working closely with the Filipinos. It's a very delicate relationship. Intell's keeping it all under wraps. That's all I know. I just do what they tell me. Just like you. That's our duty. We're on the same side. Trust me."

"I don't, sir. And I won't." Rainey shoved the man away. "Good to go, sir?"

"Yeah," Callahan said slowly, massaging his throat. "Good to go." He leaned over, retrieved his weapon.

"Everything all right?" asked Corpsman Mindano, coming slowly forward. "We've been waiting for your signal." The old man glanced suspiciously at Callahan.

"We're good to go here, Corpsman," Rainey said, then cleared his throat and keyed his mike, "Dogma Four, this is Dogma One, over."

"One, this is Four, over."

"Four, we are good to go, out." Rainey glanced to the corpsman. "Let's move." Then he sharpened his gaze on Callahan and in a scathing tone asked, "Ready, sir? That priest is waiting for you. And you're not going up there to make a confession, are you?"

Callahan shuffled away, muttering, "I already have."

II

Ramzi Janjali presumed that if the Americans had sent a rescue team, they would insert on foot and not draw near his mountain until the wee hours. The Americans would not dare fast-rope a team into the area. Their helicopter, no matter how quiet its rotors, would betray them because Janjali had at least one informant placed at nearly every military checkpoint throughout the island. Indeed, the rescue team would have to cross the mountains on foot, and Janjali had to assume that they had sifted through intelligence, had questioned as many of the locals as possible, and had narrowed down the location of his camp. Could they find a weakness in his defenses? Would they surprise him by sending in an entire company of troops instead of a small commando squad? There were just too many unknowns.

Despite his nerves, he returned early to his hut, expecting to find Garden waiting for him. But his personal guards had said that she had left to feed General Santiago, then she had gone out to feed the Americans. After she had left them, she had traveled to the caves to bring water to the men posted at the entrances. That was just like her, a strong, compassionate woman on the outside.

But Janjali knew the cunning sorceress that lay within. How naïve she thought he was. For the past few months, he had given her the freedom to roam his camp as a test of loyalty. She had not once tried to escape, and he had thought that by now she would have felt something for him. Her pleas to be killed were just her way of hiding her pain and defying him. But he knew now he should have listened to them more closely. He knew now that she was making plans with the general for an escape. With teeth grinding and hands tightening into fists, he considered jumping out of his bed. He would find her, question her, torture her.

But he just lay there, seething, breathing, waiting for her to return. And within five minutes, she did. He already had one handcuff around his wrist, and when he sat up, the other found hers in a flash of movement.

"Ramzi, what are you doing?"

"Protecting you." He pulled her onto the bed with him.

"You can do that without the handcuffs. I thought we had made an agreement."

"The Americans will be here before morning. I need you to stay close to me."

"You will use me as a shield."

"No, I will save you from yourself."

She flinched. "What are you talking about?"

He placed an index finger over her lips, then grabbed the back of her head and shoved her down toward his crotch.

"Ramzi, please . . ."

"Go to work, you lying whore. Go to work. Otherwise I will kill you right now."

She wrenched out of his grasp, tugging on the handcuffs and nearly ripping him from the bed. "Then do it! Kill me! Kill me, you bastard!"

He sat up on the bed. "You don't want to die. You never have. Now sit down, and do what I say."

Her lip trembled, and she backhanded the tears away.

"You are still my Garden."

She hesitated.

"Come now."

Lowering her gaze, she released a shivery sigh, thought a moment more, then slowly reached for his pants.

OPERATIVE OMEGA EAGLE
TOWN OF SUMAS
BASILAN ISLAND, SOUTHERN PHILIPPINES
2308 HOURS LOCAL TIME

Father Tomas Nacoda's pockmarked and wizened face brightened as he answered the door of his rectory. "Lieutenant Colonel, that is an interesting, if not painfully familiar uniform you wear."

"Yes, Father, it is," Callahan replied, then moved into the small hut as Nacoda closed the door after him. "You, as always, are fond of black."

Nacoda smiled tightly. "I thought you would come sooner."

"Not during the day." Callahan glanced at the torn cot and the dented metal desk held up on one side by stacks of books. A few candles burning from sconces mounted to the bamboo walls cast warm light on the otherwise cold squalor. "Father, we found a small water bottle in the jungle."

"Probably one of Santiago's. His men are sloppy. They always have been."

"Then he was here?"

"Yes. With a small group. They tried to bribe the men to fight you if you came looking."

"You're a good man, Father. Thank you."

"No need for thanks. Janjali and his men have terrorized us for long enough. And any man who supports him is an enemy of ours."

"You said a small group. How many?"

"His bodyguards, I remember. And maybe five or six more, I'm not sure. They stayed only long enough to take some of our food and water."

"Did they say anything else?"

"Before they left, Santiago said that if we did not pay for his help, Abu Sayyaf would come and kill everyone

in the village. Since then, I have been ready." Nacoda
reached around to the small of his back and withdrew a
.45 caliber pistol from his belt. "As I've said, the collar
is white and the bullets are black. There is no gray out
here. And there is no help. The military cannot protect
us. We must fight for ourselves."

"I'm sorry it has to be that way, Father."

"It doesn't." Nacoda gripped Callahan's shoulder.
"You Americans can put an end to this. You have the
people and the resources."

Callahan sighed in disgust. "The politics are complicated."

"They always are. But faith will carry you through."

"I believe that, Father. I do. Now, did you see Santiago leave? Was he heading southwest?"

"He was. Janjali's camp is up there, somewhere. I
thought Santiago would never go there."

"He's on the run. He's trying to get off the island.
He's gone to Janjali for help. I'm going to stop him."

"Do you need help? Every man in this village would
volunteer—including myself."

"No, Father. We have to do this alone."

"Politics again?"

"Of course. And we'll get Santiago."

He nodded. "Before you leave, we will pray together.
But first, I have a favor to ask . . ."

TEAM DOGMA

OUTSIDE TOWN OF SUMAS

BASILAN ISLAND, SOUTHERN PHILIPPINES

2315 HOURS LOCAL TIME

The rest of the team was accounted for and had taken up positions along a jagged ridge overlooking the village.

"Dogma One, this is Dogma Four, all clear, over."

"Roger that, Four. Dogma One, out."

Rainey checked his watch for the third, or was it the fourth, time. Damn it. What the hell was Callahan doing? Rainey's paranoia was already swelling. Was the guy setting them up? Would they be surrounded by Abu Sayyaf guerillas? Was Callahan being paid off by them? Rainey could already hear himself giving the order to move out, leaving the lieutenant colonel behind. He resumed his gaze through his Nightstars, kept his focus on the hut that Callahan had entered, then abruptly left some five minutes prior, following the priest around the back and out of sight. Where had they gone? Rainey was tempted to call the man. All right. He would give Callahan three more minutes. Then he would order him back.

Rainey continued crouching in the jungle, sweat dripping down his neck, his eyes straining to spot Callahan in the phosphorescent glow provided by his binoculars. A rustle of branches above sent him wheeling around as a bolt of shivers rushed through him.

"Dogma Four to Dogma Team. It's just birds," Vance said. "Just birds, over."

"Dogma Four, this is Three. Confirm birds, out."

Rainey caught his breath, lowered the binoculars, and just sat there, his attention lured up to the incredible mantle of stars. He had never seen a night sky as brilliant, and he wished Kady were with him for just a few moments so they could share the view.

"Dogma One, this is Dogma Three," Houston called. "Be advised I have Eagle Six advancing our location, over."

Jerking his head down, Rainey stared once more through his Nightstars. Callahan darted toward them, alone, thankfully. Once the lieutenant colonel had drawn close enough, Rainey worked his clicker, and the man veered toward the sound.

After a final click, Callahan ducked behind the shrubs where Rainey waited. "Do we still have a friend in Jesus?"

"As a matter of fact we do, Sergeant." The lieutenant gasped for air. "That water bottle belonged to the men with Santiago. They came up through here."

"You knew he would. Didn't you . . ."

"I thought so."

"What's your interest in him?"

"Same as yours. He's another hostage."

"And if we get him out, we're heroes with the military and government here. That it?"

"You could say that."

"Well, I'm not here on a diplomatic mission. If we can get Santiago, great. But he's not my primary concern. We're bringing Doc and Banks back home. Period. Let's go."

"Sergeant, there's a little boy. Some kind of respiratory problem. High fever. He's really sick."

Rainey closed his eyes and groaned through his teeth. "What are we now? The fucking Red Cross? I've got two men up there who are going to be executed tomorrow if we don't do something about it. Every minute counts."

"Then let's stop talking about this. Give Mindano ten minutes to go look at the boy. Ten minutes. That's all I'm asking."

"That's ten minutes too long. Let's go."

Callahan's stare grew intense. "You and your wife just had a son."

"Don't play that card with me. And by the way, that's none of your business."

"Listen. For the past year these people have been very good to us. They've been our eyes and ears. We owe them. This kid could die without our help."

"Now you're a doctor? You're sure he'll die?"

"Ten minutes. That's all I'm asking."

Rainey shut his eyes tightly, saw his son's tiny face. "I'll call Yankee Thunder. Maybe they can send a team with a corpsman up. Best I can do."

"Thank you, Sergeant."

"Dogma Team, this is Dogma One. I want Dogma Four and Firelight One to advance one hundred meters for recon of next path. Dogma Three, rally on me to contact Yankee Thunder."

Though he still burned up a minute calling in for that medical support, Rainey figured a minute wouldn't make or break them. As he and Houston dropped back onto the trail, Rainey's conscience felt a little cleaner. Demarzo was calling for a Filipino team to help the boy, and while that team wouldn't arrive for several hours, at least help was on the way.

With movements as terse as automatons, Vance and Golez picked their way along the ridge until they reached the end, where a new slope would take them across the mountain. The incline was about thirty degrees, and the ground became much rockier and less stable. Point man Vance chose his steps carefully, his boots occasionally slipping as the mud and gravel gave way. He paused to warn Golez, who, coming up from about five meters back, returned a hand signal.

They pushed farther up toward a broad stretch of land that leveled off. The canopy became much denser, and the ground returned to mud, covered here and there by mats of dead fronds. Vance checked his GPS, noting their coordinates, elevation, and direction, then he gave the signal for Golez to halt. They hunkered down and surveyed the terrain with their binoculars.

Satisfied that the path was clear, Vance issued the next signal, and they continued the hump.

As he glanced ahead, picking his next route, a sharp crack resounded from behind—

Followed by a horrific scream from Sergeant Golez.

Vance whirled. The path behind was empty, and for a second, it appeared that Sergeant Golez had been plucked off the face of the Earth.

"Golez?" Vance stage-whispered. "Golez?"

In the next heartbeat Vance realized what had happened. And his heart sank. As he got closer to Golez's position, he saw how a few mats of broad, flat fronds had dropped away into a narrow hole. Shit. There it was. A booby trap. He and Golez had been searching for toe-poppers and trip-wire-triggered grenades and mines, but it was the cheapest, most primitive form of device that had tricked them: a punji pit.

Vance had been taught that bamboo is the best piece of gear you can find in the jungle. You can build with it, cook with it, use it as a weapon and as part of a trap. Punji stakes—sharpened pieces of bamboo—were impaled in the ground below a pit concealed by dirt, leaves, fronds, whatever blended into the landscape. When a soldier stepped into the pit, the stakes, often covered by manure and urine to cause infection, would drive into the soldier's boots and incapacitate him.

Golez, however, had not been that "lucky."

Reaching the edge of the hole, Vance held his breath and looked down. The Filipino sergeant had fallen straight down for about a meter and a half, impaling both feet on stakes. Then he had fallen back onto a bed of more needle-sharp stakes, two of which sprouted up from his abdomen.

"Oh, shit. Oh, shit. Sergeant?"

Slowly, Golez's eyes opened. He stared vaguely as blood leaked from the corner of his mouth. With a half-stifled groan, he reached out for Vance, tried to say something, the words inaudible.

No matter how many times Vance had seen a buddy

get hurt—and this certainly wasn't the first time—it always freaked him out. His breath shortened, his heart thumped in his ears, and his eyes failed to focus as logic became drowned in blood. He was a Marine, a professional trained to deal with situations like this. In the face of danger, of death, he knew he was *supposed* to remain levelheaded so that he could help his fellow Marine.

He blinked hard and began pulling away some of the fronds. "I'm going to get you help, buddy. I'm going to get you help. Just hold on. Dogma One, this is Dogma Four, over."

Rainey began to lose his breath as he listened to Vance's report. "Dogma Team, rally on Dogma Four's position with extreme caution. Go! Go! Go!"

He jogged in behind Padua and Houston, who kept a brisk but guarded pace across the ridgeline.

"Dogma One, this is Dogma Four. He's bleeding out real bad. Really bad. We need Papa Two right now!"

"Roger that, Four. We're on our way, out."

It wasn't like Vance to get so emotional over the radio. Sure, he had raised his voice before, but Rainey had never heard the sniper adopt a tone this urgent. For a moment, it seemed as though the entire operation was slipping through Rainey's fingers. He broke into a sprint, reached Houston and Padua, then blew right by them.

"Sarge, wait," cried Houston.

"We got a man down!"

Bradley Houston was the last person in the world Rainey expected to be the voice of reason, but the radio operator's simple call, followed by Rainey's mad reply threw a mental switch. No, Rainey couldn't just run up there when the ground could be littered with booby traps. He was better than that. Much better. He had to shut down. Shut it all down. Then turn the situation into a math problem: add five, subtract one, carry the two, and save his injured man.

He slowed, waved the others on, told them to kick up some mud to mark their path. The act was crude, but it was the quickest and most secure way to keep Callahan and Mindano, who were pulling up the rear about fifty meters back, on a safe path. Rainey assumed point, his gaze sweeping the ground and scrutinizing every irregularity. Far ahead, Vance was already working his clicker, and Rainey homed in on the noise.

"Dogma Four, this is Dogma One," he called. "Got your clicker, over."

"Roger that, One, waiting, out."

With hairs on his neck standing on end, Rainey finally neared Vance's location, and as he came within ten meters of the corporal, he spotted a slight shadow peaking up from beneath several fronds to his left. He paused, leaned down, and with his AK's muzzle, inched the leaves aside to reveal a punji pit about a meter deep. "Got another right here," he announced, shoving more leaves aside to expose more of the trap. The hole was nearly two meters across and about as long—just big enough to prove effective, even fatal. "Watch it!"

"Where's the corpsman?" Vance asked. The corporal was on his knees beside the punji pit, holding Sergeant Golez's hand. "I didn't want to move him, but he's still bleeding, really bleeding. His chest cavity's filling up."

Leaving the pit he had discovered, Rainey continued on to Vance and reluctantly looked down. Sergeant Golez lay across the punji stakes, his arms outstretched like Jesus dying on the cross. 'Nam vets had shared horror stories of guys who bought the farm by falling into similar traps, but you couldn't connect to them until you stared down into the face of agony. Now Rainey understood all too well.

Taking Golez's other hand in his own, he said, "The corpsman's on the way, Sergeant. He's on the way."

Sergeant Padua reached the pit and dropped to his knees. "I blame only Abu Sayyaf for this. Only them. Golez lost all of his men. And now this."

"Sergeant, I want you and the lance corporal at the top of the next rise, on watch. If I were them, I'd ambush us right now, while we're distracted."

Padua bit his lip, nodded.

Houston offered his hand to the rem ng Filipino sergeant. "Good to go?"

"Yes, good to go."

As they left, Rainey told Vance to work his clicker. "Here come Callahan and Mindano."

The corporal complied, and the silhouettes of two men appeared against the broken fence of tree trunks. Vance drew them closer with a few more clicks, and finally Callahan and the corpsman hustled up. Mindano kept his expression hard as he viewed his patient, then hurriedly slipped off his rucksack and began opening compartments. "Sergeant Rainey, do you know that these pits were not built by Abu Sayyaf?"

"How do you know they weren't?"

"Many of the villages have been constructing them to keep the bandits out. And you can tell by the angle of punji stakes that they are meant for intruders approaching the village, not leaving it."

"That didn't seem to matter here."

"No, it didn't."

"Did you know about these?" Rainey asked Callahan.

"I would've mentioned them if I did," the lieutenant colonel shot back.

That tone lit Rainey's fuse. He released Golez's hand, busted to his feet, seized Callahan by the collar, and dragged him several meters away from the pit. Surprisingly, the man did little to resist.

"Sergeant, this wasn't my fault. Don't take it out on me. We're all trying to do the right thing here."

"Look at him down there," said Rainey. "He's going to die. If we weren't sidetracked here, who knows, maybe . . ."

"We're all following orders, Sergeant."

"Shit. I'm tired of losing men to this fucking place. I'm tired of it!" He glanced away, took a deep breath to recover. "Your days of 'observing' are over. Go cover our six."

Callahan gave a terse nod, jogged off.

"Hey, Mindano, he's not moving anymore," Vance said to the corpsman.

Rainey rushed back to the pit as the corpsman, who'd been kneeling, dropped back onto his haunches, his latex gloves spattered with blood. Rainey eyed Mindano, and there was no need to ask the question. The corpsman spoke quietly in Tagalog, as though issuing some prayer over Golez's body, then he looked back at Rainey as he tugged off his gloves. "What should we do with him, Sergeant?"

"Get him out of there." Rainey shifted away, keying his mike. "Dogma Three, this is Dogma One, over."

"One, this is . . . Aw, shit, fucking fire ants, man! Aw, I got bit! I got bit!"

"Dogma Three, do you copy, over?"

"Dogma One, this is Three. Sorry, I copy, over."

"Three, get me Yankee Thunder and rally back on Vance's position, over."

"Uh, yeah, uh, roger, One. Calling Yankee Thunder and rallying back, out."

Once Vance and Mindano had hoisted Golez's body out of the pit, they slowly, reverently, set it down on the mud.

Vance repeatedly wiped his hands on his pants, as though they had been contaminated. Then, with eyes red and swollen, he approached Rainey. "Hey, Sarge?"

Rainey cocked a brow.

"I must've come within inches of that pit," Vance went on. "But I didn't see it."

"The goggles can only help so much."

"I don't know how I missed it."

"You know better than to apologize, Corporal."

"I'm not apologizing. I'm just saying I got the guy killed."

"He took the step, not you. Yeah, it fucking sucks. But it always is, what it is."

"Some day it'll be my turn to make that wrong step."

"You talking about marriage or walking point?"

Vance almost smiled.

Rainey squeezed the sniper's shoulder. "Don't beat yourself up over this. Doc and that other guy, what was his name?"

Vance finally grinned. "I don't remember."

"Me neither. But they need you."

Mindano walked over, carrying Golez's ruck and RPK machine gun. "His gear, Sergeant."

"Corpsman, are you familiar with this machine gun?"

"I am."

"Outstanding. I'll take your AK."

"I heard that it is customary for your corpsman to always carry the largest weapon. Why is that, Sergeant?"

"Because fire superiority is the best combat medicine."

Mindano nodded. "Hurt them before they hurt you."

"Exactly. But they also say that if we fire a single shot, we've failed our mission."

"I think we will be firing many bullets, Sergeant."

A grimacing Houston came up with the Foxtrot's microphone in his hand. "Sergeant, I have Yankee Thunder."

"You all right, Lance Corporal?"

Houston pushed up one pantleg and shook his foot. "Damn ants. I'm all right, Sarge."

"Good. Now Vance? Mindano? Rally up on Padua's position. We'll catch up in a minute. Same line order."

"Just without Golez," Vance added gravely as he led Mindano away.

Sighing over the remark, Rainey called Yankee Thunder and reported Golez's loss. The Filipino team that was coming to treat the boy would also recover the body. Lieutenant Colonel Demarzo tried to hide the disappointment in his tone, but it leaked out when he said, "Be advised that we may receive word to abort the mission. Repeat, we may have to abort the mission."

"Yankee Thunder, be advised we are still capable of carrying out all operations. We will issue sitrep at next checkpoint. Dogma One, out."

Although Golez could have proven very valuable since he could more easily pass for an Abu Sayyaf guerilla, the team still had Padua and Mindano. Well, the corpsman's age could betray him, since most of the Tausug tribesman working for Janjali were in their late teens and early twenties. If the team needed to slip a man inside Janjali's camp, Padua was basically all they had. Rainey didn't know very much about the man, except that he was a highly capable warrior when under attack. But could Padua handle the mental strain of such an operation, especially after his morale had been torn to shreds? And he wasn't the only one feeling

Golez's loss. One of the hardest challenges Rainey faced during combat operations was to keep his men fighting, even as they watched the men next to them get riddled by bullets, cough up blood, and die. Some men would find their rage. Some would find the desire for revenge.

And some, those whom you thought were the baddest asses on the planet, those who had already given their blood, sweat, and tears for the mission, would shock the hell out of you by turning tail. Every man has a breaking point, and now it was up to Rainey to monitor each of them for the warning signs. Good old Doc used to handle that, and even old Terry McAllister, whom Rainey missed almost as much as Kady, used to advise him on the team's mental state. With them gone, Rainey would keep a careful eye on the team—but who was looking after him?

As he returned the microphone to the Foxtrot's big pack, he asked Houston, "You going to be all right?"

"Fuck these bad guys and these bugs, Sarge."

"We got a lot of ground to cover and time to make up."

"So what? Yo. Yo. Force Recon's in the house. They all going to clear a path for us."

Rainey nodded half-heartedly.

"Hey, Sarge. Are *you* going to be all right?"

Rainey gave the lance corporal's neck a solid squeeze. "I am now. And thanks for asking."

12

Ramzi Janjali awoke with a start. He had not meant to fall asleep, but after Garden had pleasured him, he had felt so relaxed that the desire to beat her had slipped away. Now she lay beside him, breathing softly and still handcuffed. Janjali dug for the key in his pocket, removed the shackle from his hand, then cuffed her to the bedpost—not that he expected the bed to actually hold her; he just wanted to make her time in his hut a little less comfortable. He wanted control.

"No, don't," she said groggily, her eyes trying to focus.

"Stay here," he said, then coyly added, "Will you?"

"Where are you going?"

He smirked, then rose, pulled up his pants, and left the hut, startling both of his guards, who had fallen asleep. He grabbed one boy by the collar, smacked him across the face, then turned to the other, who was already raising his palms. Janjali grabbed the boy's wrists, then booted him in the stomach. The guard dropped to his rump with a faint moan. "There are men here I no longer trust. So the next time you fall asleep, I will kill you."

The guards knew better than to say anything. They nodded, clutched their wounds, and resumed their positions.

"Garden's inside. Watch her."

Janjali withdrew the pistol from his belt and strode across the dark clearing, headed for General Santiago's hut. His neck tingled as he glanced over his shoulder, wondering if an assassin lay across the camouflaged roof of one of his huts. Hamsiraji had confirmed that Santiago's imprisonment had sparked unrest and resentment among those fighters who had once been Filipino Marines.

But the two Tausug tribesmen posted outside the general's hut were as alert as they were loyal. They called out to him as he approached. He put them at ease with the wave of his hand and a few words, then he stowed his pistol and pushed open the hut's door, his entrance announced by the creak of vine hinges. A sickly sweet odor wafted toward him, and it would have made him gag, but Janjali had smelled death many times before.

General Santiago lay off to the right across a dirty grass mat, only a single candle burning to cast his fat silhouette on the hut's rear wall. Although Janjali had initially allowed the man to remain in the hut without handcuffs, he had ordered the general bound in light of recent news. Santiago's eyes remained closed, though Janjali assumed that the man was awake. Too many years as a soldier had most assuredly made him a light sleeper.

Janjali eased forward, then suddenly kicked the general. "Wake up!"

"Ramzi," Santiago whined as he sat up. "You are insane."

"I didn't want you to be alone."

Janjali turned back toward the collection of heads that encircled the general's mat. Santiago's entire group—including his bodyguards—had been murdered, their heads hacked off and delivered to the general's quarters. Some of them still wore their last expressions of horror, and Janjali stared at them for a long moment, fascinated by the faces and what they represented.

"Have you come to kill me?" asked Santiago, breaking Janjali's trance.

"Tell me, General, have they amused you?"

"This is not power, Ramzi. This is the work of a coward who cannot stand up and fight his enemies. This does not inspire your men. It makes them hate you."

"Oh, really? And what would your men think if they knew you ordered Senator Allaga's execution?"

"Ramzi, you are missing the point. You are nothing without me. We could have finished you off years ago. But we made a lot of money together. I come asking for a simple favor, and you forget all about our arrangement. You would have been captured in Lamitan if I had not called off my troops. And now, you may need to escape as much as I do. You need me—even more than some of your men, who are even more corrupt than mine."

"I know there are some men working with my brother who now despise me." Janjali picked up the head of one young Filipino Marine, holding it by the hair. He spoke softly in the head's ear. "I know everything that goes on here. Isn't that right?" Janjali tipped the head, making it nod.

"You *have* gone insane."

"No, I'm just bored of people like you. Bored of this place, this life . . ."

"It is the life you chose. For you it is too late to change your mind. Now free me. And we'll work together."

Janjali smiled, glanced to the head. "What should I do? Should I let him go?" He suddenly tossed the head at Santiago, who recoiled as the thing flew into this face.

Chuckling, Janjali called for one of his guards, and as the man entered, Janjali wrenched away the guard's rifle.

Santiago's mouth fell upon. He dug in his boots and began sliding himself toward the far wall in a laughable attempt to escape. "Ramzi, you're smarter than this . . ."

"Smarter than you know." Janjali turned the rifle around, holding it by the barrel. He reared back and clubbed Santiago across one knee. As the general screamed, Janjali came down with a second blow across the general's other knee. The young guard's face widened in shock.

"Will your loyal men want to carry you out of the jungle?" Janjali asked, looming over Santiago. "Will they carry a man who can be bought as easily as you?"

Santiago just looked at him, his face creased in pain.

"Answer me!"

"No, they won't carry me!"

"Then you should get used to being here"—Janjali glanced at the heads—"with your friends. You can think about your life. Maybe you can decide if selling out your military and your government was worth the price. Good evening, General." Janjali tossed the rifle back to his guard and, with adrenaline turning his arms and legs into pulsating weapons, he slammed out of the hut, feeling as godlike as ever. Now it was time to remind the American Marines who was in control.

Doc sat in his shark cage, holding his breath and listening.

The jungle gave up nothing. No more screams.

But he had heard them. They had come from that hut across the way, and they had jerked him awake. He had not meant to doze off, but the fear of the unknown had been sapping the strength from his limbs and his mind. Doc knew two kinds of fear. The first was when you were startled by something and reacted. It all happened fast, with no time for the fear to settle in. The second kind of fear was much worse. You knew something bad was going to happen, but there was time, way too much time, to think about it. The fear would fester and grow, and if left unchecked, it could rob a Marine of his spirit.

More than three hours had passed since the woman had told them of the general's plan to escape. Three hours. And still no word from anyone. The longer the group waited, the less time they would have to exploit the dark. If the general was leading them, then he should know that. Had something gone wrong? Doc dismissed the negative thought. *Keep the faith. They're coming for us. And like they said, just be ready.*

To pass the time, Doc had put his recon skills to work. Using the heel of his boot, he had drawn in the dirt a little map of the compound. He figured the place was about the size of a football field, though broken apart by the rugged terrain. He marked their position, the positions of the guards behind them, and where the main gate lay below. He plotted out the locations of those machine-gun nests he had seen, and he hoped to God that the men leading the escape had an alternate exit in mind. If they had to bypass those nests and head down into the jungle below, those gunners could easily spot them through breaks in the canopy—breaks Doc and the others had no time to avoid while running their assess off.

During the past hour, Doc had seen a curious amount of activity in the camp. All of the children had been taken down to the southern end of the camp, and Janjali's men had been carrying dozen of crates, presumably of small ordnance, along the trail, headed in the same direction. Doc had caught a glimpse of a particularly large crate, whose side was marked ARMED FORCES OF THE PHILIPPINES. He wondered if the rebels had stolen the crate and its contents—or whether it had actually been supplied by the military. Doc wondered even more why all of the equipment was being moved south. If Janjali was preparing for an attack, he would most likely reinforce the north and northwest sides of the camp because a commando team from Isabella—especially one coming in on foot—would advance from that direction. Was Janjali second-guessing his enemy? Did he believe they would circle around to the back of his camp? If so, they would have to ascend the mountains—and that would take way too much time and limit the amount of ground they had for their own escape.

Doc had discussed the possibilities with Lance Cpl. Banks, who believed that Janjali and his men were making plans to flee the camp should the attack not go their way. That would seem reasonable if they were moving equipment to the north and northeast. But to the south? They either knew of a passage that would take them quickly across the mountains, or, as Banks had suggested, they had found some caves that cut through and wound their way down to the mountains' base.

"Doc?" Banks called, pushing forward. Although he had considered fighting the guards, he had finished eating and with a full belly had surrendered to the cuffs and noose. Banks's expression, nearly lost in the darkness, reflected his discomfort. "Hey, Doc?"

Taking a deep breath and returning his attention to the hut, Doc answered, "Yeah?"

"Did I imagine that?"

"Nope. They're torturing somebody. Pray it isn't

someone we need—you know what I'm saying?"

"Yeah. Hey, wait a minute. I think someone's coming. See him?"

"Got him. Shut up."

It was so dark that Doc could not identify the man until he had nearly reached the shark cage. Oh, shit. It was the maniac himself. Doc exchanged a quick look with Banks, who shrugged in confusion.

Holstering his pistol, Janjali called to the guards, who rushed to the cages and opened them. Wearing a strange look, his chest heaving, the terrorist stepped into Doc's cage as Doc rolled his legs sideways, about to stand.

"Stay down," Janjali growled.

"Time for interrogation?"

"Shut up." After another rapid-fire exchange, the guard jogged back to his comrade and accepted something. He returned to Janjali and handed him a syringe as another guard slipped into the cage. The first one shoved Doc onto his side while the other drove his boot into Doc's head, pressing his cheek into the ants and mud.

"Fight 'em, Doc!" Banks screamed. "Don't let them do this! You're a Marine! Semper Fi! Semper Fi!"

"Hey, Janjali? I'm a medic," Doc said. "Just tell me what it is."

"Oh, don't worry, Marine. You're going on a wonderful trip—and you're going to be so happy that I sent you."

As Janjali tested the syringe, Banks continued to scream until one of the guards shoved a rag into Banks's face.

Doc wanted to resist. More than anything. But they had pinned him to the ground. And Janjali was already looking for a vein. "What is it? Heroin?"

"Shhh. Oh, there you go. You're going to feel something now. You're going to feel—"

A chill broke across Doc's back as the drug took hold and tension in his arms and legs evaporated.

"There's a demon inside you now, eh, Marine? And now you know why so many men have killed for the demon. She controls you in a way that no flesh-and-blood woman could."

Janjali's face swam against the darkness, and his words were like notes resonating from an old flute that Doc's grandfather liked to play before bedtime. The guards released Doc, and he was unable to pick himself up. He lay there on the beach with his grandfather, who played a sad, lonely song as the breakers rolled in.

All four guards had to drive Banks against the shark cage and hold him there. But he kept struggling, kept spitting in their faces, kept cursing at them—

Until Janjali, who was about to inject him with the drug, called to one guard, handed him the syringe, then ordered the others to back away. Banks glared up at the man, who reached down, grabbed him by the shirt collar, and dragged him to his feet.

"Come on, motherfucker," Banks rasped. "You want to go at it? One on one? Me and you? Come on, motherfucker, let's go. Right here! Right now!"

Tossing a look to his guards, Janjali smiled as two men gripped Banks's arms and held him in place. "Your comrade is smart. If he ever makes it home alive, his family will recognize his face. But yours . . ."

"Come on, motherfucker. Take off my cuffs. It's me and you. Or are you just a scumbag coward like they say?"

Janjali's hand found Banks's throat and squeezed until Banks's air was gone. Then he punched Banks in the eye. Punched again. And again. Each blow sent Banks's head crashing into the bars, then whipping back—to connect once again with Janjali's fist.

Then the terrorist shifted position and came in again, delivering three more blows to Banks's other eye. As the concussions faded and Banks's head lolled to one side, he blinked, felt the stinging pain, and saw only a blurry curtain of darkness.

Janjali snickered. "Marine or not, you are just another infidel."

"Fuck you!" Banks managed.

A sudden blow sent Banks's head into the bars, and only after he made impact did he realize that he'd been punched in the mouth. Warm, salty blood poured over his tongue, and one front tooth felt wobbly.

A second punch extracted the tooth altogether, and Banks coughed, spit it out, and gasped for air. The bastard was turning Banks's face into raw hamburger, and there wasn't a damned thing he could do about it. Never in his life had Banks felt more helpless. And he was hardly used to dealing with that. He screamed in rage, barely recognizing his voice. He was a rabid rottweiler ready to bite off Janjali's head with his remaining teeth.

"I could be your death," Janjali said. "I could be. And now look at you. Your eyes are swelling shut. Your lips are fat. Your tooth is gone. I can keep going. I control the pain. How can you *not* fear me?"

Banks thought of cursing Janjali one last time, but his mouth was so full of blood that he could barely speak. He stood there, his face on fire but his spirit intact. The man had not broken him. The man could not.

"Do you fear me, Marine?" Janjali hollered, ripping his nails across the scabs on Banks's tattoo and drawing a sharp groan from Banks. "Do you fear me?"

Although he could no longer see the man, Banks imagined Janjali's dark complexion and rage-filled eyes. Banks smiled against them, blood pouring from his mouth until he spit hard, hopefully drenching the terrorist.

Janjali answered with a smack across Banks's bloody face, a smack that sent more blood spattering from his mouth. "Fear me, Marine! I am your death! Fear me!"

And then . . . silence for a few heartbeats. Boots shuffled. One guard murmured something. More boots. Banks tried in vain to open his eyes. The dizziness was coming on strong, and his legs were beginning to give out. Another murmur, this one from Janjali, then—

Banks jerked his arm at the stinging pain as someone wrestled to hold him still. Damn it, they had injected him. He shivered against the chill spidering up his arm. "Doc?" he called, sounding like a seven-year-old with a lisp. "Doc? It's me and you, Marines till the end! He can't beat us. He can't!"

On the opposite end of the camp, Hamsiraji followed Charti down a long tunnel whose ceiling abruptly rose some four meters. The tunnel jogged right, then left, then straight away again, and Hamsiraji could hardly believe that the skinny boy who was barely seventeen had alone discovered a passage so deep and so broad. Only a day prior Charti had also found the new cave, and with a little digging, had squeezed his way into this new tunnel. Hamsiraji's flashlight shone into a grotto ahead, where Charti stood to the left, waving him over and pointing at the wall, which was in truth a section of rubble where the ceiling and part of another wall had caved in. Abutting the rubble stood a section of rock upon which dust-covered Japanese characters had been drawn with black paint.

"Look here," Charti said. "Is this important enough to wake you?"

Hamsiraji ran his fingers over the markings. "They were here, all right."

"And after they left, maybe years later, the ceiling came down. Maybe this is why no one has found the treasure yet. If we can clear this path, the gold could be on the other side! It is all pointing to here."

Hamsiraji's breath quickened as he sized up the excavation job. He would need fifteen or twenty men to begin clearing all the rubble. Some of the rocks probably weighed three to five hundred pounds. The more men he could sneak down into the tunnel, the faster they would reach the other side. Time was running out, he knew. His brother was fast making preparations to abandon the camp, should the Americans and Filipinos surprise everyone by sending in a large force. If Hamsiraji was going to learn once and for all if the gold existed on Basilan, the time was now.

"Charti, go up and tell the others that I want twenty-five men down here! Twenty-five! No less."

"But Hamsiraji, the Americans are coming, and your brother will—"

"Forget the Americans. Forget my brother. Get me the men. I don't care if you pull them from the gate or the machine-gun nests. Just get them."

"I will. I will! This is the closest we've ever come! I believe the gold is here! I really do!" The boy waved his fists as he sprinted away.

Hamsiraji stroked his beard for a few seconds, then set down his flashlight and began removing some of the smaller stones as he imagined Ramzi yelling in his ear, *"You fool! You fool!"* Hamsiraji had already decided that if he found the gold, he would not tell Ramzi. Like a grand, old pirate he would sail away from the island a rich man who was no longer kept by his brother.

13

TEAM DOGMA
JUNGLE SOUTHEAST OF SUMAS
BASILAN ISLAND, SOUTHERN PHILIPPINES
0220 HOURS LOCAL TIME

"Four, can you see the river yet, over?"

"Dogma One, be advised we're approaching now, out."

As Vance neared a row of shrubs a few meters from the shoreline, he gave the signal to halt, then shoved himself into the foliage. With his Nightstars he studied the dark pockets of growth on the opposite bank. The river was about fifteen meters across and who knew how deep, although Vance had heard during the briefing that most of the central jungle rivers were pretty shallow. The current was nearly nonexistent, but the water was too stained to make any assessment about depth.

Vance continued his observation, panning left with his binoculars until he came upon a remarkable sight: an Abu Sayyaf guerilla seated beneath a tree, his rifle in his lap, his head hanging down. For a moment, Vance thought the man was dead, but then he zoomed in until the image nearly blurred. The guy's chest was rising and falling. Vance activated the Nightstars' laser range finder. "Dogma One, be advised I have spotted a single scout to our left, opposite riverbank, range approximately sixteen meters, over."

"Roger that, Four. Continue threat scan. He's not alone, over."

"Roger, One. Continuing scan, wait, over,"

Sergeant Padua, who had crouched down a few meters behind Vance, had his own binoculars pressed to his eyes. "Dogma One, this is Crossbow One. Be advised I have spotted second guerilla to our right, range approximately eighteen meters, over."

Vance turned back, flashed Padua a quick thumbs-up, then zoomed in to find the second bad guy. Wouldn't you know, he too, had fallen asleep on the job. These guys could be the first of many long-range scouts hiding in the jungle. Vance wouldn't bet that every one of them had fallen asleep, but you took the lucky breaks as they came—and you took them cautiously. Those two guys could be decoys trying to lure the team into an ambush.

Probing every inch of the jungle before them, Vance knew that at the moment, good eyes meant the difference between life and death.

And he wasn't going to miss something again—especially after what had happened to Sergeant Golez.

His breath quickening, Vance shifted position for a look down their own bank. "Where are you?" he whispered to himself. "Come on . . ."

"Dogma Four, this is One, sitrep, over."

"One, this is Four, wait, over."

Vance thought he spotted a shirt sleeve, zoomed in, saw only a thick branch. Shit. He was getting paranoid already. Tensing as a tremor woke in his hands, he switched his attention back to the opposite bank. One more look. Only two guys? Not three? Maybe. It made sense to spread them out in small teams. One shot would boom across the mountains and alert the other scouts. Pair them up.

So Vance concluded with a heavy sigh that there were, in fact, only two guys out there. He was staking his life and lives of the others on that. "Dogma One, this is Dogma Four. Be advised we have spotted only two bad guys, over."

"Roger that, Four. Dogma Three? Rally with me on Dogma Four's position, over."

"Roger that, One. Rallying forward, out," Houston replied.

Vance shifted gingerly back toward Sergeant Padua and whispered, "Got them both?"

"Yes, I do," Padua answered, his Nightstars locked over his eyes. "Moving between one and the other."

"Outstanding. Now Force Recon is going to give you a little show that demonstrates our motto."

"I am ready for the show."

The sarge and Houston came skulking up, and while Houston slid out of his ruck, Rainey borrowed Vance's binoculars and took a look for himself. "One and two," he muttered. "A nice little package. So long as the water is deep enough."

"And I was worried about it being too deep to cross," Vance said.

"All we need is two feet max. What do you think, Mr. bass fisherman? Do we have that?" Rainey asked.

Vance unsheathed his K-bar. "I think so." He clenched the knife between his teeth, then signaled to Houston, who already had his K-bar jutting from his fist.

As Rainey gave orders to Callahan and Mindano to establish supporting fire positions should the ambush go south, Vance and Houston entered the water with movements so slow, so carefully executed that they were almost excruciating.

With a little gasp, Vance lowered himself to his hands and knees, then he dropped slowly forward, letting the water swell around him. He pushed along the rocky bottom, and suddenly the river dropped away from his hands. Awesome. They had the depth they needed. He took in a long breath and dove under, swimming hard to right while Houston branched off to the left. It was all about one sense now, all about what he felt. Occasionally, he dropped his left boot a little deeper, trying to feel his way along the bottom. After about thirty seconds of swimming, his boot dragged along rocks. He was nearing the shore, but he wouldn't come up, wouldn't take a breath until the bottom was nearly at his nose. And then, he would surface like a big

old Florida gator targeting some old lady's poodle who
had wandered down to the lake from his little dog-
house. Vance would come in all quiet like, and then . . .
chomp!

Houston didn't mind getting into the water. No bugs in
there, right?

Yet as he swam, he thought about leeches and imagined other strange, insectlike flesh-eating creatures
who lived in the river.

What the hell was the matter with him? He was a
United States Marine, for God's sake. He had been shot
at, stabbed, and shot at some more. He needed to focus
on the job. He needed to cross the river, move up
silently on the sleeping guard, and give him one to the
heart with the K-bar.

Then his recon fire would be more than lit; it'd be
blazing.

So, to help rekindle that fire, he played a little game.
He imagined he was a green Marine and didn't know
jack about sneaking up on a guy and whacking him. He
concentrated on the swim, drew a mental picture of his
prey, and planned every step from the riverbank to the
tree where the Abu Sayyaf fighter had dozed off to
dream of screwing the American girls he'd seen once
on satellite TV. That was one pervert who needed a
super-sized dose of killing. Houston had blade, did
travel, would oblige.

After moving a few more meters, Houston's hands
abruptly smacked into the bottom. Now working his

arms as though they were wings, he kept himself as low as possible to the bottom. Once the water had crept down to his ears and the bottom was just a few inches from his chin, he slowly lifted his head from the water, allowing only his eyes and nose to clear the surface. He opened his eyes. Blinked. Focused. And found his target.

Rainey knew he had to put Vance and Houston in harm's way to take out the guerillas. Padua had to stay back in case they needed him at the camp, and Mindano's medical skills were invaluable. Well, Rainey could have sent Callahan. The guy was the most expendable member of the team . . .

However, you never sent a pogue to do a man's job—especially a pogue who claimed to be only an observer.

So Vance and Houston had drawn the short straws. Those boys were all that was left of Team Dogma. If something happened to one or both of them, Rainey might very well abort the mission. He knew that the fear he had about getting killed, about leaving Kady and his son alone in the world, was affecting the way he managed the team. While he loved his men, he was usually able to recognize the importance of the mission, the importance of the big picture.

But everything was different now. Doc and Banks were already in danger, and part of Rainey wanted to spare the rest, even spare himself. But you couldn't have it both ways. And as he had told Demarzo, his team was the best for the job.

So Rainey had to deal with the risks and with the

possibility of losing Vance and Houston. He couldn't
protect them. He wasn't their father. He was their sergeant, a fellow Marine, a brother charged with sending
them out there to live or die. And deep down, even
though he knew as team leader he must hold back to
conduct the operation, he cursed the logic and wisdom
of command. No, he didn't want to get himself killed.
And yes, he was afraid of that. But he wanted more than
ever to be out there with his boys. He could help them.
And he could prove to himself that he still had what it
takes, that this new fear brought on by becoming a father had not undermined his esprit de corps.

Or maybe it had.

He fingered a dial on his Nightstars and watched as
Vance crawled slowly out of the water, heading for the
trees. Then Rainey did a quick pan to the right, spotting
Houston, just as the lance corporal disappeared behind
a rubber plant.

Lieutenant Colonel Charles Callahan had Vance's bad
guy in his sights, though he kept his finger very light on
the AK's trigger. One shot would send everything to
hell; Callahan's warrior instincts were too well-honed
to make an error as grave as that.

The guerilla still sat under his tree, his head hanging,
and Callahan was going to watch it all unfold through
the night-vision scope.

Steadying his arms, Callahan wondered why Vance
hadn't already made his move.

Then Callahan blinked.

In the next instant, an arm appeared from behind the tree and came down toward the thug's chest. Callahan could almost hear the K-bar popping flesh. The guy toppled.

"Dogma One, this is Dogma Four, over," Vance called in a hushed voice.

"Four, this is One, I confirm your kill. Hold your position, over."

"Roger that, holding, out."

Callahan switched his aim to Houston's bad guy, who had also not moved since they had first found him. Okay, where was the beach boy with the knife? After nearly thirty seconds, Callahan began to curse under his breath . . .

Houston's boots had crackled too loudly on the dried fronds lying along the riverbank, so he had taken a moment to veer around them and track soundlessly toward his bad guy's tree. He had circled wide and was coming around the back. The tree was about four meters ahead. He saw the scout's knee jutting out to one side, saw the butt of his rifle lying in his lap. As he narrowed the gap to two meters, he thought he heard snoring.

Damn, the guy's rifle was awfully close. Houston considered pulling it away first, then gutting the man. But if he was good—very, very, good—then the weapon would mean nothing. The terrorist would die before his fingers reached the stock.

With the tension practically crackling in his ears, Houston took in a long breath and put himself into his killing zone, a state of complete relaxation where he moved with ease because his muscles had become a part of his surroundings. He neared the tree, came down to his knees, glanced at the K-bar in his fist. Then he leaned forward and paused. The guy wasn't snoring anymore, but his breathing sounded heavy and rhythmic.

Houston reached around the tree, about to make the punch—

And a long, black caterpillar dropped onto his arm. "Fuck!"

He swatted the bug, started to reach again, but the bad guy had awakened and was already jerking forward, his hands going for the rifle.

Houston got up on one foot, lunged around the tree, and crashed into his enemy, a bleary-eyed guy of about twenty. Though still half asleep, the guy used his rifle like a fighting stick, bringing the butt up into Houston's jaw.

Gasping at the sharp pain, Houston lost his balance and fell back onto his ass. By the time he looked up, the guy was already tucking the rifle's stock into his chest, about to fire.

With the better part of a second before getting shot, Houston reacted.

Callahan wanted so badly to take the shot that he could taste the hot lead. Lance Corporal Houston was about to get it point-blank in the chest. Callahan knew he could save the guy, but if he fired and Houston was somehow able to save himself, then Callahan would have given up the team's location for nothing. And giving up that location could ruin the entire mission.

But if Callahan just sat there, a bright, talented, young man might die.

With a stifled groan, Houston dropped his K-bar and threw himself at the terrorist, his hands going for the AK's muzzle. He locked on, bent the rifle sideways, then rolled, pulling the guy closer so he could boot him in the neck. One kick—

And the bad guy suddenly released the weapon, sending Houston recoiling like a rubber band.

The guy shouted something, probably a call to his friend, then he clambered to his feet as Houston turned the rifle around, aimed it at the guerilla. "Don't move."

Raising his hands, the terrorist took a step back, his gaze flicking between Houston and the rifle.

Then, a knowing smile came over his face. He turned. Bolted.

The son of a bitch knew Houston wouldn't fire. Damn it. After scrambling to his feet, Houston snatched up his K-bar and took off after the bastard.

Callahan saw the terrorist scout running off. Maybe he wouldn't shoot the guy, but he wasn't going to sit around any longer. He exploded from the brush, trounced down the muddy bank, then splashed into the river. The water rose quickly to his knees. He figured that if he could make it to the other side in time, he would cut off the bad guy. In fact, Houston would drive him directly into the trap.

Now hip deep in the river, Callahan wondered why Rainey wasn't calling over the radio, freaking out and ordering him to return to his position.

A glance back provided the answer.

Padua, Mindano, and the sergeant himself were joining him, rifles held high, legs working hard as they stumbled over the rocks and slid into the muck.

While all of them should have advanced as silently as Houston and Vance had, it was either make the mad dash or let the guerilla escape. Callahan felt confident that there were only two scouts in the area, but he knew old Murphy as well as Sergeant Rainey did. If more guerillas were nearby, then maybe the situation had already gone to hell. They just didn't know it yet.

For the life of him, Rainey could not figure out what the hell had just happened. Taking out two scouts was, for the most part, a routine operation, especially for seasoned operators like Vance and Houston. How Houston's man had managed to escape was a story Rainey couldn't wait to hear.

With his teeth clenched, he finished crossing the river, then flashed a hand signal to Vance, who left his position and joined them in pursuit of Callahan, Houston, and the fleeing guerilla.

Houston rounded a palm tree—

And lost the bad guy.

"Oh, shit . . ."

He spun around, felt the whole weight of the mission come crashing down on his shoulders, and then . . .

There he was, fucking thug, right there, slipping between a pair of trees. Houston should call the sarge. Damn. There wasn't time. He had to get this guy. If he escaped, told his friends . . . shit! Houston had fucked up big time. And it was all because of a stupid bug. He could never tell the sarge the truth. He would never live it down.

"What's your problem, Houston? Little competition got you worried? Never had anyone really push you?"

Fuck you, Banks!

After shoving his way through the rubber plants, he leaped over a thorny bush and came down into a small clearing—just as his bad guy was slipping under the fronds ahead. At least the little runt was running parallel to the river instead of taking them up higher into mountains. The guy knew the faster escape route was along the river. *Way to go, bro. You're making it easier for me to make you dead.*

With branches and fronds smacking into and groping at him, Houston closed the distance between himself and his prey. Three meters now. The little guy repeatedly looked over his shoulder, darted right, darted left, then suddenly dropped into a long ditch that had come out of nowhere.

Damn, Houston had been running too fast and couldn't slow himself before his boots left the mud. He slipped about a meter straight down and stumbled as the guerrilla scaled the opposite mud wall.

Biting back a curse, Houston took another step—and his boot sank into calf-deep mud. He tried to pull forward, took another step, flopped onto his gut. He realized only then that the thug had taken a wider path across the trench, where the water had not pooled. The guy was getting away.

As Houston hauled himself up, something whirred past his ear. He turned back.

Callahan stood on the edge of the trench, his hand coming down toward his side.

Up ahead, the guerilla emitted a brief cry, drawing Houston's gaze.

A K-bar jutted from between the scout's shoulder blades as he hit the mud, his legs writhing a second before his entire body grew still.

Houston just looked at Callahan, awed. "You're no pogue."

"Here," Callahan whispered, reaching down, offering his hand.

Accepting, Houston pursed his lips and climbed free of the trench. As he brushed himself off, Rainey arrived with Mindano, Padua, and Vance, who had retrieved the bad guy's rifle.

"Very sloppy, Lance Corporal," Rainey said. "If we had time, I'd ask you what happened. Let's move. After we bring home Doc and Banks, you owe us all a round."

"Okay, Sarge."

"And you?" Rainey said, cocking a brow at Callahan. "You killed him? You hide him."

"What? No thank you?" Callahan asked.

Rainey smirked, then waved the others on.

"Hold up, Sergeant. I thought I saw a radio on his belt." Callahan crossed to the shallow end of the trench, splashed across the mud, then reached the guerilla's body.

Houston bit his lip as Callahan held up a small walkie-talkie. "It's still on."

The sergeant turned a blistering gaze on Houston. "Lance Corporal, did he make a call?"

"Now way, Sarge. I would've heard. He never got very far from me. He was probably reaching for it when he saw me get stuck down here."

"I'm praying you're right," Rainey snapped. "I suggest you do the same."

"I will, Sarge."

"But when these guys fail to check in, the ball will drop," Callahan said.

"But the mountains cause interference," Padua interjected. "They might not become suspicious at first. And when they do use radios, which is not often, they will dial to police frequencies, and sometimes there is confusion."

"Whatever the case, the clock's ticking faster. It's oh-two-fifty, and this took way too long. No more delays. No more mistakes." Rainey shoved the Foxtrot radio into Houston's hands. "Callahan, give that radio to Sergeant Padua. He'll monitor for us."

"Here," Callahan said, tossing the walkie-talkie to the Filipino sergeant. "They shop at Radio Shack."

Padua frowned and examined the device.

As Houston strapped on the radio, he noticed that some kind of long, dark worm, similar to the centipede that had landed on his arm, was slithering across the mud. He lifted his boot and stomped on the thing with a vengeance. He would have stomped again if the sarge and Mindano hadn't been watching.

TEAM DOGMA HOSTAGES
ABU SAYYAF STRONGHOLD
SOMEWHERE IN THE CENTRAL MOUNTAINS
BASILAN ISLAND, SOUTHERN PHILIPPINES
0252 HOURS LOCAL TIME

The angelic woman with long, dark hair, the one who had come to Doc and Banks with the plan to escape, was leaning over Doc and wiping his forehead and the corners of his mouth with a damp rag. Doc wanted to say something, but he felt entirely drained. The drug, heroin probably, was still wreaking some havoc with his system. Since being taken from the shark cage, he had had several hallucinations in which the trees had come alive and had strangled him to death. Then he had gone from being cold to soaking his utilities with sweat. And for a while, it felt as though ants were crawling over his entire body. The itching was intense and drove him mad since he couldn't use his hands. He wasn't sure, but he believed he had vomited several times. And then . . . a blackout for some time.

But now he felt a little better and seemed reasonably

aware of his surroundings. He was not in the jungle anymore, that was for sure. Walls of brown rock swept up around him, and shadows flickered across the stone ceiling. Had Banks been right? Had Janjali and his men found some tunnels they planned to use for an escape?

"Don't try to talk," the woman said. "He's done this before. He only gave you a small dose. You'll feel better by morning. He doesn't want you or your friend to give him trouble."

Doc sat up, his wrists still cuffed, the noose still on. The floor listed violently. He wanted to clutch the dirt and hang on, but he fell back onto his side. Was that Banks lying off to his right? His eyes wouldn't focus that far.

"No, stay down. Take the rest while you can. He's going to move us. I know it. I heard them talking about Jolo Island. And he can do it, too. He's going to leave his men here to defend the camp while he takes us to the coast."

That was good. And that was bad. If they were moved, a rescue team might never find them. But such a move might provide an opportunity to escape. Then again, how were Doc and Banks supposed to seize such an opportunity when they were as incapacitated as a couple of ghetto junkies? "The general," Doc forced out. "What happened?"

"I'm sorry, but I don't think General Santiago and his men will be coming for us. Ramzi broke the general's legs, and some of his men have already fled. Again, I am so sorry."

"Can you help?"

"I don't think so. I'm a prisoner like you. When you

came here, I thought you could help me. I thought we could leave before he drugged you." She wiped a tear from her cheek.

"We'll get you out. I promise."

"Don't make promises like that." The sound of a man retching diverted her gaze. "Your friend needs help."

"Thank you," Doc said as she wiped his head once more, then set down the rag and went to Banks.

"Well, Garden, I expected to find you here," said Janjali from across the cave.

Wearing a cruel grin, Janjali came forward, grabbed Garden by the wrist, and yanked her away from Banks. "I told you not to go near these men. Do I have to cuff you again?"

"No, Ramzi. The guards allowed me to make sure these men were all right—"

"And you wanted to see if they can help you escape."

She closed her eyes. "I know that will never happen."

"Is this life so terrible? It is a simple life, really. Out there, the world is complicated and miserable." Janjali raised a hand in the air and shouted to several guards in the cave, two of whom broke from their posts and strode toward Doc.

"Doc?" Banks called. "I'm so itchy."

"It'll pass, man."

"They're moving us?"

The guards wrested Doc from the floor, and his legs felt rubbery. "Hang in there, Banks. Doesn't matter where we go. We're always Force Recon."

14

Point man Vance signaled yet another halt, and as Rainey dropped in close to the base of a tree, the corporal's voice came low and even over the radio. "Dogma One, this is Dogma Four. Be advised I have found another wire. Will mark, over."

That booby trap was the third one Vance had located in the past twenty minutes. The terrorists could afford the more expensive methods of defense, though they had probably constructed the requisite punji pit or two. After discovering the first two wires, Vance had sounded a bit more confident, and now by locating a third, Rainey hoped the sniper's confidence had soared. You had to be damned good to spot a wire as carefully hidden as the ones Jimmy Vance had found. And you had to be even better to do that at night while wearing a pair of Night Vision Goggles.

As the signal to resume worked down the line, Rainey slid up his sleeve, checked his wrist-mounted GPS. They were nearing Mohajid Mountain, and if the intell had been correct, Janjali's camp could lie beyond the next rise. By now he thought his lack of sleep would be wearing on him, but the closer they got, the more alert he had become. The anticipation of what they would find and what they would need to do to rescue Doc and Banks was in his veins like caffeine. He wasn't just overtired. He knew the difference.

They resumed their pace, each stepping carefully over the wire, and when Rainey's turn came, he spotted the small circle in the mud and the twigs Vance had arranged to identify the trap. He lifted his leg, but then he hesitated, pricking up his ears and listening to the jungle behind him. A click. A slight cry from some bird. A far-off shuffle of fronds. His senses told him they were being watched, being followed. He wanted to call a halt, run a sweep back. But they had to keep going.

"Dogma Four, this is Dogma One, over," he called softly.

"One this is Four, over."

"They got us looking down. What does that mean, over?"

"Roger that, One. Crossbow has the SOPHIE on the trees, over."

"Outstanding," Rainey said, smiling to himself as he imagined the thermal images flashing across the SO-PHIE's LCD as the unit displayed heat sources in glowing white among the shadows. "Dogma One, out."

The presence of trip wires suggested that the enemy might post snipers in the trees so that while you were looking down to avoid the wires, they would whack you from above. Vance had already accounted for that by enlisting Padua's help. However, even the most sharp-eyed point men using the best thermal imager could miss a guy perched on a thick limb who had covered himself with branches and who waited with the patience and cunning of any other nocturnal predator. The best you could do was survey the treetops from within imaging range and try to spot a sniper before you got close enough for him to spot you. Their current grade was about thirty-five degrees, and that angle helped to reveal more of the foliage that would otherwise be hidden in a flat stretch of forest.

Three meters ahead, corpsman Mindano rounded a tree, paused, and removed his glasses to clean them. "Sergeant?"

"Come on, corpsman. We can't stop."

"We're being followed."

"I know. And we don't need Padua and his SOPHIE to confirm. They're back there."

"If Janjali's men are behind us, they're driving us into the killing zone."

"No, we're headed there on purpose."

"I see."

"Too late for second thoughts."

"I don't mind dying. I've had a good life. I just hate to see others suffer. For me, that's worse than death."

Rainey thought of the faces of those people in Tipo-

Tipo. Perhaps his time on this Earth was drawing to a close, and no matter how much he worried about leaving his family behind, there was nothing he could do. Mindano would watch him die.

No. He shook off the thought. "Corpsman, when we get close, I have a couple of ideas to get rid of those guys behind us. You just roll with the punches, all right?"

"I will, Sergeant."

Rainey's earpiece clicked, then Vance's voice came over the channel. "Dogma One, this is Dogma Four, over."

"Four, this is One, over."

"We're coming up on a big ridge. Can't get over it. Have to work parallel until we reach the far edge, over."

"Roger that, One, out."

For the next ten minutes they slipped their way beneath a huge outcropping whose back was covered by vines and shrubs. Beneath the stone lay empty Coke bottles, wrappers from all kinds of candy bars and other snacks, along with empty AK magazines and a sprinkling of shell casings.

"Dogma One, this is Crossbow One. Be advised we have movement ahead. Five, six, possibly seven individuals on the SOPHIE. Range approximately ninety-five meters. They are moving east our location, over."

That was odd. If those were the same men who had been tailing them, they had veered east and ahead so that they were in front of the team. "Crossbow One, sweep our six o'clock, over."

"Roger that, One. Sweeping, wait, over."

Rainey stepped closer to the ridge wall as the call to halt reached him from Mindano. Water trickled down over the stone and puddled at his boots. The sound would have relaxed him were he not anxiously awaiting Padua's report. He panned the jungle with his own Nightstars, the terrain rushing down from him and bearing a strong resemblance to the mountains back home in Colorado.

"Dogma One, this is Crossbow One. Be advised zero detection our six o'clock, over. Still reading movement east, range now approximately one hundred and twenty meters, over."

"Roger that. Dogma Four, let's keep that gap, over."

Vance acknowledged, and they continued along the ridge for another few minutes, until Mindano passed down another call to halt.

Cursing under his breath at the delay, Rainey waited for Vance to explain.

But thirty seconds passed with nothing from the corporal. "Dogma Four, this is Dogma One, sitrep, over."

No response.

Rainey repeated the call.

Ten seconds after, Vance finally replied, "Dogma One, this is Dogma Four, be advised—"

The corporal cut himself short as a single gunshot boomed.

Rainey hit the mud, elbows down, rifle at the ready, boots digging in and keeping him ready to spring up. Distance on the shot? Not close. Way up the mountain. Away from Vance.

The gunshot echoed away into the chatter of bugs and Rainey's huffing. "Dogma Team? Wait . . ."

ABU SAYYAF STRONGHOLD
SOMEWHERE IN THE CENTRAL MOUNTAINS
BASILAN ISLAND, SOUTHERN PHILIPPINES
0401 HOURS LOCAL TIME

General Romeo Santiago had, despite his excruciating pain, managed to convince the young guard to remove the handcuffs. "I'm not going anywhere," Santiago had pointed out, glancing at his swollen legs, his kneecaps shattered by Janjali's blows. As the guard had removed the cuffs, Santiago had made his move, snatching the naïve boy's rifle. Before the guard could react, Santiago had shot him in the chest—

But now, as he flopped onto his back, the second guard burst into the hut, swung his rifle on the general—

Who shot him before he could get off a round.

Then, with eyes tearing over the pain, Santiago crawled toward the hut's door and retrieved the second guard's rifle. He clung to the hope that his act of defiance would inspire the men who had once been under his command. Now lying behind the dead guard, he screamed, "I'm General Santiago! I'm here! Come and free me!"

"General!" came a voice from a hut across the clearing. "I'm coming for you! Don't shoot!"

A young man in fatigues jogged from the darkness,

his AK held high across his chest. As he neared the hut, Santiago watched him bring his rifle to bear.

Was he just being cautious, or was he going to . . .

The guerilla's rifle winked orange and spat a half dozen rounds that ripped through the bamboo a few inches from Santiago's head. Even as the splinters dropped and the report stung the general's ears, he sighted the young man and squeezed the trigger.

Charti came dashing down the tunnel, just as Hamsiraji was getting the new men started on the next section of rubble. "Didn't you hear it?" the boy asked.

With nearly twenty men digging around him, Hamsiraji could barely hear his own thoughts, let alone anything else. "What?"

"Gunshots in the camp! Maybe the Americans are here."

"Go up there. See what's happening. Then come back."

"But these men . . . They need to get back. Two of the machine-gun nests are empty!"

Hamsiraji dismissed the boy with a wave. "When I can get through to the other side, I'll send these men back."

"Who knows how long that will take?"

With an index finger poised near the boy's nose, Hamsiraji tightened his gaze. "This is all my brother's fault. He's ruined almost everything. But not this. Not now. These men will stay. Go see what's happening!"

* * *

The young tribesman making his report was so excited that Janjali could barely understand him. Something about Santiago killing his guards, killing another guerilla, and now holing up inside his hut.

"Tell the men they must take the general alive, then return to their posts. Tell them if the military comes, they will fight until every infidel is dead."

Nodding, the bare-chested guerilla ran off.

Janjali was already smiling. He did not care if Santiago lived or died. The truth was, the general, along with the rest of Janjali's men, would provide an excellent diversion, should a rescue team be nearby. Hopefully, Santiago's capture would be a long, drawn-out affair. And then Janjali had another plan to further confuse the Americans.

In the meantime, Janjali, Garden, the two Marines, and a party of ten of his best warriors would now flee through the tunnels Hamsiraji had discovered during his quest for the gold. Janjali whispered a good-bye to his obsessed brother and felt no remorse as he hurried away, his flashlight peeling back the darkness.

"Why can't this end?" Garden asked, struggling to keep up with him.

"The jihad never ends."

"You don't care about that."

"You would know?"

"I know you don't have to take me. I'm worth nothing. Aren't you sick of me?"

"Quiet." Janjali glanced over his shoulder to make sure he wasn't moving too quickly for the others.

"Just let me go. You can find another woman."

"Shut up!"

"Did you think I would learn to love you?"

"Shut up!" Suddenly, Janjali found himself falling. "Bitch!"

Although he had cuffed her again, she had thrust out her leg and tripped him. He hit the ground, felt her bare foot pressing on his neck. As he rolled over, she increased the pressure, cutting off his air. A demon looked out from behind her eyes. "Die," she screamed. "Die!"

This is it, thought Lance Cpl. Ricardo Banks. Despite the come-and-go euphoria, the nausea, the itchiness, and a face as swollen and ripe as a melon, he was conscious enough to realize that Janjali was down and that he and Doc needed to make a break. Were he not drugged, not battered and bruised, he might have thought twice about the attempt, since he was cuffed and surrounded by ten heavily armed men. Well, he still would have thought twice—but he still would have tried, no matter the odds. Bravery? Insanity? Was there a difference?

"Doc!" Banks twisted free from his guards, only to stumble and fall flat on his face. "Doc, come on, man!"

From somewhere behind him, the medic answered, "Let it go, Banks. Let it go."

Hands found Banks's arms, and once he was ripped

to his feet, he felt like a bobble head glued to a four-by-four's dashboard.

"Patience," Doc said as his guards escorted him away. "Patience . . ."

Banks glanced lazily ahead to Janjali, and through one eye he caught a blurry image of the terrorist, who was smacking the dark-haired woman across the face. After receiving the blow, she held her chin high and cursed him.

As the guards hauled him along, Banks suddenly felt a little giddy and broke into a Force Recon cadence, "Paint my face black and green, you won't see me, I'm a Recon Marine. I slip and slither into the night, won't see me till I'm ready to fight . . ."

One of the guards rolled his rifle, gave Banks a crack in the head. Feeling no pain, Banks kept on singing—until the second blow sent him to his knees.

WOLF NEWS CREW

CAMP BALIKATAN

TOWN OF ISABELLA

BASILAN ISLAND, SOUTHERN PHILIPPINES

0410 HOURS LOCAL TIME

Celebrity news reporter Rick Navarro sat in Lieutenant Colonel Demarzo's hut, staring across a huge mahogany desk that barely fit in the tiny quarters. The office chair was equally ornate and equally out of place. Bored after fifteen minutes of waiting for the man,

Navarro thumbed through the folder in his lap. Watertown had printed out the images of the captured Marines, and Navarro couldn't wait to hand them over to this Demarzo guy.

By the time Navarro had glanced at the last photo, the colonel arrived, squeezed his muscular frame behind the big desk, and dropped exhausted into his chair. He looked like any of the other middle-aged, macho clones. Even his crewcut betrayed his arrogance. "Well, well, well, Mr. Navarro. A lot of big talk got you this far, but if you're blowing smoke and wasting my time, your relationship with the United States Marine Corps will be severed here and now. I can guarantee that. Do I make myself clear?"

Grinning smugly, Navarro placed the folder on Demarzo's desk, then shoved it across the polished wood. "I understand. And by the way, my compliments to your interior designer."

"I requested new furniture," Demarzo said. "They went a little overboard . . ." He opened the folder, flipped quickly through the images. "Where did you get these?"

"They were couriered directly from Janjali."

"He's made contact with you?"

Navarro leaned back, stifled a yawn. "It's an ungodly hour, sir. Let's slow down. Those photos were made from digital images, and they confirm that members of Team Dogma have been captured by the Abu Sayyaf Group. Janjali wants me to show these pictures to the world so that he can flaunt what he's done and make us look bad here in the Philippines. Of course, I would never do anything to compromise the lives of these men, or our national security."

"Our relationship with the government here is tenuous at best. That's why no one's going to see these photos. We'll need to confiscate everything you have."

"See, that's the thing that bothers me. I do for you, but you do nothing for me."

Demarzo raised an index finger. "I'll tell you what I'll do, mister, if you don't turn over that evidence—"

"You don't have to threaten me, Colonel. I'm a patriot. I've been to hell and back with your boys, fought alongside them. I watched Mohammed al-Zumar die right before my eyes. I love my country."

"What do you want?"

"Have you sent in a rescue team?"

"That's classified."

"Not for long, I'm sure. In any event, I want complete and exclusive access to information as it becomes declassified. No other reporters will be allowed inside the camp. I'll be the only one."

"You want me to shut down the major networks and all the cable guys?"

"Not shut down. Just shut out. For a short time. I get the exclusive—"

"Or what? You'll broadcast these pictures? This is a hell of a lot worse than that stunt you pulled at Nova. That bordered on conspiracy. This is blackmail, plain and simple. And if you do this, we'll get you under the Patriot Act. Your career will be over. You'll be in and out of federal court, and probably do some jail time."

"Colonel, you don't seem to understand. My contract's up for renewal. Unless I can scoop something big here, I'm done with Wolf News. If you can't play, I understand. But I *will* show those pictures. I'll say these are the images your own military didn't want you to see. These are the photos of American Marines being held captive by one of the most brutal terrorists on the planet. And you know, the families of these men will see their loved ones for the first time on national television. They'll say the Marines never notified them that their loved ones had been captured. They had to see it on Wolf News to learn the truth."

One of the lieutenant colonel's aides appeared at the door, gave the colonel a knowing look, then went over to whisper something in the man's ear. The aide gave Navarro a polite nod, then quickly left.

"Navarro, they said you were a gutless scumbag, a leech who feeds off of other people's misery. But I didn't want to believe you were that cruel. After seeing the reports you made from Pakistan and Korea, I thought you were as gung ho as some of the other journalists. I figured you for a wannabe Marine who got stuck with a microphone instead of a carbine."

"You figured wrong. It's a cruel world, Colonel. In this business, only cruel people survive."

"Correction. Only *careful* people. Make no mistake,

this is a very small island, and we have folks from intell tagging the media." Demarzo waved toward someone at the door.

Navarro's producer, Watertown, shuffled resignedly into the hut. "Sorry, Rick. They got us. Confiscated everything."

Navarro beat his fist on the desk. "You can't do this."

"Yes, I can, Mr. Navarro. And off the record, you of all people should know that you do not fuck with the United States Marine Corps. Now then. You, sir, are dismissed."

TEAM DOGMA
NEAR MOHAJID MOUNTAIN
BASILAN ISLAND, SOUTHERN PHILIPPINES
0412 HOURS LOCAL TIME

"Dogma One, this is Dogma Four, be advised the fire originates from above us. Also be advised I have found one individual here, KIA, knife wound to the chest, over."

"Stand by, Dogma Four, I'm coming up, out." Rainey jogged past the rest of the team and reached Vance, who was crouching over a young man's bloody body. The kid was Abu Sayyaf all the way, his bandanna lying near his head.

"This just happened," Rainey concluded, using his palm to shield the penlight in his other hand as he examined the fresh wounds. "Man, they butchered him."

Vance frowned at the carnage. "We got help?"

"I'm not sure what we got. I am sure we need to find out A-SAP." Rainey glanced up, listened. The gunfire had ceased. He keyed his mike. "Eagle Six, this is Dogma One, rally up here, out."

"Too many delays," Vance said.

"No shit. Get over this ridge."

"Aye-aye."

Rainey swung around to Padua, gave the Filipino sergeant a hand signal indicating he should join Vance. While those two left, Callahan lowered himself to a knee and examined the dead rebel.

"I'm waiting for my next surprise," Rainey said darkly.

"You think I know something about this? Maybe one of our guys killed him. Maybe they escaped."

"That's not the work of my men."

"Maybe one of his buddies did it. They were fighting over drugs or something."

"Maybe there's someone else out here, someone you know? More *observers*?"

"Sergeant, I—"

"Dogma One, this is Dogma Four. Be advised we have picked all six. Repeat, we have picked all six, over."

"Roger that, Dogma Four. Dogma Team, rally on Dogma Four. Dogma Three, establish uplink with Yankee Thunder at rally point, over."

"Dogma One, this is Dogma Three. Establishing uplink at rally point, out."

Rainey craned his head to Callahan, who self-consciously glanced away and stepped over the body as Houston and Mindano trotted by.

After a last look at the forest along the ridge, a look that left him even more uneasy, Rainey beat a path after his men.

For another five minutes they scaled a steep rock wall, though good purchase was easy to find. Once they reached the mountainside proper, Vance called the halt, and they dispersed into a wide line, with the flank men setting up about ten meters from Rainey's position at the center. The mountain towered above like a medieval fortress defended by hundreds of bowmen.

AK fire popped and rattled off. A single shot. Another. Then a triplet, all from within the compound. The jungle fell silent, then, after a few more seconds, the cry of distant birds returned.

"Dogma One, this is Dogma Three," called Houston, who had taken the east flank. "I make at least ten nests, over."

"Dogma One, this is Dogma Four," echoed Vance from his spot on the west flank. "They're dug in pretty deep over here. Multiple foxholes and a fence line up there, over."

"Dogma One, this is Crossbow One," came Padua's voice. "Be advised I have at least two nests with no thermal readings. Repeat, two nests with no readings. Range on the nearest one approximately one hundred ten meters, over."

Two machine gun nests empty? Rainey rolled his eyes to the dark sky. *What're are you doing now, Murphy?*

"Dogma One, this is Eagle Six. Be advised I have movement to our east, range two hundred and twenty meters. Count ten, maybe fifteen individuals. Maybe more, over."

As the information streamed in, Rainey sorted through it, analyzed it, tried to calculate what the hell was going on and what the team's next move should be. Empty machine-gun nests. Movement to their east again. Up to fifteen combatants or more. Gunfire from within Janjali's stronghold.

Of course, the most obvious path would be to head toward those empty nests, slip on by and push deeper toward the fence line. But was the enemy baiting them in that direction? If Rainey could get Vance and Padua onto the higher ground to the north, he might get his answer without having to call back to Demarzo and rely on Yankee Thunder's sketchy and sometimes misinterpreted satellite imagery. He gave the order, and the two men swept to the right flank, darkness and trees consuming them a few moments later.

"Dogma Three, this is Dogma One, report uplink, over," Rainey called to Houston.

"Dogma One, this is Dogma Three. Be advised uplink in progress. Yankee Thunder confirms receipt of Nightstar images and GPS coordinates. Uplink networked to Crossbow One's SOPHIE and Dogma Four's GPS, over."

"Roger that. Maintain link, out."

"Dogma One, this is Dogma Three. Be advised Oscar Five Delta requests contact, over."

Rainey breathed a curse. He would be calling Demarzo after all.

As Charles Callahan lay on his stomach, continuing his observation of the mountain, he heard the footfalls behind him. By the time he swung around, the figure was right there—

But then, as the soldier moved forward and the faint moonlight picked out his features, Callahan's mouth fell open. "What are you doing here?"

With a grunt, Rainey got up, hunched over, and half slid, half ran along the mountain to Houston, who lay on his belly at the foot of a leaning tree. Rainey took up the Foxtrot's microphone. "Yankee Thunder, this is Dogma One, over."

"Dogma One, this is Yankee Thunder. Stand by for Oscar Five Delta, over."

Oscar Five was the call sign for a lieutenant colonel. Delta stood for the D in Demarzo. Rainey added a P to the call sign, which stood for Demarzo being a pain in the ass to call now.

"Dogma One, this is Oscar Five Delta. Be advised we have received GPS coordinates and imagery. Eyes in the Sky have been adjusted. We count twenty-two huts and a few supporting structures. We estimate troop numbers to be ninety to one hundred individuals. You are authorized to advance, over."

"Roger that, Oscar Five Delta. Advancing, out."

Rainey would not count on the troop numbers report until the team actually encountered the enemy. Satellite was a beautiful thing—until your life depended upon it. Then you had best double-check with an old-fashioned pair of binoculars.

Out of nowhere, gunfire from maybe a half dozen AKs resounded from the east side of the mountain. And right behind that racket came the report of at least three or four of those big machine guns resting in their nests.

"What the fuck?" Houston mumbled.

"Just stay put," Rainey said, then darted away, steering back toward his original position. There, he dove to his gut, fished out his Nightstars, and just as he zoomed in on the muzzle flashes dancing around the trees, a hand came down hard on his shoulder, startling the hell out of him.

He looked up, saw Callahan, accompanied by a priest, who was hunkered down and holding an AK. "Sergeant—"

"What the hell is this?"

"They knew we wouldn't accept help," Callahan explained quickly. "They tailed us. Father Nacoda has about twenty men down there, and they're staging a diversion."

"Sergeant," the priest said emphatically. "Get your men into the camp. We will draw them to the east."

"Somebody's been firing inside the camp," Rainey said to the priest. "Do you know who it is?"

"No."

"We were supposed to slip in and slip out. Now we have a full-blown attack."

"Sergeant, you should move quickly," said Nacoda. "Janjali will not be here for long."

Rainey's cheeks flushed. He wanted to scream against the unknown variables.

"They did what they did," said Callahan. "Now we react."

Vance and Padua had scaled the mountain behind the camp, and from their vantage point atop a narrow ledge, Vance worked his Nightstars while Padua sent thermal images to Camp Balikatan.

About twenty or thirty guys were rushing to the east side, where the gunfire from the nests continued to erupt, directed toward that unknown attacking force in the lower forest.

"Who *is* that down there?" Padua asked.

"Don't know. But I doubt they're Abu Sayyaf, unless Janjali's got a civil war going on. You see that hut down there? A few guys are trading fire with someone inside. I'd bet my best flippin' stick that our hostages are in there."

"Flippin' stick?"

"A fishing rod. Just look again."

Padua directed the thermal imager down toward the hut. "Just one heat signature. Just one."

"That could be Doc or Banks."

"Or another hostage."

Vance keyed his mike. "Dogma One, this is Dogma Four, over."

Rainey shook his head in disgust. "All right, Father. Keep your men there and continue to draw their fire. Callahan? We rally on Houston. Let's go!"

As Rainey made the mad dash, he answered Vance's call and listened as the corporal relayed his observation of defensive positions along the perimeter as well as his discovery of a single combatant holed up in a hut.

"Dogma Four? Use Crossbow One as your spotter. Stand by for my mark, over."

"Standing by, out."

"Papa Two, this is Dogma One. Rally on Dogma Three's position, over."

"Rallying on Three, out," replied Mindano.

Squinting through his Nightstars, Houston saw a scrawny, unarmed man flit behind an outcropping and into a dark shadow that had to be a cave entrance. He lowered the binoculars as Callahan, Mindano, and the sarge came charging up.

"How we looking?" Rainey asked.

"Those nests are still empty," Houston reported. "But Sarge, I think we got a cave entrance over there. Saw a guy go in. There could be caves beneath the entire camp. Man, I'm flashing back to Pakistan."

"Don't."

"If there's a tunnel in there, it could run under the

fence," Houston guessed. "We wouldn't have to go head-to-head with those guys along the wire."

"Or it could be a dead end," Rainey said.

"Could be. What do you think, Lieutenant Colonel?" Houston asked Callahan.

"He's not being paid to think," Rainey snapped. "Just observe."

"But I do have an opinion," Callahan retorted. "I say me and the sergeant hit the fence. Vance and Padua will keep the bad guys ducking. Houston? You and Mindano will check out the cave. If it's a dead end, you rally back on us."

"I'm not wasting two men to go cave exploring," Rainey said. "What we're going to do—"

The sarge broke off as Callahan launched away from the group, charging toward the empty machine-gun nests.

Rainey swore, got to his feet. "Fucking pogue."

"Not a pogue. A live wire," muttered Houston.

15

Charles Callahan had been a loner for too long, and his patience had finally worn thin. No matter what Sergeant Rainey decided, Callahan could find a way to search for and find General Santiago. They were so close, and Callahan could no longer abide the Sergeant's practiced, calculated style of command. Callahan was the kind of Beret who would size up the situation in five seconds or less and go in, guns blazing. For him, it was all about input, interpretation, and reaction—all in the same breath. Rainey was far more analytical, much to his credit, but Callahan had grown used to worrying about only himself.

With legs growing sore from the incline, he reached the first machine-gun nest and swept his AK over the sandbags. The big gun sat there, unmanned and harmless. Good. Ahead stood a pair of trees. He high-tailed it for them, ducked behind the trunks, then surveyed the fence line until he found the gate. In front of it lay two men, arms locked, rifles aimed straightaway, range about twenty meters. The next pair of guards lay about fifteen meters west of the gate.

As the rifle fire from the east grew more intense, Callahan produced a fragmentation grenade and lobbed it at the guys to the west. He was already moving before the grenade exploded. When it did, the guerillas to the west screamed as the guys near the gate suddenly got to their feet.

Perfect.

Callahan's first triplet of fire leveled the thug on the right. His second fell a bit wide, but one round caught the second guy's shoulder, hammering him to the ground. Dead? Not yet. Callahan charged toward him, squeezing off another volley that sent a wave through the guy's chest. Done deal.

At the gate, Callahan didn't bother shooting the lock connected to the heavy chain wrapped between the bamboo doors. Instead, he fired point-blank at the bamboo itself, shattering the wood enough so that he could yank the chain away. He pushed open the gate and burst inside the compound.

Janjali and his men had taken Doc and Banks through a series of tunnels, the last of which terminated more than halfway down the mountain. With more than an hour's worth of darkness to exploit and a path winding downward under the heavy canopy, Doc feared that Janjali would gain a significant lead on any rescue team.

All the gunfire coming from behind might have lifted Doc's spirits—if he could tell who was attacking. He listened for a carbine amid all the popping, then reminded himself that a rescue team could be carrying the enemy's weapons to keep them confused and maintain the team's security. The grenade that had just exploded could have been anyone's. If he could just get some confirmation, just hear anything that would let him know . . . Doc prayed for the thumping of a chopper and the whooshing of rockets. There was no mistaking those sounds and the force behind them. But those guys weren't the only ones looking for them. Maybe some keen-eyed geek back at Camp Balikatan would spot them via satellite.

Or maybe they would reach the coast. Then what? How did Janjali plan to get them to Jolo Island? Did he actually have air support or access to boats? Would he try to hijack a ferry? Or was his entire escape so carefully orchestrated that even U.S. Navy forces could not stop him?

No. Doc couldn't let it go that far. He and Banks had

to fight back. And if he couldn't swing a fist, then he would make life for his captors as miserable as possible. With a jerk and a gasp he collapsed, sending the two guards at his arms into a frantic attempt to haul him up. Doc Leblanc became dead weight. The line slowed, and from ahead Janjali shouted in Tagalog.

In the meantime, Banks had looked back through his puffy and blackened eyes, and had taken Doc's cue.

"They'll carry us home on our shields, Doc," the lance corporal cried, going limp as his guards hollered at him.

"Hoo-rah. United States Marines do not give up."

"You know it, Doc. United States Marines resist till the end. We are the baddest motherfuckers on the planet."

"You know it. They are weak. And we are strong."

That last remark elicited a blow to the mouth from one guard, and as Doc swallowed back blood, his back cracked as one guy took his legs, while the other two grabbed his arms and lifted.

They had him. He couldn't escape. He had known that, but slowing them down felt damned good for at least a few moments. Then he choked up. He was afraid again. For his family. For their future.

As they carried him along, Doc glanced up at the sweeping landscape, treetops rising along the slope, then breaking off as huge outcroppings divided their paths. He could see the camp, the ledges along the mountain that staggered down. Then the trail cut sharply right, and the canopy stole his view, zipping him into the utter darkness of a body bag.

"I saw something to the south. Just for a second," Vance told Sergeant Padua, who had been using his Nightstars to help the sniper spot targets.

Padua directed his binoculars to the southern jungle. "I don't see anything, but the SOPHIE's still warmed up. Just a moment." Padua switched to the cylindrical thermal imager. "Okay, I have something. There. Maybe twelve to fourteen individuals moving in a line down the mountain. They're not moving too fast. Looks like they're carrying two people."

"Shit, man, that has to be them." Trembling over the discovery, Vance lowered his Dragunov, keyed his mike. "Dogma One, this is Dogma Four, over."

"Dogma Four, this is Dogma One, wait, over."

"Sarge, this can't wait!"

"Bead window, over." The sergeant was admonishing him for mentioning rank over the radio.

"You still got them?" Vance asked Padua.

"Yes, I have them. But if we don't get down there soon, they will get away."

Rainey was just smashing past the gate, with Mindano and Houston behind and at his flanks. Callahan had widened his lead and was shifting between the trees, running parallel to a narrow, well-worn path. Two pairs of huts stood at the end.

As Rainey broke left, tracking the lieutenant colonel, Vance called once more, and Rainey finally acknowledged. "Dogma Four, sitrep, over."

"Dogma One, be advised we have a small party carrying two individuals down from the southwest mountain face. Believe we have found our package, over."

Rainey charged up to a tree and remained there as Mindano and Houston ran like maniacs to reach him. "Dogma Four, maintain your position with Crossbow One. Dogma Three? Notify Yankee Thunder to focus eyes on retreating group. Dogma Team, be advised we're about to enter the camp and will rally toward the southwest side. Need covering fire on my mark, over."

"Roger that, One."

"Dogma Four, also be advised Eagle Six has entered the camp alone. I'm sure he's after Santiago. Spot him, over."

"Will spot, out."

"All right," Rainey said, catching his breath and facing Houston and Mindano. "Much as I'd like to, we can't abandon Callahan. I'm going after him. Just hold back a few yards and cover me. We're not wasting more than a few minutes on this. Get the RPGs ready for a little good-bye bang on the way out. Are we good to go?"

They nodded.

Rainey was about to dash off when a tremendous

burst of automatic-weapons fire tore through the trees ahead. He rolled around a tree, breathing hard. *Son of a bitch. Pinned down already?*

"I see 'em, Sarge. Two guys," said Houston, resting on one knee and squinting through his rifle's sight.

"Kill those annoying bastards, will you?"

"Wait," said Mindano, setting up the bipod of his light machine gun. "There are two more."

"Very well. Mindano, stay here and suppress. Houston? You come with me. Ready? Go now!"

Stooped over, Callahan worked his way to the corner of the hut, peered around it, then recoiled as gunfire chewed into the bamboo where his head had been. "You, inside! Who are you?"

"I'm General Santiago. Who are you?"

Callahan eyed the sky, whispered a thank-you. At least finding Santiago had been easy; getting him out was another story. "Hold on, General! I can't get to you yet."

"My legs are broken. I can't walk!"

"Just hang on."

If Callahan could get Santiago out of there and put about a kilometer between them and the camp, then he could call for a chopper extraction, courtesy of the Agency. He could already see it unfolding in his mind: the litter kit coming down, Santiago being strapped into it, the signal being given to haul him up, then the next rope coming down for Callahan. But could he abandon Rainey and the others?

Still unsure what he would do, Callahan pulled the pin on another of his grenades, let it fly. He readied a second one, had it in the air as the first boomed and heaved a cloud up toward the fronds. Then he charged around the front of the hut and crashed through the half open door as the second grenade detonated.

He didn't see Santiago lying there beside a dead guerilla until he was already falling over the man. Callahan hit the dirt, rolled, met the general's gaze.

"You?" Santiago said, his eyes swelling.

"Yeah, me. Ready to get out of here?"

The general looked to the clearing. "I'd rather face *them*."

A second wave of machine-gun fire rattled in the distance, and Callahan wondered if that was Mindano on the RP-46. If so, he was probably covering the others, who were on their way. "Listen, General. You're getting out of here with me and not the other Marines. We'll work out a deal. It's the best you can hope for now."

"I don't trust spies."

"But you trust terrorists? Look where that got you."

"Who are you? NSA? CIA?"

Callahan grabbed Santiago by the collar. "I'm your only friend in the world."

"No, you want to kill me."

"Doesn't matter." Callahan shoved the general. "And by the way, your friend Senator Allaga? He's still alive. Next time you want to kill someone, hire professionals."

* * *

"Papa Two, this is Dogma One," Rainey called, still on the run toward the hut where Callahan had stopped. "Break off and rally on us, over."

"Roger that," answered Mindano, his voice nearly drowned out by his rattling gun. "Papa Two, out."

Stealing their way along shrubs where the tree line tapered off, Rainey and Houston suddenly hit the deck as two men came charging into the clearing to their right, rifles churning out rounds. "Dogma Four—"

Vance's big Dragunov woke a pair of thunderclaps over the mountain. The first round punched a gaping hole in one guerilla's head, while the second turned his buddy's chest into a tangled mess of dark viscera.

"Damn," Houston whispered. "Thought he hated that rifle. Works for him."

"Dogma One, this is Dogma Four. Capped two, over."

"Confirmed two down," Rainey said. "Outstanding."

"Roger that. Weather up here is just fine. Still tracking package, over."

"Understood. Keep covering, out."

Mindano came thumping from behind, the barrel of his machine gun still smoking. Rainey waved him over.

"Sarge, look," Houston called, pointing toward Callahan's hut, where a man, presumably the lieutenant colonel, had slung another man over his shoulders.

"Come on," Rainey barked, sprinting off.

As he neared the back of the hut, he caught Callahan starting off for the forest and the fence line beyond. The lieutenant colonel turned, his teeth bared under the heavy load across his back. "Sergeant, let me talk."

"Hold it right there."

"The general's legs are broken. I'm getting him down past the fence line."

"No!" Santiago cried. "Let me go!"

Callahan tugged hard on one of the general's arms. "Shut up."

"Sergeant," Mindano called. "Let me treat the general."

"Not now."

From the corner of his eye, Rainey picked up a half dozen guerillas running along the opposite side of the clearing, heading toward the increasing gunfire supplied by the priest's men. Rainey dropped to his haunches, raised his rifle.

Houston saw the men, too, and he lifted his AK to track them without firing.

"Sergeant Rainey, is that you?" the general asked.

"Yes, sir. We spoke briefly."

"And you're on Dogma Team?"

"That's right, sir. But we need to leave now. Janjali's on the run—and he has my men. Callahan, you're not going down to the fence. You're not going anywhere by yourself. You're sticking with us. Let's move."

"Sergeant," the general gasped as Callahan shifted his hands. "I want to go with you—but not with this man."

"Shut up!" barked Callahan.

Rainey lifted his voice. "What did you say, General?"

"This man is a traitor! He gave your training schedule to Senator Allaga, who is in bed with Janjali. That's why your men were captured. Callahan is not a Marine. He can't be. He set you up."

"Holy shit," Houston blurted out. "And hey, Sarge, they're moving up across the clearing. We boogie now—or we don't boogie at all."

Rainey wasn't sure what to believe, who to believe. He looked at Callahan, read the man's face.

And the truth came.

Feeling the heat, Callahan made a lopsided grin. "Sergeant, this piece of shit on my back is your traitor. And we're bringing him home. Come on . . ."

"We got a few seconds," Rainey said. "You set us up . . ."

"I'm not at liberty to discuss this operation."

"You set us up!"

Callahan stood there, straining under the general's weight.

"Motherfucker," Rainey said, then he craned his head toward Houston. "Lance Corporal? You and Mindano take the general."

"I have him, Sergeant," Callahan said, his tone steely, his gaze unflinching.

"You're a fucking spook," said Rainey. "And you've been playing the Corps like we're a bunch of idiots."

"Sergeant, please . . ."

"You ran off and came here just for him, huh? And you got lucky. He's the only one you care about. He's got what you need. You just came along, used us as bodyguards to get you here, that right?"

Callahan took a step back as Mindano and Houston approached. "Sergeant, you have no idea the position I'm in. I could tell you that I wanted no part in this, but that wouldn't matter. Our goals are the same. And you can thank me for Father Nacoda's help."

"Shoot him, Sarge," Houston said. "No one's going to say anything. Fucking routine training exercise goes to hell. We lose Doc and Banks. And it's all because of him."

With burning eyes and trembling hands, Rainey put pressure on the trigger. He wasn't sure if he had ever felt as much hatred for another human being. Just a little more pressure, and justice would be served.

God, he wished he were ten, fifteen years younger, reacting from the gut and literally shooting from the hip. He wouldn't have thought it out. He wouldn't have remembered his career, his reputation, his family. He would've taken the shot.

Instead he poked Callahan with his rifle, then, muttered another curse and stepped back.

"I'll do it *for* you, Sarge," Houston said, pushing toward Callahan.

Rainey forced down the lance corporal's weapon, took a deep breath, then glowered at Callahan. "You're getting out with us, not with your spook buddies. And maybe I'll get lucky, and one of those scumbags out there will do the job for me."

"All right, Sergeant. Have it your way. But the general is mine."

"No offense to the general, but I don't give a flying fuck about him. We're going to get my men. Move out!"

* * *

The guy came out of nowhere and hit the new ledge where Vance and Padua lay, overlooking the camp.

Vance swung his head, saw the wide-eyed guerilla lifting his rifle.

Sergeant Padua had šeen the man a half second earlier. He rolled onto his back, hit the guerilla's ankles—

When both of their rifles went off.

The guerilla went down, and Vance wasn't sure if Padua had been shot. He didn't have time to look. He brought his Dragunov around as another guerilla dropped from the ledge above and fired at Vance, just as he returned fire and dropped the bastard.

But suddenly, Vance was sliding over the edge, having failed to realize how close he had come. He reached out with one hand, felt a sharp sting in his bicep, lost his grip on the rifle, and it tumbled over the side. He searched frantically for something to hold, found a heavy branch growing from within the rock, locked on. Vance swung down, over the ledge, suspended by one hand, the jungle floor some thirty meters below.

Then he heard movement above. Went for the .45 tucked into his waistband. His sleeve was torn and bloody. No surprise. He'd been shot. The wound didn't feel too bad—ached like hell, though. He freed the pistol and pulled himself up, spotted yet another thug getting read to shoot Padua, and fired. Fired again. Again.

A bare foot as rough as sandpaper came down on his arm. He glanced up. A young guerilla with missing teeth literally howled at him. The guy had his rifle

pointing down at Vance, who hung there, two possible
fates hitting him at the same instant: He would get shot
in the face, then fall to his grave, or he would fall and
die on impact.

However, the kid had taken a moment to gloat. A fatal mistake.

Boom. Vance shot him in the head. The guy fell forward and silently plunged into the shadows below.

Vance shivered through his breath, felt a warm rush
of relief. But Padua was up there, groaning. Vance
searched for a foothold in the mountainside. Nothing.
He would have to haul himself over via the single
branch. He tucked away his pistol and grimaced as he
reached out with his wounded arm.

Big mistake. The branch suddenly came loose from
its rocky crevice, and Vance started sliding. "Oh, shit.
Sergeant?"

"Here," said Padua, reaching over the edge.

Vance strained with everything he had, found the
hand, gripped it tightly. Padua began pulling. The sounds
coming out of his throat were nearly inhuman. He had to
be in tremendous agony, but he did not give up.

Once Vance's elbows reached the ledge, he dug in,
crawled over the side, grunting and groaning as loud as
Padua. "Sergeant . . ."

Padua collapsed onto his back, his shirt blood
soaked. He stared blankly at the early morning sky.
With his own shirt sleeve now drenched, Vance crawled
over to the man, started unbuttoning Padua's shirt. He
could at least bandage the wounds.

"Corporal," the sergeant began, seizing Vance's wrist. "Corporal . . ." Padua's grip slackened, and his head dropped to one side.

Vance shut his eyes tightly. "Not another one, man. Another one on my fucking watch."

"Dogma Four, this is Dogma One. Need you to draw sniper fire away from us. We are on the west side of the camp, near the last two huts before the fence line, over."

Vance sniffled, opened his eyes. Shit, he was crying. A fucking Marine crying. *Don't do it, man.* "Dogma One, this is Dogma Four. Be advised Crossbow One is down, KIA, over."

A pause. Then: "Roger that, Four. Draw what fire you can and rally down our position, over."

"Will draw and rally, out."

Breathing a shivery sigh, Vance searched for his sniper rifle, then he remembered it had gone over the side. He took Padua's rifle, RPG, and the SOPHIE, shoving the latter into his ruck.

The Sarge wanted him to draw fire? Well, Vance would eliminate that fire altogether with a vengeance. He kneeled down before Sergeant Padua, gripped the man's hand. "*Semper Fi*, brother. The Marines will be back for you. I promise."

"The sergeant's going to kill you," said Santiago as Callahan set him on the ground behind the last hut, near the fence line. "You wait. He's going to kill you."

"He won't do you the favor."

Rounds tore into the hut's thatched roof, sending

Callahan to the mud. He waited. Another volley thumped into the bamboo. He got onto his elbows.

Across the forest, a thin trail had been cut through and would take them down about a hundred yards to the fence. Who knew what kind of resistance they would meet there? At least for now the incoming was concentrated directly ahead.

"Get up and shoot them, you fool!" hollered Santiago. "They still teach spies how to shoot, don't they?"

Callahan wanted to tell the idiot that the guerillas who had climbed to the high ground were just firing blindly and that if he returned fire, he would not only give up his position but the positions of the other men, who were lying at the foot of the other hut. It had obviously been a long time since the general had been in a real combat situation. A bullet to one of his vital organs might refresh his memory.

"Eagle Six, this is Dogma One, over," Rainey called.

"One, this is Eagle Six, over."

"Get eyes on our break to the clearing. If they're off to our flanks or on the high ground to the north, I want to know about it. Can you handle that, over?"

Callahan ground his teeth; he had already been inspecting their back door. "Affirmative, Dogma One, out."

Nightstars in hand, Callahan began his surveillance of the forest perimeter and the northern slopes. The thinner cover up there might allow him to single out those snipers.

As he studied the terrain, he was tempted to grab Santiago and take off. In the grand scheme of things, the lives of two American Marines hardly mattered. It was highly likely that General Santiago could tap them into the entire network of corruption within the Philippine government and military—and he was the only solid link they had left. Rescuing the general was simply far more important to the United States. Callahan fully recognized that now.

But was Callahan sticking around because he felt guilty over setting up Rainey and his men? Certainly that was part of it. He had been cut from the same cloth, and it had grown increasingly harder to detach himself. He had also reasoned that now he had a better chance of escape if he had help. If he stuck to the original plan, he might put some distance between himself and the camp, but carrying Santiago would render them slow and vulnerable. The escape would be the longest kilometer of Callahan's life. Those Tausug tribesmen would hunt them down and kill them before the extraction helo arrived.

From the corner of his lens he saw a figure dart from one tree to the next. He zoomed in. Corporal Jimmy Vance was about to gut an unsuspecting sniper who had set up near a tree.

The grim reaper had cometh in the form of a Recon Marine named Cpl. Jimmy Vance, and the sniper, who was just turning his head at Vance's approach, realized in the last nanosecond of his life that he was looking into the face of death. The shock in his expression conveyed nothing less.

The knife went in, turned, came out. The sniper fell,

tucked himself into a fetal position, and bled.

Vance was all rabid animal now, his heart hard and black.

He ran. Hard. Next tree. Right there. Another guy. Thin face. Guy looked up. Opened his mouth. Bam. Got it in the heart. *Die, motherfucker.*

On to the next. Rally home. Powerful now. The wounded arm did not matter. Numb. Nothing.

There he was. Guy with an RPG. Waiting. Vance could have stabbed him. Didn't. Grabbed the RPG, wrenched it from the little fucker's hands, turned it around. Clubbed him over the head. Split his skull. Clubbed him again. Again.

Caught his breath, looked up—

And then, as he gazed across the mountain, spotting the last two huts, he sighed deeply, as though exhaling some of the rage. He was almost human again. He had to *think.* "Dogma One, this is Dogma Four. Am approaching from your north. I have acquired an RPG. Suggest I rally on you at the trail, over."

"Roger that, Dogma Four. But hold for now. Dogma Team, listen up. I want our own RPGs up. I will designate targets, and you will fire on my mark. Stand by . . ."

After a quick threat scan of the area, Vance remained tight to a nearby tree and slid the Rocket Propelled Grenade's strap from his shoulder. The RPG-7's wooden heat guard had been beat up to shit, as had the rest of the barrel, but Vance felt confident that everything else was in order.

Fronds rustled from somewhere behind him. He froze. Listened. Then, ever so slowly, he pulled out his binoculars. Waited a moment more. Had a look. He focused on the edges of shrubs and trees where the smallest outline of a human form might appear. Damn, he was wasting time. He needed to get the RPG ready.

Trying to calm down, he took up the weapon, shouldered it, sighted in on several huts. With eyes focused ahead and ears taking in every hum and snap to his rear, he made his adjustments, tried to get comfortable despite his throbbing arm, tried to anticipate the kickback that hit you like a punching bag. He steadied his finger on the weapon's long trigger, felt the weight of the tail-end blast shield tugging down a little, then he corrected his aim.

"Dogma Team, I have your targets. Dogma Three, you have the main group of huts to the east. Papa Two, you got the ones to the north. Eagle Six, you will stand by to move with your package. Dogma Four, target our location on second mark, over."

Had Vance misheard the Sarge? "Dogma One, this is Dogma Four, repeat my target, over."

"Dogma Four, you will target our position—*on my second mark,* over."

Ah, it clicked now. The sergeant did not have a death wish, nor did he want to take the others with him to his grave.

Vance concentrated on his breathing, turned his aim on the two huts, sighted in, found one corner that would heave an explosion powerful enough to level both structures.

"Dogma Team? Stand by . . ."

The fronds rustled again, and Vance could not help but turn his head.

16

The guns still boomed from somewhere above as Hamsiraji wriggled himself into the gap between the two boulders. Half of the men who had been helping to clear the rubble had already deserted him. They feared his brother's wrath and had gone up to fight the infidels.

No matter. In fact, Hamsiraji would dismiss all but Charti once he learned what was on the other side. He leaned forward, pushed a little farther, then came through the crack and tumbled onto the dirt floor. He got up, wrenched his flashlight from a pocket, thumbed it on, and let the beam play over this new tunnel's damp walls. He swung to his right, and the flashlight revealed a wall of dusty wooden crates, maybe fifty in all, with Japanese characters stenciled across their sides.

Hamsiraji began to pant as he tucked the flashlight

under his arm, reached up to a stack, and hauled down a crate the size of footlocker.

"You found it?" Charti called, his head jutting out from the gap between boulders.

"Send the others to their posts now. Right now."

"You *did* find it."

"Do as I say!"

The young man slipped back into the hole as Hamsiraji struggled with the crate's lid. The thing had been nailed shut, and even after all these years, it would hardly budge. He turned over the flashlight, began banging on one corner of the lid, trying to pry it up. After a half dozen blows, the lid popped, and the flashlight began to flicker.

Inside, stuffed between heavy wood shavings, lay several golden goblets affixed with brightly colored jewels. Hamsiraji lifted one, surprised by its weight.

"A toast to you, General Yamashita. A toast to you!"

The flashlight flickered out. Hamsiraji shook the thing. It flickered once more, died. Another shake. Nothing. He began to unscrew the light and screamed for Charti.

As his voice echoed off, something exploded above, something so powerful that it shook the entire tunnel. Dust began dropping onto Hamsiraji's head and nose.

Then, only a few meters away, a sickening rumble— as though the tunnel's ceiling were caving in—resounded and sent a gust tugging through his curly hair.

Hamsiraji looked up and realized he had lost his bearings. He was not sure where the boulders were and could not navigate in the darkness. "Charti!"

The rumble grew louder. A heavy piece of stone struck his arm. Another smaller piece bounced off his shoulder, nearly knocking him to the floor. Frantic but keeping the golden cup in his hand, he reached out, searching for a wall. More pieces of rock rained over him, and the roar grew so loud that it seemed to go through him. He ducked, groaned, felt a huge blow to his head, felt the ground smack him in the face and chest.

He squeezed the golden chalice, even as the air was squeezed from his lungs.

TEAM DOGMA

ABU SAYYAF STRONGHOLD

MOHAJID MOUNTAIN

BASILAN ISLAND, SOUTHERN PHILIPPINES

0503 HOURS LOCAL TIME

"Yeah," whispered Houston as he tossed down his RPG and raised his Nightstars. "That's what I'm talking about!"

His grenade had left the launcher, fins had folded out to stabilize the rocket's flight, then the motor had ignited at a range of thirty-six feet to carry the glistening bomb nearly three hundred meters to its target. Not only had the huts been leveled, but a long fissure had opened up in the earth, exposing tunnels below. "Dogma One, this is Dogma Three. Direct hit, over."

"Dogma One, this is Papa Two, confirm Three's hit and my own, over."

"Dogma One, this Eagle Six standing by with my package, over."

"Roger that, Dogma Team. Dogma Four, stand by for second mark, over."

Vance did not reply.

"Dogma Four, sitrep, over."

Nada. Though it would be well-nigh impossible to actually spot the sniper, Houston searched the forest from where Vance had last checked in. *Shit, where are you buddy?*

Behind Houston, the priest's men were on the move, drawing more of the ASG guerillas to the east fence line. The bad guys shouted to each other, and the shifting, sporadic gunfire drifted across the mountain as the attacking force drove on. Their movement sent the clock hands racing around the dial. Vance had about two more seconds to acknowledge, then the sarge would give the word to move out.

Damn, every time someone on the team failed to check in, Houston usually thought the worst. And his mind always raced to figure out how he would deal with the loss of that particular operator. Then he would curse himself for putting out the negative vibe and jinxing the guy, should he still be alive.

Of all the operators on the team, past and present, Vance was the only one who really understood Houston. They were opposites to be sure, but Vance had always thrown that aside and had helped Houston no matter what funk had plagued him. And even when Vance knew that Houston wasn't up for a task, he would never go squealing to the sarge. He was decent enough to protect Houston's dignity and ego. He made the kinds of sacrifices and took the kinds of chances you would not expect from even a fellow operator. A guy like Banks would never do anything like that. And Houston had always told himself that Vance was the one guy on the team whose loss would strike him as hard as losing his father. That dumb redneck was family.

"Dogma Four, key your mike, over."

Goddamn it, Jimmy. Key your mike!

Vance had set down his RPG and had moved about ten meters to the right of his position to investigate a rustling of fronds that had unnerved him.

As he peered out from behind a shrub, he spotted a guerilla crouched down among the rubber plants, his face masked by soot. Vance knew that if he returned to his tree, the guy would continue to close on him. With Vance's back turned and his eyes and thoughts focused on his target, the guerilla might get off an unobstructed shot or even go for the bolder move of slashing Vance's throat.

Vance needed to take this guy out.

But there wasn't time.

"Dogma Four, we are rallying toward the trail. If you can hear me, count thirty seconds and execute, out."

Thirty, twenty-nine, twenty-eight . . .

Vance keyed his mike twice and slipped off, winding around the rubber plants and back toward his tree. He could hardly breathe, he was so nervous. He nearly lost his footing as he sidestepped down, reached his gear, and got slowly onto his haunches, back into his original position.

Twenty, nineteen, eighteen, seventeen . . .

He lifted the RPG, sighted the huts, saw the team dashing across the perimeter toward the trail and dense jungle. His neck tingled. A drop of sweat fell from the tip of his nose. A crunching sound erupted, suddenly died. The bad guy was on the move over the dead fronds.

Vance tossed a look over his shoulder, still counting: *Twelve, eleven, ten . . .*

A snap. Nothing. Vance wanted to look back, but he had the target. He would not lose it.

Three, two, one . . .

As the rocket exploded from his launcher, Vance let the recoil carry him onto his back. As he hit the ground, tossing the RPG aside and reaching for his AK, a shot rang out and bored into the tree.

Vance could not see the guerilla, but he fired anyway, a full automatic burst.

The second his finger relaxed on the trigger, he grabbed his ruck and dove for the next stand of trees, dropping behind thick, exposed roots. He buried his head in his chest, expecting a grenade.

And damn if he wasn't a fortune teller. The bang pierced his ears, and the blast, out near his first tree, tossed up a huge wave of mud that crashed on top of him as those tiny pieces of shrapnel—the pieces that doctors would be removing from your body for the rest of your natural life—pierced the leaves and branches like a billion insects chewing their way toward freedom. All of that happened as the powerful rush of hot air tugged at Vance's utilities. The roots should have protected him from the grenade, but shrapnel had a way of getting through Kevlar, let alone tree roots. Anything was possible.

As the jungle was beginning to fall silent, Vance was up and out of there, sewing a wide receiver's path across the mountain and taking sharp turns at nearly every tree.

Once he reached the trail he would stop then—and only then—to see if he had been hit and if he had lost his shadow.

Once the team had breached the forest perimeter, Rainey put Houston on point with Mindano behind him, followed by Callahan and his package. Rainey sent them off at a painfully slow pace, while he hung back, blinking sweat out of his eyes as he waited for Vance. Maybe the young fisherman had patience, but the old sergeant did not. And worse, that young man had sent Rainey's blood pressure through the roof. In the second that Rainey was about to write him off as dead, a pair of clicks had come over the tactical frequency, and though Rainey would never admit it openly, they were pure music.

A similar clicking came from the forest to the northeast, and Rainey returned the call. Then Vance came jogging hard between the trees, his Dragunov gone, his right sleeve stained heavily with blood, his eyes sore and obviously burning. "Sarge—"

"Direct hit on your target, outstanding," Rainey interjected, then smacked Vance hard across the shoulders as they crouched among clusters of wet shrubs. "You're wounded."

"I haven't looked. But Sarge, I got a shadow."

"And when there's one . . ." Rainey sang, quickly rolling up the corporal's sleeve. He took one look at the wound, saw the clean entry and exit. "Looks yummy. And yeah, you're going to live."

"I thought so. But what about that shadow? I can hang back and take him."

"No, you catch up to Callahan. You keep him and his package safe."

"Let me take point."

"Not with that arm. Houston's got it."

"All right. But I have the SOPHIE. Let me get it to him."

Rainey nodded. "Good to go?"

"Good to go, Sarge." Vance rubbed the corners of his eyes, felt Rainey taking one of his wrists. "What?"

"We'll talk later. But no matter what happened, you didn't get him killed, either. Do you understand?"

"Yeah." The corporal's tone was less then convincing, and Rainey wished they had time to talk. Still, he trusted that Vance would maintain his composure and get the job done. He had rarely done otherwise.

Rainey waited until the sniper had about a twenty-yard lead before he fell in, moving sideways, with his AK sweeping their rear as he imagined not one, not two, but a hundred guerillas suddenly rushing to attack.

Getting past the fence line proved suspiciously easy. A gate hung wide open, and the team passed through without incident. As they descended farther down the mountain, a fog rolled in that was so thick that visibility shrank to just a few meters. Anyone back on the higher ground had yet another advantage.

"You trying to tell me something, Murphy?" Rainey muttered as he shuffled on. "You're still not done with us?"

The nerves in his neck began working overtime as he anticipated a single crack that would send him flinching and ducking. That one shot, now born in all the gray vapor, would soon drive him mad.

Time to switch mental gears and contact Houston again. Rainey had been keeping in close contact with the radio operator and point man, who, during his first call to halt, had caught a glimpse of the fleeing group with the SOPHIE. The group had about a half kilometer lead, but the gap was quickly widening. How they were able to maintain such a vigorous pace through terrain as hairy as the mountains was beyond Rainey. Lance Corporal Banks had said something about them navigating the trails with their eyes closed. Maybe that wasn't far from the truth.

"Dogma Three, this is Dogma One, over."

"Dogma One, this is Three, over."

"Call halt. Get me Yankee Thunder. Dogma Four, cover rear, I'm heading up, out."

Vance gave Rainey a curt nod as they passed.

"Stay tight," Rainey warned.

"Aye-aye."

The sniper was anxious to ferret out his shadow and get a little closure with bullets, knives, whatever worked. But if he strayed too far from the line, he might leave the others vulnerable.

Rainey was equally anxious to see if Demarzo and company could fly in those two teams of Filipino Marines standing by in Maluso. Those men could be dropped in front of the bad guys to effectively cut them off. Houston was already holding out the Foxtrot's mike when Rainey arrived. "Yankee Thunder, this is Dogma One, over."

"Dogma One, this is Yankee Thunder. Be advised we have your coordinates and the coordinates of your package. Unable to positively identify package with Eyes in the Sky, over."

"Fog of war," Houston quipped.

Rainey nodded. "Yankee Thunder, at this time you should have projected course of our package. Request Indigo Alpha and Indigo Bravo for immediate assault, over."

"Dogma One, wait, over."

"This is the part where Demarzo starts raising hell with those Filipino colonels," Rainey told Houston. " 'Cause it'll be their men—but it'll be our helos. They still have to make it look like we're training them— even now."

"Then they should send along a few instructors."

Rainey shook his head. "Demarzo won't put any more Americans out here. Not till this is over."

Houston's grin soured. "Hey, listen."

"What?"

"They stopped firing at the camp. Those other guys helping us out must be on the run. And the guys not chasing them might be coming for us."

"Well, don't let that *bug* you out."

Houston smirked. "Come on, Sarge, I just—"

"Dogma One, this is Yankee Thunder, over."

Rainey lifted a palm, quieting Houston.

The team was being followed by just one guy, a thug Vance had caught a glimpse of, a second before he had vanished into the brush and fog.

Knowing that the weather could be as much to his advantage as his enemy's, Vance did not maintain his position to cover the team's six, despite Rainey's warning. Blame it on the faces of Golez and Padua flashing through his mind. Blame it on a desire for payback that you just couldn't help when you watched fellow Marines die. It didn't matter whether they had been Filipinos; they were Marines through and through.

And so, with the ghosts of fallen comrades whispering advice in his ears, Vance veered about ten yards left and ascended about twice as many yards, only to double back, falling into the team's trail.

A real scout would know better than to follow the exact path of his enemy. You always kept parallel in case they had booby trapped the path or had stopped so that you'd walk right into them. Vance had figured the guy on his tail was an amateur, inexperienced, and predictable. He would be dead on their boot prints.

But no, the guy was a couple of meters off, and Vance had wondered if his opponent was one of the Tausug tribesmen that Banks had described. He was good. Vance was better.

As Vance neared him, he confirmed that the guerilla was the same guy with a soot-covered face. He squatted in a ditch created by runoff. If he had brought friends, Vance had not detected them, but he was talking softly into a cell phone whose signal could be easily tracked. He was probably cashing in on his unlimited nights and weekends minutes and was taking a moment to call his woman to say he'd be late for the pig roast. He had no idea how late . . .

Vance slipped up behind the guy, then drove his K-bar home, into the man's heart. His shadow went down, rolled onto his back, the cell phone with glowing display dropping from his hand.

Now Vance took the cell phone, brought it to his ear, and listened as a man's voice came through. "Hello?" Vance called.

"Who is this?" asked the other man, speaking good English but with a familiar Filipino accent.

"Dogma Four, this is Dogma One, over," barked the radio.

"Hang on, buddy," Vance said into the cell phone. "I got another call coming in." He pulled up his boom mike. "Dogma One, this is Dogma Four. Be advised my shadow is down, over."

"Roger that. Rally back. We're moving out, over."

"Dogma Four, rallying back, out." Vance brought the cell phone back up to his lips. "You there?"

"Who is this? Tell me now!"

Knowing it was wrong, just plain wrong, but needing a grin too badly to resist, Vance replied, "This is a representative of the United States government."

"You lie!"

"No, seriously. I'm the secretary of defense. And right now, we suggest you lay down your weapons and move to the center of the camp with your hands raised. We have two battalions out here. And we have you surrounded."

"We don't see you! You lie again!"

"Do it now. Or we will take you by force."

The man barked to someone in Tagalog. Grinning, Vance took the phone and chucked it back up the mountain.

TEAM DOGMA HOSTAGES
SOMEWHERE IN THE SOUTHWEST JUNGLE
BASILAN ISLAND, SOUTHERN PHILIPPINES
0547 HOURS LOCAL TIME

Being in a world of hurt suited Lance Cpl. Ricardo Banks just fine. While some weaker operators might wallow in self-pity, he kept the faith because he knew that his suffering would turn him into an even more for-midable Marine. There *was* gain in pain. It *did* let you know you were alive. Scars made you stronger—when they didn't ruin perfectly good tattoos . . .

When Banks got back, the guys in his old unit would look at him differently. Their jealousy would turn to awe. They would know that he had been captured, been tortured, and had survived to tell the tale. He would have been to "the other side," while they were just chil-dren playing behind the fence. The more Janjali and his guerillas beat him, the stronger Banks would become. No question about it.

Still, Banks needed to turn strong thoughts into strong actions. Force of will was one thing. Force of fist was another. Yet he and Doc had not pulled any stunts since their last collapse. Janjali's men had grown used to carrying them down the trails and paused only briefly to freshen their grips.

It was, at times, actually nice to be hauled along, though Banks's arms and legs had become even stiffer than his neck. He found it a little easier to see as the swelling began to subside, though with the fog, that didn't matter much. He also found it nearly impossible to keep his tongue away from the gap where his tooth had been knocked out. He kept probing the soft tissue, almost unconsciously. Ah, the hell with it. He was still the most handsome Puerto Rican hillbilly on the island.

"Banks?" Doc called.

"Yo."

"How we doing?"

"No talking," growled one of he guards.

"We're doing," Banks said, ignoring the scrawny fool who thought he was a big man with his popcorn gun.

"Do you hear that?"

"Oh, yeah," Banks said, as the thumping of distant helicopters drew nearer. "Hueys. Maybe two or three."

"Hopefully ten."

"Don't get greedy, Doc. Hey, listen, you idiots. You're all going to die."

Strange thing was, Janjali's men did not react to the approaching choppers. The group continued filing through the jungle at the same pace. There was no ducking, no hiding—no evasive maneuvers. Was Janjali so cocky to believe that he and a handful of guerillas could take on those choppers and the teams on board?

An order relayed back, and finally the men picked up the pace. Banks shut his eyes and concentrated on the thwacking of those rotors. Was it his imagination, or was the sound beginning to fade?

OPERATIVE OMEGA EAGLE
NORTHWEST JUNGLE
BASILAN ISLAND, SOUTHERN PHILIPPINES
0550 HOURS LOCAL TIME

"It's almost over," Callahan told General Santiago as he dropped to his knees and slowly slid the general from his back, easing him onto the dirt along a heavily wooded ridge. "We're going to stay here."

"I need the medic. I need more painkillers."

"Shut up."

"You're feeling pretty good about yourself now, huh?"

"I said shut up." Callahan sat back, palmed the sweat from his forehead, and heaved a terribly exhausted sigh. "You've already broken my back. Don't bust my balls."

The general's gaze turned skyward. "There is no place for your helicopter to put down."

Callahan pulled a canteen from his ruck, took a quick sip, then said, "Those guys don't need an LZ. They'll fast rope in."

"It's going to be a bloodbath, you know. Janjali will take the Americans, cut off their heads, and then escape."

"You may be right. But you played with fire. Now what do you got? Broken legs and a career as a government informant, because if you don't cut a deal, they'll either execute you or put you away for the rest of your life."

"I understand that perfectly."

"I don't think you do."

"You're wrong. When Allaga was arrested, I should have turned myself in."

"The devil repents . . ."

"Not the devil. I'm just a man like you, underpaid by his government while the politicians get rich. Who is the real enemy, Colonel?"

Callahan didn't want to think about that. He took another sip on his canteen, screwed on the cap, and was putting it away when Rainey called over the radio: "Eagle Six, this is Dogma One, sitrep, over."

"Dogma One, this is Eagle Six. I am in hold position

with my package, standing by to advance, over."

"Roger that. On my mark, out."

"He's a good man, that sergeant," mused Santiago. "I was once a lot like him."

"General? I seriously doubt that."

TEAM DOGMA
NORTHWEST JUNGLE
BASILAN ISLAND, SOUTHERN PHILIPPINES
0550 HOURS LOCAL TIME

As Mindano finished bandaging Vance's arm, Rainey watched the pair of Hueys hovering over the jungle canopy.

"Delta Eagle One-One, this is Dogma One," he called. "We have you and Delta Eagle One-Two our eleven o'clock, with enemy and package at your two o'clock. Proceed ahead. Have marked our position. Unable to mark landing zone at this time, over."

"Dogma One, this is Delta Eagle One-One. Have your smoke in sight, have enemy in sight. No discernable LZ established at this time. Will hover with Delta Eagle One-Two for insertion to intercept, out."

Once the helos were in position, ropes were dropped, and the Filipino Marines, easily identifiable in their standard-issue camouflage and orange armbands, began their descent, vanishing behind the fog and treetops. Rainey could almost feel that green, braided, polypropylene rope in his own fingers. Fast-roping was simply about signals, about hands and feet on a rope, and about sliding down. There was really nothing to it. But some operators did not have their lock-out techniques perfected, as evidenced by one Filipino who rocketed down the rope so quickly that Rainey knew the guy had never braked and had probably broken a leg.

Gunfire sounded from the jungle ahead, and the sparks from ricocheting rounds lit up the fuselages of both choppers. The pilots coolly reported they were taking fire, and with the last men out, immediately broke off, indicating that they would set down in the nearest available LZ to the west, where the jungle thinned into the beach.

"All right, Dogma Team. Make sure you're wearing your tape. Now we're pushing in to surround. Stand by, over." Rainey switched to the Filipino Marines' channel. "Indigo Alpha One, this is Dogma One, over."

"Dogma One, this is Indigo Alpha One. Have package spotted ahead. Moving in to flush, over."

"Roger that, Indigo Alpha One. We are good for Sierra Kill. Drive them right toward us, out."

Rainey slung his AK over his shoulder, tugged one of his K-bars from a calf sheath, then started through the shrubs. In order to eliminate the bad guys without accidentally killing the Filipino Marines or the hostages, Rainey had called for a "Sierra Kill," or silent kill. Just knives and reflexes.

Mindano was about ten yards to his left, Vance about ten yards to his right, luminescent tape flashing on their arms. Houston was directly ahead, about twenty yards up, ready to jump anyone who came running his way, save for Doc and Banks.

As the fog thinned out, the big mahogany trees appeared to grow out of the vapor, and voices seemed to come directly from those trees—screams in Tagalog followed by salvos of automatic fire.

"Dogma One, this is Dogma Three," Houston cried. "Here they come!"

"Roger that, Three. Dogma Team, widen the flanks. Papa Two, stand by for call up. We are Sierra Kill, out."

With a thick tree trunk at his left shoulder, Rainey balanced on a knee, Nightstars in one hand, K-bar in the other. The shouting and gunfire gave way to sounds of his breathing, his pulse, his stomach. He tensed, waited. Waited some more.

"Dogma Three, this is Dogma One. Where are they, over?"

"Dogma One, this is Dogma Three," Houston replied in a half whisper. "Still coming. But slow. I think they're on to us."

17

With Callahan and General Santiago in a safe position, Houston, the rest of the team, and the Filipino Marines were pushing in to surround Janjali and recover the hostages. Houston couldn't wait to draw some terrorist blood. As a guerilla neared the brush ahead, he sprang, reached around the guy's head, covered his mouth, and jerked back. The guerilla was about to bite Houston when he punched the K-bar into the money spot.

As he turned the blade, Houston kneed the guerilla's AK so that the guy's finger slipped from the trigger. The guerilla went limp, and Houston dragged him beneath a bush. "Now that's textbook, thank you." He keyed his mike. "Dogma One, this is Dogma Three. One down. See two more heading back for you, over."

"Roger that. Hold position, out."

Houston squatted and wiped off his K-bar on his pant

leg. He wanted so badly to see Doc and Banks running toward him that for a second he thought he did, only to realize that two Filipino Marines were pushing silently forward. He worked his clicker, drawing their attention. One man returned a click, then Houston slowly emerged from his bush, making sure his silvery luminescent tape was in plain sight. "U.S. Marine right here. Lance Corporal Bradley Houston."

One of the Filipinos, a sergeant with a thin moustache, spoke up. "Lance Corporal, only three got back here. We believe we have accounted for the rest, but some may have escaped into the jungle."

"But you have the hostages?"

The sergeant winced. "The rebels were carrying two men in stretchers, but they were not hurt, not Americans. Just a decoy. The hostages are not here."

Houston grabbed the man's shoulders. "Are you kidding me?"

"No, I am not."

Houston wanted to collapse right there. He released the sergeant, turned, stared into nowhere. "Dogma One, this is Dogma Three, over."

"Dogma Three, wait." Rainey was about to jump one of the guerillas, who turned, gave an appraising glance at the tree beside Rainey, then suddenly bolted.

On his feet, Rainey tracked the man. He had the K-bar's tip between his fingers. He wound up, let the knife fly.

With a hollow thump, the blade stuck in a tree just behind the fleeing guerilla.

Wrenching another K-bar from the sheath on his belt, Rainey was about to charge off in pursuit, when the guerilla dropped to the leaves and got off three rounds. As Rainey hit the deck, Houston called emphatically over the channel: "Dogma One, this is Dogma Three. Cannot wait, over."

"Dogma Three, you will *wait*."

"Dogma One, this is Dogma Four. Coming up on your six, stand by, over."

After a pair of clicks, Vance slid into home plate beside Rainey as the guerilla fired another burst. "What's going on, Sarge?"

"Same old shit. Taking fire from some meathead."

Vance drew his knife. "Mind if I kill him?"

"Nah, go ahead."

Vance rose to his hands and knees, then abruptly drove himself into a sprint toward the next cluster of trees.

"Dogma Three, this is Dogma One, sitrep, over."

"Dogma One, this is Three. I am here with Indigo operators. Be advised they have secured the area and we have captured or killed all but two rebels, but this was a decoy team. Repeat. Decoy team. No package found. No package found, over."

"Say again, Dogma Three?"

"Repeat. This was a decoy team. No package found, over."

Rainey closed his eyes. "Roger that, Three. Get me Yankee Thunder and tell them to stand by, out."

No package found. Shit! Janjali had divided the group and escaped.

A report came in from Vance: "Dogma One, this is Dogma Four. Be advised our shooter is down, over."

"Roger that, Dogma Four. Dogma Team, Sierra Kill is over. Fire if needed and rally on Dogma Three, out."

Rainey got up and jogged through the jungle toward Houston, his thoughts consumed by the one big question: Where were Janjali and the hostages? If Janjali had sent a decoy team toward the west coast, had he gone to the east? It was safe to assume that he wanted to flee the island and had made preparations. Where would he go? Jolo Island? How would he get there? Boat? Chopper? Where along Basilan's coast was the best point of departure? Even if Rainey weighed all of the variables and put together the most likely scenario, the fact remained that he and the others had still failed the mission. And to rub salt in the wound, the damned spook who had set them up would return with his prize.

Feeling the frustration begin to mix with sheer panic, Rainey started running with everything he had, reaching Houston in just a minute. The lance corporal stood among a group of Filipino Marines. "Sarge, I have Yankee Thunder."

Snatching up the mike, Rainey took a few seconds to measure his words. "Yankee Thunder, this is Dogma One. Be advised we have captured or killed all but two members of fleeing group. Package is not here. Repeat. Package is not here, over."

"Roger that, Dogma One. Stand by, over."

"Sarge, you all right?" Houston asked, keeping his voice down.

"I'll be all right when I can put a bullet between that maniac's eyes. He's heading toward the coast, trying to get off the island. We just have to find him. We can do it."

"Dogma One, this is Yankee Thunder. You are ordered to abort mission and rally on Delta Eagle One-One for extraction. Repeat. Abort mission and rally on Delta Eagle One-One for extraction, over."

"They're writing off Doc and Banks," Houston said. "How can they do that? *Can* they do that?"

"Yankee Thunder, this is Dogma One. Aborting mission. Rallying back to Delta Eagle, out."

"Sarge?"

"Hey, they're not writing off Doc and Banks, and neither are we. But this is a dead end. And we're getting the hell out of here," said Rainey.

"So we're aborting?" asked Callahan, who had just handed off General Santiago to two Filipino medics.

"It quacked like a duck. We chased it. And it turned out to be a fucking poodle," Houston groaned.

"Callahan, if we don't recover my men, I'm going to . . ." Rainey broke off, losing his breath. He was ready to drop the guy right there. "You can hide from some people, but not from Force Recon. Not us."

"I'm not hiding from anyone."

"But you got what you wanted," said Houston. "What do you care?"

"Once upon a time, gentlemen, I was just like you."

"I don't think so." Rainey waved over Mindano and Vance. "Gentlemen, we are aborting and—"

"Dogma One, this is Delta Eagle One-One, over."

"—saddling up for the beach. Hold on. Delta Eagle One-One, this is Dogma One, over."

"Dogma One, be advised I made a pass along the coast before setting down and may have spotted your package approximately four kilometers south your position and heading west, over."

"Bingo!" Rainey cried, then keyed his mike. "Delta Eagle One-One, we are on our way!"

JANJALI GROUP
TWO KILOMETERS NORTH OF SUMISIP
BASILAN ISLAND, SOUTHERN PHILIPPINES
0645 HOURS LOCAL TIME

Ramzi Janjali had never been one to rely too heavily on misdirection and diversion. His years in the jungle had taught him that for every clever move he made, the enemy could respond with equal creativity and ingenuity. Sometimes the simplest plans worked because his opponents were expecting something much more elaborate. Thus, he had created a simple diversion of smoke and mirrors that had shocked him by actually working. The Americans had followed the decoy group all the way up the coast. Now those helicopters had landed, but it wouldn't be long before the Americans learned the truth.

Janjali shouted to his men on the dock, who said they had checked the route for commercial and military traffic and that there would not be any problems. The Filipino Navy boats were off the coast of Kabingbing and would never be able to intercept in time. The two American amphibious assault ships were still off the coast of Isabella, and they could send Cobra attack helicopters and Harrier jets. Though Janjali could use the hostages as shields against such a force, the Americans could call his bluff and fire anyway, despite the risk to their men. He needed to move quickly and avoid any such confrontations.

Beyond him, the inlet's cool, calm waters waited, and just seventy miles beyond, Jolo Island rose up from the emerald waves, its dense jungles promising sanctuary. Janjali had more men stationed there to help smuggle him and others to his secondary base in the north central mountains. All right. Everything was in place. He turned and jogged back along the dock.

Several years prior, Janjali had paid handsomely for the construction of the two boathouses standing ahead of him. Four more of his men were waiting there, and they had reported that the fueling and loading had gone smoothly. He liked to brag that his pair of thirty-foot-long speedboats were two of the fastest watercraft on the entire island, and he was about to make good on that boast.

Janjali entered one house and jumped into the back of his boat, where Garden and the black U.S. Marine had been placed. The Hispanic Marine was in the other boat. Beaten again and still suffering from the lingering effects of the heroin, Janjali's hostages were docile, just the way he liked them.

Unfortunately, they could still use their mouths.

"They're going to catch us," said the Marine named Doc. "And when they do . . ."

"Haven't you had enough? If I decide to cut you from the seat and throw you overboard, you will drown with your feet tied and the cuffs still on. And I will do that if they catch us."

"Just to spite them?"

"As a Marine you should know that we all go down fighting. They will not take me alive. Nor will they survive the attempt." Janjali hollered in Tagalog for his boat's captain to take off. The five hulking Volvo engines roared so loudly that Janjali, Garden, and some of his other men were forced to cover their ears. Then, as the captain engaged the throttle, they hit their seats and the boat raced from the boathouses, leaving a massive wake.

The second boat joined them a few seconds later, trailing just behind, then revving up and riding beside them, about twenty-five meters out. With the wind whipping through his hair, Janjali stood and waved his AK at the others in the second boat. They raised their own weapons and let off a cheer.

"Even if you do get away, they won't pay you this time," Garden cried from her seat next to him. "Not this time."

"They always pay. But you know, I don't care any-more. I was making up excuses why I needed to stay. But I don't. Not anymore. I can live without the money."

"Then let me and the two men go."

Janjali closed his eyes, turned his face toward the sun, and ignored her.

TEAM DOGMA
DELTA EAGLE II LANDING ZONE
BASILAN ISLAND, SOUTHERN PHILIPPINES
0705 HOURS LOCAL TIME

By the time Rainey and the others reached the landing zone on the beach, the Filipino Marines had already jammed aboard Delta-Eagle 12 and were just dusting off. Because the enemy contact was still unconfirmed, Yankee Thunder had already ordered that helo back to Camp Balikatan and given Delta Eagle 11's pilot au-thorization for a single pass over the contact zone to identify the package.

"Too bad you missed your ride," Rainey yelled to Callahan over the whine of the helo's engine and the howl of prop wash.

"What're you talking about?"

"You and Santiago are staying here. I'll call for an-other helo to pick you up."

"Bullshit!" Callahan pointed to the general, who lay

on a portable stretcher and was now heavily sedated. "He needs surgery A-SAP! And what about Janjali's men? We didn't get them all! You know that!"

"What can I say? You got bad timing, Colonel."

Callahan seized Rainey's shirt. "You know what? You're right. My mission is all about Santiago. He's going to help us bring down these terrorist motherfuckers. We need to get him out of here now. Do not test me, Sergeant."

"I'm doing this for your own safety, asshole! If Janjali's out there, he won't go down without a fight. You want to be riding around in a helo with the general—while they're taking shots at us?"

"No, we're going straight back to camp."

"The fuck we are. I have authorization for a single pass over the contact zone."

"In five seconds, you'll have nothing. Houston? Over here!" Callahan waved over the radio operator. "Get me Yankee Thunder!"

Callahan should not have turned his head. If he had not, he would've seen Rainey reaching for and producing his MEU pistol. He would have watched as Rainey lifted that pistol and aimed it at his forehead.

But when Callahan saw the odd look on Houston's face, he finally turned back—

Right into the .45's barrel.

"What kind of fucking nonsense is this?" asked Callahan, unfazed by the weapon. "You looking to end your career, right here, right now?"

"No. I'm looking to end yours."

"Hey, Sarge . . . come on, man . . ." Houston began.

"Shut up!" Rainey screamed, then he jammed the pistol against Callahan's head. "I got two men out there. And I'm going after them. Do you read me, Colonel?"

Callahan did not flinch. "I read you, Sergeant. You can look for your men—but you're not leaving here without me and the general. Do *you* read *me*?"

Rainey lowered the pistol. "Completely. Now get your fucking package and get on board that helo."

As Callahan moved off to enlist Mindano's help in loading the general, Houston came over to Rainey. "Jesus Christ, Sarge. I never seen you like that. Fuckin' insubordination, man."

"It's only insubordination when you're dealing with a real officer. Come on. And by the way, you forgot about attempted murder."

"Yeah, I did. But he won't."

"I don't care. We have to find Doc and Banks. That's all that really matters."

Once they were on board and strapped in, the pilot's voice came over the radio: "Dogma Team, this is Delta Eagle One-One in the cockpit. Stand by for dust off . . ."

"Hey, Sarge?" Vance called over the rising whine of rotors. "Fast-ropes are good to go."

Rainey held up his thumb, then eyed Houston, who returned the thumb, as did Mindano. Callahan, who was seated beside Santiago, wasn't paying attention and wouldn't have raised a thumb, anyway.

"Yankee Thunder, this is Delta Eagle One-One, dusting off with Team Dogma and Oscar Gamma Sierra on board," reported the pilot. "Will make slow pass over coastline southwest our position for possible enemy contact, over."

"Delta Eagle One-One, this is Yankee Thunder, confirm your coordinates. You are authorized for single pass, then return to Balikatan, over."

"Roger that, Yankee Thunder. Delta Eagle One-One, out."

"Well, there it is," Rainey moaned. "A single pass. We got one round in the magazine, and it had better count."

TEAM DOGMA HOSTAGES
EN ROUTE TO JOLO ISLAND
BASILAN ISLAND, SOUTHERN PHILIPPINES
0709 HOURS LOCAL TIME

Lance Corporal Ricardo Banks wanted to throw himself overboard, but the bastards had tied his arms and legs, then they had tied him to his seat. He was locked into his fun ride and sitting next to a guerilla who smelled like dog shit and freshly mowed grass. Through the one eye that wasn't as swollen as the other, Banks made out the occasional clear image, though he would almost rather be blind. The smelly guy had an

RPG balanced on his shoulder and a horrible grin on his face.

Prior to boarding the boats, Doc and Banks had put up a pretty good fight, but there had been too many guerillas. New bruises from being punched, kicked, and pistol-whipped were forming all over Banks's body, and another tooth had been knocked loose. The only weapon he had left was his spit, and he intended to use it, should the guerilla with the RPG get close enough.

Banks glanced back at the five big engines that sent them rocketing across the sea. He had never been in a boat as fast, and he wondered if the old Filipino skipper with the sunburned pate was really capable of piloting such a craft. He seemed at odds with the controls, jerking the big boat abruptly as he course-corrected. With little else to do but watch the skipper and try to loosen his bonds, Banks's thoughts wandered, and for a few moments, he began to feel sorry for himself. This was supposed to be the opportunity of a lifetime. He had had his chance to become part of not just any Force Recon team, but part of the famed Force Five. And what had happened? He had been captured. Now look at him. Beaten into raw meat. Tied. Helpless. Probably going to die. And what did he have to show for his efforts? Not a damned thing. He stopped pulling at his bonds.

Then, as Banks lowered his head, about to let the depression wash over him like a rogue wave, the sound of a distant helicopter gripped him. He craned his head and squinted toward the coastline as the RPG guy yelled to his comrades.

Like Vance, Houston, and Mindano, Callahan was seated on the chopper's deck and gripping the bulkhead straps. He didn't mind that position, so long as no one began shooting at them. They didn't have helmets to sit on and protect their family jewels like regular infantry. However, they did have a door gunner perched behind his 7.62 mm machine gun, as well as a pair of seven-shot rocket pods mounted up front.

Sitting there, he took a moment to reflect on what had just happened with Sergeant Rainey. They were both doing what they understood was best. Callahan actually admired the man's fortitude, but he still wondered what he would do if they made contact with Janjali.

He pushed himself a little closer to the door's edge, drawing the door gunner's attention. "Sir?"

"Relax. I'm good." Callahan raised his binoculars.

"Dogma Team, we are approaching zone. Make two speedboats off the coast, heading south, over."

"That has to be them," Callahan said. "It is."

Rainey, who was hunched over and spying the water

with his own Nightstars, suddenly shouted, "Delta Eagle, get us there now!"

Callahan looked at Rainey, who returned a warning look. Callahan opened his mouth, about to tell Rainey it was all right—

Just as the pilot banked hard right, descending at a nauseating rate before leveling off, sweeping just a hundred feet above the water. "Yankee Thunder, this is Delta Eagle One-One. Be advised we have confirmed contact with our package. They are aboard two speedboats heading south southeast toward Jolo Island. Request Charlie Bravo and medevac support, over."

"Delta Eagle One-One, this is Yankee Thunder, confirm your sighting. Dispatching Charlie Bravo and medevac support. ETA nineteen minutes, over."

"Roger that, Yankee Thunder, will keep package in sight until support arrives, out."

"Whoa, whoa, whoa," Callahan hollered, watching an RPG ignite from one of the speedboats. "Incoming!"

The pilot rolled left, the prop wash buffeting the airborne grenade as it flashed by.

"Get us in close before they reload," Rainey shouted as the pilot leveled off, then wheeled back, coming up behind the boats once more. "Get us close enough to drop."

"I can do it. But I can't hold for more than a few seconds."

"That's all I'll need."

As they came in at full throttle, Callahan gripped his strap with one hand while pulling a pistol from his holster. They sped over the right speedboat's wake, the one carrying Banks, the one with the RPG guy who was busy reloading his weapon. Another guy with an RPG stood on the left boat, along with Janjali, Doc, a woman, and three more of Janjali's guerillas.

"Hey, Sergeant, we got another clown with an RPG," Callahan cried.

"Vance? Houston?" Rainey shouted. "Stand by. Callahan? Back away from the door."

Callahan shook his head. "This one's mine, Sergeant."

"He's on his feet, getting ready to launch," yelled the door gunner. "I have to take him out."

"No! Our man's too close," Rainey screamed.

Callahan nodded to Rainey, then looked down as the chopper descended to just fifteen feet above the speedboat. The guerilla with the RPG was about to fire point-blank into the hold while the other guys on board opened up with their AKs.

For Callahan, everything about the moment seemed familiar, as though he were just remembering it. Was that fate working? Déjà vu? Destiny? He didn't know, didn't care. All he knew was that if he didn't stop that son of a bitch, everyone was going to die.

And so . . . he threw himself from the Huey, plummeted down toward the guy while firing his pistol. Callahan's rounds struck the guy in the chest as he hit the deck and crashed into the man, knocking the RPG aside. The rocket blasted from the launcher and arrowed away like an errant firework streaking into the white foam.

As Callahan smashed into one of the seats, he heard the AKs popping, felt the rounds ripping into his flesh. His time had finally come, and that was okay. Rainey would probably still hate him for setting up the team, and Callahan's own life was still not enough to pay off the debt. That was okay, too. At least he had proven to himself that beneath all of the bogus titles and uniforms, he was a warrior. And Valhalla called.

TEAM DOGMA HOSTAGES
EN ROUTE TO JOLO ISLAND
BASILAN ISLAND, SOUTHERN PHILIPPINES
0715 HOURS LOCAL TIME

The woman named Garden, whose hands were cuffed behind her back but whose feet were free, got up from her seat. Doc had thought she had been tied down, but apparently Janjali didn't see her as much of a threat. She was.

Like a defensive lineman, Garden came across the deck, lowered her shoulder, and plowed into the guerilla getting ready to shoot the Huey with his comrade's reloaded RPG. He and his weapon toppled overboard—

But in that same instant, one of the guerillas up front near the captain, swung his AK away from the chopper and fired.

Garden's head exploded, blood spattering over Doc's face as she hit his lap.

"Garden!" Janjali howled as she rolled across the deck, more blood pouring from the side of her head.

"Garden!" Janjali was about to lean down when he suddenly spun and shot his own man, rounds punching the guy onto the gunwales, then over the side.

The captain and the remaining two guerillas were hollering at each other as Janjali turned back to the woman, got to his knees, and touched her cheek.

Doc glowered at the man. "She died for nothing!"

Janjali grabbed Doc by the neck. "And so will you!"

TEAM DOGMA
ONBOARD DELTA EAGLE II
BASILAN ISLAND, SOUTHERN PHILIPPINES
0716 HOURS LOCAL TIME

"They shot Callahan," Vance screamed as he and Houston were about to bail out of the chopper. The door gunner suddenly opened fire, raking the bow of the speedboat, instantly killing the captain and another guerilla. Then, with shell casings rattling off the deck, he swung back, firing on the engines.

"I told you my man is too close!" Rainey boomed.

"He's all right!"

As the door gunner brought more hell to the boat, the remaining guerilla decided to do the right thing: bail out. Now there was just Banks, tied to his seat aboard a runaway speedboat.

"Vance? Go!" Rainey ordered.

Vance bailed out, hit the speedboat's deck. Houston

was right behind him, but he hit the gunwale and fell away, into the waves, cursing.

"Oh, shit. Don't worry, buddy, I'm coming back for you," Vance said as he watched Houston shrink away into the boat's wake. Then he crawled past Callahan's body and toward the controls. The boat slapped hard against the waves, two of the engines coughing up black smoke and reeking of gasoline.

"You going to wet a line or save my ass?" Banks called from his seat.

Vance reached the throttle and eased it down as the Huey roared away, heading for the other boat. He switched off the engines and gagged as the stench of gas grew even stronger.

Then, as the bow dropped down into the water, Vance realized they were taking on water through holes blasted by the door gunner. In fact, they were sinking fast. And one spark could ignite the still smoking engines.

"We're going to drown or explode. Which one you like?" he asked Banks as he reached the lance corporal and began sawing his K-bar across the heavy twine binding Banks to the seat.

A wave of heat passed across Vance's cheek. Shit. One of the engines had already caught fire.

Banks cocked his head at the flames. "Hurry up, dude!"

The fire spread quickly to the next engine as the twine finally came free. Banks stood, and Vance was about to cut through the twine around the guy's ankles

when Banks threw himself over the side, handcuffs
and all.

The flames spread quickly across the deck and
reached Vance's boots. He dove in after Banks, grimaced as the salt water made it past his lips, then he
broke the surface and swam toward the lance corporal.
Then he dove again, came under Banks, and worked
frantically to saw through that twine around Banks's
ankles, but the damned stuff was thick. Banks was
doing his best to hold his breath, but he started
writhing frantically. Vance had expected him to hang
on much longer, but his ass had been thoroughly
kicked, and it was clear now that he didn't have much
strength left. Abandoning the twine, Vance came up
again, wrapped an arm around Banks's head, and hauled
him to the surface. The lance corporal coughed hard
and gasped.

The boat was engulfed in flames now, and Vance did
his best to move them away. He could see Houston in
the distance, his pants removed, the legs tied, the whole
affair filled with air and tied around his neck. Houston
had relied on the old survival trick of turning your pants
into a life preserver, and Vance wished he could do the
same, but he needed to keep Banks's head above the
surface. He couldn't even pull off his boots, and he was
quickly running out of breath.

Janjali and his men were firing at the chopper, and despite the incoming, the pilot was taking them in, fangs
out. Rainey braced himself.

"I got a clean shot on their engines," said the door gunner. "I have the shots."

"My man is still too close," Rainey said as they thundered up behind the speedboat.

"I won't hit him," argued the door gunner. "I won't!"

Rainey tightened his lips, shuddered, then cried, "Take the shots."

The door gunner's machine gun drummed hard, chewing into the back of the boat. Smoke billowed from one engine, then another, then a third, as Janjali and the two remaining guerillas on board kept firing, rounds ricocheting or puncturing the Huey's armor.

"Get the skipper," Rainey ordered, and the door gunner swiveled his gun and opened fire. Rounds punched bloody holes along the skipper's back, and he dropped away from the boat's wheel. One of the guerillas ceased fire and took control of the boat while the other continued shooting with Janjali.

Rainey wasn't sure if Doc was even still alive. The medic was hunched over, his head hanging low, his arms cuffed behind his back. The pilot suddenly veered away, leaving a trail of smoke behind him.

"We got a little rotor damage," he reported over the intercom.

"Get me back in there," Rainey cried.

"I'll try. You got one chance to drop, Sergeant. Here it comes . . ."

Rainey nearly fell out of the hold as the pilot rolled back and dove toward the speedboat. As they leveled off, Rainey found a smoke grenade in his ruck, pulled the pin, and let it drop onto the boat's deck, up near the bow so that the smoke would blow over the men in back. A red cloud jetted from the canister as the pilot got them down again to just ten feet.

"I'm right behind you," Mindano said, pistol in hand.

"That's all right."

"I'm right behind you," the Filipino medic insisted.

As he slid his legs over the side, Rainey spotted Janjali using a rag to pick up the hot smoke grenade and toss it overboard. Still, the smoke was thick enough to have disoriented the men. Time to strike.

With his own pistol ready, Rainy pushed off, and even as he dropped he fired at the two guerillas, who had moved away from the bow. He capped one and hit the other in the shoulder. He hit the deck so hard that he lost his footing, went sliding into one side, then looked up—

Janjali was right there, lowering his AK to fire.

18

"Sergeant!" Doc yelled.

Despite having the muzzle of an AK-47 poised near his head, Rainey felt tremendous relief that old Doc was alive—even though, in the next few seconds, they both might buy the proverbial farm.

Janjali's bloodshot eyes swelled, then he craned his head just as Mindano came flying down and hit the deck. The medic stumbled into Janjali, knocking him aside as the AK discharged a triplet that passed harmlessly over Rainey's shoulder.

At once Rainey lifted his pistol, about to fire, when the guerilla he had shot in the shoulder clambered to the rail and got off a one-handed round that pierced Rainey's bicep and knocked the pistol from his grasp.

The next discharge from that guerilla's AK pounded

into Mindano's back, and the old medic looked at Rainey, gave a slight nod, and surrendered to death.

But then, mustering what had to be his last ounce of strength, the medic shifted around and fired his pistol at the guerilla, finishing the man—

As Janjali simultaneously finished Mindano with two more rounds, point-blank to the heart.

Seeing that Janjali was his only comrade left, the boat's captain decided enough was enough. He throttled down the remaining engines, which were coughing and sputtering, then he leaped out.

At the same time, Rainey grabbed the barrel of Janjali's AK, driving the man back and pulling himself to his feet. As the boat jolted against the backwash, Rainey shoved Janjali toward the rail as the terrorist emptied his clip, trying to ward off the Huey.

Behind them, Doc began hacking, and Rainey stole a glance there as smoke from the engines nearly swallowed the corpsman. Damn it. Doc might suffocate if he remained in his seat. But Doc couldn't get up, and Rainey couldn't get to him.

"I got him!" cried the door gunner from the hovering Huey.

Janjali glanced up at the gunner, then in a flash of movement released the empty AK, grabbed Rainey by the collar—

And dragged both of them over the side, crying, "We die together!"

As they crashed into the waves, Rainey let go of the rifle and wrenched Janjali's hands from his uniform.

With a couple of kicks he breached the surface, then he paddled back toward the boat, screaming for the door gunner to hold his fire. The trigger-happy bastard would kill him before Janjali did. The Huey gained altitude and slid right to evade the smoke billowing from the boat.

As Rainey reached the gunwale, Janjali came up beside him, a gleaming blade sticking from his hand. He reared back, came down, and it was all Rainey could do to hold back the knife with both hands, his one arm now aching and throbbing from his gunshot wound.

Janjali forced him below the surface. Holding his breath, Rainey tried to pry the blade from Janjali's fingers, but the terrorist knew that if Rainey didn't let go, he could hold him there until Rainey lost consciousness and drowned.

Steeling himself, Rainey rolled, exploiting the water to give Janjali a boot to the upper chest as he freed the terrorist's arm. Janjali fell back and a wave crashed over his head. Rainey kicked hard for the boat, the railing just out of reach. He could get back on board and grab one of the AKs there, or he could at least put enough distance between himself and Janjali to get that door gunner back in the game . . .

Rainey slung his arm over the rail, began hauling himself up. His wet utilities weighed a ton, and with his boots still on, he couldn't kick hard enough to do much good. He groaned loudly and pulled. Shit, he couldn't do it.

Where was the Huey? Still coming around.

And Janjali was swimming toward him now, knife

still in hand. Rainey tried swinging one leg onto the gunwale, but to no avail. Janjali was about to reach him when Rainey shoved himself away from the burning boat—

But he wasn't quick enough. Janjali made a swipe, slashing into Rainey's thigh. The water quickly turned red, and the sight of all that blood at once scared and enraged Rainey. Only his mean genes would save him now. Hissing, he grabbed Janjali's wrist with the hand of his wounded arm, then seized Janjali's throat with the other.

Knowing he couldn't hold back the knife for more than a few seconds with his faltering grip, Rainey dug his fingers into Janjali's throat, while the man dug his fingers into Rainey's wrist. Shutting his eyes in exertion, Rainey saw Kady holding their baby boy.

My son . . . I'm going to teach him how to be a man.

As the Huey thundered overhead, Rainey shoved Janjali beneath the water, continuing to choke him with his good arm as his wounded arm gave way.

The blade came down into Rainey's right shoulder, sending hot lightning through his arm and chest and driving him under with Janjali.

They hung there in a submerged death embrace, Rainey still clutching the fanatic while Janjali kept a fist wrapped around his blade, the long nails of his other hand drawing blood from Rainey's wrist.

With the water clouding up with spilled fuel and more blood, Rainey's eyes began to sting, and his grip on Janjali's throat faltered.

A scream formed in the back of his throat.

Then . . . Janjali's grip went slack, and the most feared man on Basilan Island floated soundlessly away.

Dragging himself to the surface, Rainey took in a huge breath and stroked with one arm, thankful he could keep his mouth above water. He was drifting away from the boat, with Doc still tied to his chair and the engines still smoking. Without looking back and with the knife still jutting from his shoulder, Rainey started kicking, but his legs were cramping up.

The Huey banked hard as though riding on rails, then it swooped down to hover once more over the speedboat. A fast-rope dropped to the boat's deck, and the door-gunner came sliding down, detached himself from the rope, and immediately went to Doc.

Rainey's grin hurt, but he couldn't stop smiling. Banks would be okay. Doc would be okay. He pushed on, but he never reached the boat.

TEAM DOGMA

CAMP BALIKATAN

TOWN OF ISABELLA

BASILAN ISLAND, SOUTHERN PHILIPPINES

1900 HOURS LOCAL TIME

"I knew you guys would come for me," Banks said, lisping slightly and lying in his bed inside the field hospital. He was truly enjoying some company that didn't want to stick a needle in him or listen to his breath sounds.

"We wanted to rescue Doc, but we figured, what the hell, we'll save Banks's conceited ass as well," Houston said.

Banks smirked. "So how's Doc?"

"Better," Vance answered. "But he's still in the other hut, won't leave the sarge."

"Rainey's not going to make it, is he?" Banks said.

Houston gave the lance corporal an incredulous look. "That's Mac Rainey. It takes a hell of a lot more than some jungle-boy terrorist to do him in. He's been there, done that, got the scars to prove it. And he'll do it again."

"I hope you're right. Because if he buys it, I get the blame—and that, right there, is the curse of Dogma Five."

Vance looked at Houston and their lips remained zipped, proving Banks's suspicions.

But then Vance offered his hand, and Banks took it. "No matter what happens, you won't get the blame. You would've done the same as him."

"That go for you, too, Houston?" Banks asked.

"I won't blame you. And you know, I figured something out. I thought maybe I was getting soft, kind of like what you said about nobody pushing me. But I'm not. I still got the fire. And you know who reminded me? You did, you asshole."

"So you want to thank me?"

Houston smiled. "Fuck you."

Vance looked at Banks's bandaged arm. "Hey, man, I didn't realize he ruined your art."

"I thought he did, too, but then I got to thinking about

how the scars across the tattoo make it look even cooler."

"Yeah, they go great with your missing teeth," Houston said.

Banks forced his tongue into the spaces. That second tooth that had been knocked loose had also fallen out. "I'm not worried. Shit, they got all kinds of implants these days. They do teeth, boobs, whatever you want."

"Yeah, Houston tried to get an implant for his little buddy down there, but the docs had never seen one that small, and the implants were all too big."

"Hey, I'm not the guy who plays with his worm—"

"Wait, don't move," Vance said, staring at Houston's shoulder. "You got a bug on you."

"Where? Where?"

Vance tapped Houston's temple. "Right there."

"Jerk."

Feeling a little left out of the joke, Banks quickly changed the subject. "So what about Callahan? What was up with him? I never figured him for a hero."

"He was a spook. He wanted Santiago, and he got him," Houston explained. "Turns out Callahan was the guy who set us up. Then he goes and sacrifices himself. Guy was just full of contradictions. But I'll tell you one thing. He was no pogue. He was just . . . Maybe he was just caught in the middle, and he did what he could."

"Sometimes that's all you can do," Vance said. "I don't hate him. I just hate what they asked him to do— use us as bait. I prefer to be on the other end of the line, if you know what I'm saying . . ."

* * *

Doc had been holding Rainey's hand for the past hour. The knife and gunshot wounds had not posed the greatest threat to the sarge's life. He had lost consciousness in the water, and he had sunk. By the time the door gunner pulled him out, he had gone into cardiac arrest. Doc performed CPR and restored Rainey's pulse, but by the time they had flown him back to Camp Balikatan, he had slipped into a coma. Doc was worried that Rainey might have aspirated water, which can lead to secondary drowning or massive pneumonia. Rainey had needed a well-equipped ICU, and Doc was uncertain whether the new field hospital at the camp could meet the challenge of his injuries. Surprisingly, the camp turned out to be nearly as well equipped as the sick bays aboard the amphibious assault ships that were still off the coast of Isabella. And the field hospital had been thirty minutes closer. Rainey was intubated, on a ventilator, and getting blood and antibiotics.

"You know, Sarge, with all that's gone on, I've forgotten to just say thanks. But I have to tell you, you're really pissing me off now. You just had a kid. It isn't time to check out. There's too much to do, all right? Don't be a stubborn asshole this time. That's all I'm saying."

"Doc?" Houston called from the doorway. "We're going to get something to eat. You coming?"

"No."

"You have to eat, man. You look like shit on a stick."

"Feel like it, too."

Houston approached the bed. "Kind of scary. I've never seen him like this. I'm usually the one who gets stabbed or shot. Not him."

"And I'll be the one calling Kady."

"You haven't already?"

"I've been waiting to see what happens. I just don't want to make the call if he's like this, you know?"

"You can't wait forever, Doc. Come on. Let's get something to eat." Houston gripped Doc's arm and tugged him away.

TEAM DOGMA

CAMP BALIKATAN

BASILAN ISLAND, SOUTHERN PHILIPPINES

2 DAYS POST MISSION

0921 HOURS LOCAL TIME

The second he heard the news, Cpl. Jimmy Vance streaked like ball lightning across the compound and through rows of huts. He nearly tripped over several infantrymen heading back to their billets.

A few wild turns later, he burst into the field hospital, ran down the line of beds, and found Doc, several doctors, and Banks and Houston gathered around the sarge's bed. He pushed his way past Banks and gaped at the sarge, who had an arm draped over his forehead as he picked his nose. "What?" Rainey asked. "You want to kiss me?"

The others broke up as Vance said, "No, Sarge. No

way. I just can't believe you're back. Thought we lost you."

Rainey lifted a pair of fingers. "I got two words for sad endings: Fuck 'em."

"You're damn right," Houston seconded.

"All right, Marines, let's let the doctors do their jobs," Doc said.

"Yeah, everybody out except Jimmy," Rainey said.

The others cleared away, and the doctors said they would stop by before lights out. Vance felt a little awkward standing before the sarge's bed. "What's up?"

"Well, it looks like I'll be on my back for a few weeks, maybe more. But after that, I was thinking we might take a little trip before we ship out. I'll get Demarzo's approval."

"Where we going?"

"You'll see."

TOWN OF SUMAS

BASILAN ISLAND, SOUTHERN PHILIPPINES

30 DAYS POST MISSION

1115 HOURS LOCAL TIME

"Do you speak English?" Rainey asked the barefoot boy of about twelve who had greeted them near the edge of town.

"I don't think he does, Sarge," Vance said.

"I learn English in school," the boy said. "Do you have something for us?"

"No, we're just looking for Father Nacoda. Is he here?"

"He is here. I will take you."

They followed the boy past several pig pens, then took a rocky trail leading up to several huts. The boy knocked on a door, and the priest appeared. The boy uttered something quickly in Tagalog, then Nacoda stepped outside and brightened as he came over. "Ah, gentlemen. This is a surprise."

"How's that sick boy?" Rainey asked.

"Oh, he's made a full recovery, thanks to the team you sent. Come inside. I'll make us some tea."

"Actually, it's kind of nice out here, if you don't mind," Rainey said, glancing down into a narrow yard where about a dozen children were seated on small wooden crates and being taught by a young woman standing before a chalkboard.

"It *is* nice this morning, but you're not here for the weather."

Rainey nodded slowly. "How many of your men died?"

The priest took in a long breath. "Too many."

"Why did you do it? What did you owe Callahan?"

"With his help I was able to build my church and school. Everything came through him, and he paid for it himself. I confronted him, and he said, 'What else I'm going to do with all my money?' But he's dead, isn't he . . . ?"

"I'm sorry, Father."

"The Lord has a special place for men like him."

"We weren't as fond of him as you are, Father. But in

the end, you're right. He was a good man. And he died like a man. And he died for something. I'm sure you've heard that we got Janjali."

"I did. And I read about how General Santiago confessed that the cabinet secretary was helping Abu Sayyaf. You know, there is an amazing sense of peace here now. Thank you."

"Actually, I wanted to thank you myself. I thought you and your men would get us all killed. I was wrong."

Father Nacoda extended a hand. "You're welcome."

Rainey glanced at Vance and realized he had not introduced him. "Father, this is Cpl. Jimmy Vance."

Vance shook hands with the priest, then said, "I want to thank you, too."

"Tell me, Corporal, are you a Christian?"

"Yes, Father. Catholic, as a matter of fact."

"When was your last confession?"

"Been a long time."

"Come on, then. You're carrying a heavy burden. Let's go up to my church . . ."

"I don't know, Father . . ."

Rainey slung his arm over Vance's shoulders. "Corporal, the man is giving you an order."

"Aye-aye."

UFFA HEADQUARTERS
JAMBA, SOUTHEAST ANGOLA
SIX MONTHS POST MISSION
2315 HOURS LOCAL TIME

After being out of the field for nearly six months, Sgt. Mac Rainey was more than ready to get back into the shit. He and the rest of Team Dogma had made a HALO drop into Jamba, where the United Freedom Front Alliance's headquarters were carefully hidden among a ramshackle block of tin-roofed residences and storefronts. The UFFA was responsible for disrupting Angolan oil production, consequently sparking yet another civil war in the war-ravaged country. Rainey, Vance, Houston, Doc, and the team's newest official member, Lance Cpl. Ricardo Banks, had moved in on a section of the street and were transmitting digital photographs as well as intelligence reports regarding troop numbers and movements back to Patriot Seven, their headquarters aboard the USS *Iwo Jima*.

"Dogma One, this is Dogma Five, over," Banks called.

"Dogma Five, this is One, sitrep over."

"One, be advised I count twenty-one combatants on the perimeter armed with AKs. Be advised I have also spotted three individuals with RPGs. No more observed, over."

"Dogma One, this is Dogma Four. Confirm Five's count from my position, over."

"Dogma One, this is Dogma Three. Count is accurate from my position. Uplink good. Patriot Seven data transmitted and received, over."

"Roger that, Dogma Team. Continue observation, and stand by to rally my position, out."

Love him or hate him, that kid Ricardo Banks had managed to smooth-talk his way onto the team with a rec letter from Doc and an actual endorsement from Rainey. Funny, Rainey had never known a Marine who wanted it more badly than Banks. The kid's desire had reminded Rainey of his own excitement when he had first been accepted into Force Recon some nine hundred years ago—or at least it felt so. Lance Corporal Ricardo Banks would always be an asshole, but he would be all right, as would Rainey.

"Dogma Team, this is Dogma One. Rally back my position. Our work here is finished, out."